A NEW LOVE FOR JOY

"It'll be better soon," Uriah promised. "When we get the *dawdihaus* finished. And not just because we'll be out of your way, but because Johnny B will have freedom of movement. He'll be able to care for himself. That will take so much from your shoulders. That's why I'm doing this, you know. To help with the burden."

She had been doing and caring and running everything by herself for so long that she had forgotten what it felt like to have someone there other than her daughter to lend a hand.

Joy's palm itched to touch Uriah's face, run her fingers down his rusty blond beard. But that action was too familiar. It was the touch of a wife to a husband when they were alone. Not that of a sister-in-law to her brother-in-law. Not at all.

Could he feel her emotions? Her thoughts? She had to get a handle on herself. She couldn't go around like this. What was wrong with her today?

She missed it, she realized. She missed the companionship of a husband and helpmate. She missed having someone to share her day with, to talk to when the lights were out. To sleep next to and take comfort in their steady breathing all through the night. She didn't just miss Rudy; she missed all that he gave her as well. . . .

Books by Amy Lillard

Published by Kensington Publishing Corporation

ONE MORE TIME FOR JOY

AMY LILLARD

ZEBRA BOOKS
KENSINGTON PUBLISHING CORP.
www.kensingtonbooks.com

ZEBRA BOOKS are published by

Kensington Publishing Corp.
119 West 40th Street
New York, NY 10018

All Kensington titles, imprints, and distributed lines are available at special quantity discounts for bulk purchases for sales promotion, premiums, fund-raising, and educational or institutional use.

Special book excerpts or customized printings can also be created to fit specific needs. For details, write or phone the office of the Kensington Sales Manager: Kensington Publishing Corp., 119 West 40th Street, New York, NY 10018. Attn. Sales Department. Phone: 1-800-221-2647.

First Printing: April 2023
ISBN-13: 978-1-4201-5524-2
ISBN-13: 978-1-4201-5525-9 (eBook)

10 9 8 7 6 5 4 3 2 1

Printed in the United States of America

To Addy and Chayton
I love you both so much!

A friend loveth at all times, and a brother is born for adversity.

Proverbs 17:17

Chapter 1

They were wrong. No two ways about it. The doctors were wrong. They had to be.

Joy Lehman rolled onto her back and stared up at the ceiling, though she couldn't see it. It was impossible to see anything in the pitch black of the night. The house was quiet, the night was dark, and yet she couldn't sleep. Too many thoughts from the day kept swirling around inside her head.

Today the doctors had told them that Johnny B's healing had stalled, and he wouldn't improve beyond where he was now. He wouldn't be able to walk. He wouldn't gain any more feeling in his legs. He would be in a wheelchair for the rest of his life.

She refused to believe them. She refused to give up hope.

It wasn't like doctors hadn't been wrong before.

She rolled onto her side and sighed. She needed to shut off her thoughts. Three thirty came mighty early in the morning. Bread needed time to rise. She could make some of the dough up in the afternoons. But by then her feet were dragging she was so tired. It was easier to just go to bed and get up early again to make it. She was that tired now, but her thoughts were too restless to allow her to rest.

She could hear every sound the old house made. From the sighing in the attic loft to the ticking of the ancient grandfather clock that sat near the entrance to the living room. For a moment she held her breath, listening. She thought she heard someone stirring around upstairs. Maybe one of the younger children getting up to go to the bathroom. The house was quiet and not quiet and oh—so dark.

Hope. She needed hope. She had to have hope. Especially when no one else around her held any for her son. She would continue to pray that God's will be done. It was all she could do and accept it as it came. But that didn't mean she had to give up hope. That didn't mean that she couldn't pray that it *be* God's will that her son would walk again.

It was even more important now that the doctors had crushed all the hope that Johnny B had had going into this afternoon's appointment. She had seen the downward turn of his mouth, the bitterness that had settled in his eyes. Whatever hope he had clung to had been ground underneath the heel of their fancy *Englisch* shoes.

Stop! she told herself sternly. She wasn't about to go down that road. She wasn't about to allow herself to turn bitter as well. She couldn't. Even if she had wanted to. Someone had to remain positive, and that someone had to be her.

Johnny B would walk again. She couldn't allow thoughts of anything else.

The small beam of a flashlight verified what she had earlier suspected. One of the smaller children was up and about. Most likely the youngest, Jane, who flitted around during the day as if nothing was wrong but allowed the night to bring in doubts with it. Just like someone else she knew.

"Mamm?"

Joy smiled a little into the night at the sound of her sweet daughter's voice. Jane had been only a year old when her father had died. She had no memories of him whatsoever, no inkling of what life might have been like before his death. All she knew was her *mamm* ran a bakery in the basement, where her older sister and a couple of girls from their church district worked.

Joy was secretly glad that Jane had none of those memories. It made the "now" somehow easier to accept. *Jah*, children were resilient. Yet some more than others. Jane carried with her whatever she experienced. She hid it during the day, but at night, it rose back up to haunt her.

Jane could remember when Johnny B was able walk. Her sweet, caring heart hated that he was suffering. Though she was too young to know that was the reason. Just as Joy couldn't tell her.

"*Jah*?"

"Are you awake?"

"*Jah, liebschdi.*" She waited until Jane made her way completely into the room, stopping beside the bed next to her. "Are you *allrecht*?"

Jane nodded, a motion Joy could detect from the bobbing of the flashlight beam.

"What's wrong?"

"Leah's snoring, and she's keeping me awake."

Joy was glad the darkness hid her smile. Leah didn't snore, but Joy wasn't about to argue with an eight-year-old over the fact. "You want to come sleep with me?"

It was a bad habit to get into, but the truth was Joy needed the nighttime comfort as badly as Jane did.

"Please."

Joy scooted over in the bed, patting the spot next to her.

Jane jumped in beside her, turning off the flashlight after she had snuggled down safely in the covers.

Joy wrapped her youngest into her arms and kissed the top of her head.

Jane sighed contentedly.

She shouldn't give in. She shouldn't allow Jane to sleep with her. Or allow her to give in to her fears, but it was one of the few things she seemed to have control over these days.

Ten-year old Chris was acting like . . . well, she didn't know what to call how he was acting, but it wasn't proper behavior. He seemed angry all the time. Sullen, as if he had been the one to lose use of his legs. He didn't like the fact that he and his brother no longer shared a room, though he wouldn't admit as much.

Johnny B couldn't navigate the stairs in his wheelchair, so they had moved his bed into the living room. That of course threw a monkey wrench into the dynamics of the entire household. The couch had to be moved into another part of the house. It had been on the back porch for a while, but with winter approaching that plan would have to be altered. And with only three bedrooms, the idea of allowing him to take over her downstairs room would have her sharing with the two girls or her youngest son. Neither prospect seemed doable long term. And the basement was where her bakery was located. Without that . . .

And then there was Leah; Joy might be worried about Leah most of all. Leah smiled too much, was too accommodating. Joy swore to herself that if she asked Leah to go into town barefoot in the snow, the child would do it with an unwavering smile on her face. That wasn't healthy. Her family wasn't healthy. She had no idea what to do to get everyone back on track. And it was worse at night, like this. The darkness always seemed to bring with it doubts and fears.

She pressed her face into Jane's sweet-smelling hair, perfumed with apple shampoo and the fresh scent of her cotton nightgown.

Everything would look bright again in the morning. She just had to make it until then.

Thoughts stilled, Joy closed her eyes and finally fell asleep.

"Joy."

She looked up as Millie Bauman called her name. Millie was standing at the top of the stairs that led down to the barn below. Joy and the members of the Whoopie Pie Widows Club—officially the Paradise Springs Widows Group—had gathered for one last day of cleaning before church tomorrow.

This was the first time that Joy would host church in her home since Johnny B had fallen, though she didn't actually host it in her house itself. Like a lot of the Amish had begun doing, Joy had built a new barn with a bonus room on the second floor. Her brother-in-law, Uriah, had come up with the plans and helped with it shortly after Rudy, her husband, had died.

The previous barn had been about to fall down around their ears, so Rudy and Uriah had been discussing the new barn for almost a year. Then Rudy up and died, and Uriah continued on in his memory, building the large structure with three stalls, enough room for two buggies plus storage, and the upstairs bonus room. She didn't keep farm animals, just her buggy horse and the retired buggy horse she was allowing to live out his days in comfort in the second stall. There was no need for a hay loft. That space was better suited for light storage, a place for the children to play on rainy days, and church. Plus it was a lot easier to clean.

Uriah and Rudy had made certain to add a couple of bathrooms in the barn plans to keep people from having to come through the house for any reason at all. Now she was eternally grateful for that decision. It took so much pressure off for the service. It was as if God had known that something was going to happen, and she would need this ease on her chores in order to get through.

"How is Johnny B going to get up here for the service?" Millie continued.

Joy pushed herself to her feet, her knees popping in the process, and made her way over to where Millie stood. Around the room, the women had all stopped cleaning, wiping down, and polishing whatever it was they were cleaning, wiping down, and polishing to watch her.

"He'll have to come up the stairs, *jah*?" Millie asked with a small nod toward the narrow wooden staircase. It wasn't a space created to be wheelchair friendly. It was narrow, not too steep, but steep enough, and of course it was *stairs*. Not suited to a wheelchair at all.

Joy felt something inside her start to wither. How was she going to get his wheelchair to the second floor for the service? How? How? How?

The question poked at her like a broken mattress spring. She chewed her lip, so very aware of everyone's eyes watching her. Judging her. Well, maybe not harshly judging, but judging all the same. How was she going to solve this? They wanted to know. *She* wanted to know.

Sylvie Yoder, Millie's aunt, bustled over. Sylvie ran the

Paradise B&B in town. "Could you move the service? I mean I know that's what this space was created for, but when I have a wheelchair-bound guest at the inn, I have a room downstairs especially for them." She didn't have any way for a physically handicapped person to get up her stairs either.

Elsie Miller, co-owner of Poppin' Paradise, the local popcorn shop, stopped wiping down the wood-paneled walls and made her way over to where Sylvie, Millie, and Joy stood. "You can't move the service downstairs. You'd have to move all the stuff you have stored down there to somewhere else, and the horses."

"Not to mention that there's no time to get it clean enough for the service," Lillian Lambert added. Lillian worked at Paradise Variety Store, and Joy had been a little surprised to see her today. Her father-in-law was her boss and somehow seemed to have Lillian too busy with work every time something like this cropped up. Joy supposed some people would think that Lillian was trying to get out of helping, but they all knew her father-in-law. They all knew his nature. He owned the variety store and liked things his own way. Liked as in demanded his way or everyone around him suffered. Lillian had managed to become so wedged under his thumb that Joy was surprised she even knew her own mind.

But she did about this. Which showed exactly how obvious it was that they faced a problem.

"Well, this many heads is better than one," Hattie Schrock, the eternal optimist, chimed in. Hattie was the voice of hope and exactly what Joy needed in that moment. Hope. Never give up hope. Never surrender. Never let them see they got to you.

Joy smoothed her hands down the front of her deep-blue day dress and black apron. There was a way. There was always a way. She wouldn't admit to anything else. She stared at the steep staircase. "There's a way," she told them, her tone emphatic, confident, and sure, though she felt none of those things. "There is a way." Now all she had to do was think of it.

Uriah did his best to listen to the words that Aaron Lapp was saying. Funny how just because Uriah owned the lumberyard everyone wanted to talk wood to him, like he had no mind for anything else. He nodded politely at Aaron, who owned the Paradise Amish Buffet—not to be confused with the Paradise *Chinese* Buffet. It was owned by a nice Asian family who had recently built a new house at the edge of town, in that no-man's-land between Paradise Springs and Paradise Hill. And who he didn't feel the need to discuss fried rice with every time he saw them.

Everyone was standing around outside Joy Lehman's house, waiting on church to start, milling in the yard and pretty much freezing. Yesterday had been a beautiful fall day, warm sun and just enough of a breeze. Now . . . *brrrr.* But that was late October in Missouri. At least it wasn't snowing yet. Though they were calling for a bad winter.

Movement out of the corner of his eye drew his attention. His sister-in-law, Joy. Joy was a good woman. Made of tough material, Uriah thought. She had definitely kicked it in when his brother died. All the widows in Paradise Springs seemed made of sterner stuff. Maybe because they had formed a group. They stuck together, supported each other. Met once a week and gabbed and ate whoopie pies and whatever else women tended to do when they flocked to one place. Uriah wouldn't know. He might be surrounded by daughters, but none were old enough to even be out of the house yet, and his own wife had been gone for four years now. But the widowers of the valley hadn't banded together or formed a club. Well, they didn't bake whoopie pies either. So there was that.

Aaron continued to talk, and Uriah continued to pretend to listen politely, though his focus had shifted.

What was Joy saying? She had approached Zebadiah Miller, the bishop for their district, as he was about to enter the barn where church was to be held. Uriah wasn't sure why her presence captured his attention. Just suddenly she was there.

He caught the words "baby monitor" right before Joy gestured toward the upstairs part of her barn.

Zebadiah stroked his beard and listened to her. Then he shook his head.

"What do you think?" Aaron asked Uriah.

Uriah roused himself out of his stupor. "Excuse me," he muttered to the other man, and went to see what was happening with his sister-in-law.

"Zebadiah." He nodded to the bishop, then turned to his brother's widow. "Hello, Joy."

She smiled at him in return, though the action was overshadowed by the sadness in her eyes and the tired slant of her lips.

"What's going on?" Uriah asked. Because something was going on. He could sense it in the air between them.

Zebadiah looked to Joy. It was her story to tell.

"It's Johnny B," she finally said. "This is the first time that I've hosted church since his accident, and I never thought about the stairs." She shook her head. "Once he can walk again, it won't matter so much, but right now, I can't get his chair into the bonus room. And Zebadiah doesn't think it a good idea to have his baby monitor in the service."

"Baby monitor?" Uriah looked from Joy to the bishop.

"I use it in case he needs me while I'm working. It's a two-way, and he calls me if he needs to, and I can hear him. He hates it of course, but until he can walk again, what other options do we have?"

"For the service?" Uriah asked. "Or for every day?" Suddenly he was swamped with guilt. After Rudy had died, he had done his part, maybe even more than his part, to help his brother's widow. He had built the barn, helped renovate the basement into the flourishing bakery that it was today, and secured a dependable lessee for her farmland. But after that . . .

"Not every day," she told him, with a small shake of her head. She closed her eyes when she said it, as if praying that it was true. "He'll walk again. We just need him upstairs for the service."

"He's fine missing this worship," Zebadiah told her. That was old Zeb: laid back, didn't get upset about much. "I think the baby monitor will be too much of a distraction in the service."

"I just—" she started.

"Mamm." Joy's youngest boy appeared out of nowhere and tugged on her arm.

"Chris, we've talked about this. I am in an adult conversation, and I can't run to whatever it is you need."

"Topher," he said with a frown, though Uriah had no idea what that meant. "I want to be called Topher."

Oh.

"I'm not going to have this conversation right now. Go get ready for service." She nudged him away, and he went, though Uriah could tell that every step was performed with the utmost unwillingness.

"So you agree that it will be distracting?" Zebadiah asked.

Joy nodded reluctantly.

Zeb was probably right.

Tears started in Joy's eyes, but just as quickly disappeared again. "I don't want him to feel different. He needs to be at the service."

Uriah remembered a couple of services that Johnny B hadn't been able to attend, but he wasn't sure what made those different than this one today. Because it was his own house? Or something else?

"I can help." The words slipped out easy as pie. Of course he would help. He would be there for his brother's family. Always.

"You can't get that chair up the stairs without help, and it's too narrow for more than one person to go up and down at a time," Joy protested.

That was true and partially his fault, but who knew this was going to happen when he and Rudy had drawn up the plans for the building? Who knew that they would need a wider, less inclined stairwell to help a wheelchair-bound boy make it to church?

"Mamm."

The three of them turned as a new voice entered the conversation. Johnny B rolled up, his expression as hard as a gravestone and twice as solemn.

"It's fine," he said. "I can miss church today. As long as Zebadiah understands."

The other man nodded. "And the Lord understands."

But Uriah could tell that the idea of Johnny B not being at church was breaking Joy's heart.

She sucked in a trembling breath. Maybe it was to steady her nerves, maybe it was to wash down the tears that she seemed determined not to shed.

Uriah held up one hand to stay the conversation. Then he turned to Johnny B. "A minute?"

For a moment he thought the young man was going to deny him, but he nodded, one stern jerk of his chin.

Uriah stepped away from the bishop and his sister-in-law, following Johnny B a few feet away so they could talk.

"I think it means a lot to your mother that you be at church today."

"I don't know why," he grumbled.

Honestly, Uriah didn't either. But apparently it did. And if it meant that much to her, then it was a problem that needed a satisfactory solution.

"As I see it," Uriah continued, "we have two ways of getting you there, aside from hurriedly building an elevator and powering it with the windmill. And truthfully, that's not something I would put my faith into."

He wasn't certain, but he thought he saw a shadow of a smile flicker on Johnny B's hard mouth. Good. That was good.

"First way: I get someone to carry your chair up the stairs and I carry you up the stairs myself." The boy wasn't quite fifteen and hadn't had that growing spurt where one day he was a child and the next a man. It wouldn't be an easy task to carry him up the staircase, but it wouldn't be impossible either.

"In front of everybody? No way."

"Or we could tie a rope to your chair. Someone could push and someone else could pull, and we could bump you up the stairs that way."

"That's just as bad." Johnny B shook his head. "Everyone will be watching."

"And they'll be watching if you turn around and go back to the house. Face it: No matter what you do now, everyone will be talking about you. So do you want them talking about you good things or bad?"

"How is me going back inside my house where no one will bother me a bad thing?"

Uriah shrugged. "I'm just thinking that determination to get to church might give you some street cred."

Johnny B frowned. "What is that?"

"Something the *Englisch* guys at the lumberyard talk about. It's like bonus points in the community. You know, like with the girls."

There was a flash of interest in Johnny B's eyes, but it was gone in an instant. "I'm not going to date."

"*Jah*, not until you're sixteen at least."

"Not even then."

"You don't know that."

"I'm never going to walk again," Johnny B said, his voice full of derision. "Who wants to date a cripple in a wheelchair?"

Uriah didn't know how to answer that. Hadn't his mother just said he would walk again? Who was right? Who was wrong?

And there was a part of him that wanted to tell Johnny B not to talk about himself that way. Words were hurtful even if a person said them about their own self.

"Okay, then. I didn't want it to have to come to this, but you need to do it for your mother."

Johnny B opened his mouth to protest, but Uriah shook his head, effectively cutting him off. "Do it for Joy."

In the end, Uriah gathered two lengths of rope and tied each to one wheel on Johnny B's chair. Then he pressed Thomas Kurtz into helping.

Thomas stood at the top of the stairs with both ropes—

tied together now—in hand. Uriah pushed and Thomas pulled and after a few grunts and a little sweat despite the late-fall chill, the two of them managed to get the boy upstairs.

Everyone watched, just as Johnny B had predicted they would, and once he was safely on the second floor, everyone clapped. It was an unusual start for a Sunday service, but Uriah supposed that some days were just like that.

Johnny B's face turned pink, and he ducked his head. No one wanted to be different. At least not so different that people noticed right off.

Soon everyone settled down and the service started. Uriah found his gaze resting more and more often on Joy. She was faced front, watching intently as Leroy Lambright, the deacon of their district delivered the second sermon. Jane, her youngest sat next to her. Leah was twelve or so, if he was remembering correctly, and she was seated with the other girls, as was the custom. He couldn't remember, but he didn't think Jane had turned nine yet. That was when the girls stopped sitting with their *mamms* and instead sat in a little gaggle of aprons and prayer *kapps*.

He thought that Jane had been about a year old when Rudy died, and his brother had been gone for seven years now. He counted them in his head. How was that possible? Where had the time gone? And what had he done for Joy in these last few years?

Nothing. He'd been too busy with his own family. After Dinah died, he'd been left with four girls and no idea what to do with them. Dinah had been sick for a while, but he had held out hope for a miracle until the day came when it was obvious no miracle was going to arrive. Since then, it had been Joy who was doing for him. Baking bread, sending over two-day-old cookies and birthday cakes for the girls, and in general being a kind and caring person. He had thought perhaps she had managed to put everything in line for herself and her family, but after today . . .

Well, today he had noticed things he hadn't noticed before. Probably because he had been too caught up in his own self, and he was ashamed of that. He hadn't noticed the desperation in Joy's face. Or how tired she looked. The bags under her eyes, the droop to her shoulders. The sadness that hovered around her like a cloud. He needed to check on her more, make sure she had everything she needed, even if that was only familial support. And he needed to start right now.

Chapter 2

The baby monitor that Joy had stored behind the cash counter crackled as Johnny B's voice sounded. "Mamm, there's some men here to see you."

Joy looked down at her hands. She was elbow deep in bread dough. It was Monday, a baking day for her. A day she used to restock the items she sold there in the shop. Normally she would have help this time on a Monday morning, but her only worker had only just decided that she didn't want to work any longer. She was a young girl, recently married and using the part-time job as extra money for her budding household. She hadn't said as much, but Joy had a feeling that she was already pregnant and didn't want to stand on her feet for so long if she didn't have to. Not that Joy could blame her for that. Some people didn't have the luxury to up and quit like that.

She supposed she was being a little unfair. The girl had given notice, two full weeks, but Joy had been too busy lately to find someone to take her place. An oversight she was regretting more and more as Monday unfolded.

"Mamm?" Johnny B asked again. He hated the baby monitor, and she had been more than surprised when she had heard him use it. Usually he turned it off when he found it in his vicinity, but she supposed that he had no choice but to use it now. His wheelchair wouldn't fit down the hallway, and he couldn't make it into the kitchen where the door to the basement was located.

She found a dish towel and wiped her hands on it, then she retrieved the two-way monitor from its resting place. "Who is it?"

"Uriah and Thomas Kurtz and this other man I don't know."

Joy sighed. She really didn't have time for this today. "Send them down."

"They want you to come up."

Of course they did. But only because she was behind and alone. At least it was early enough that there weren't many shoppers wandering in. She put up her honor sign, checked the loaves she already had baking, and started up the stairs. She was in kitchen when she noticed that she was covered in flour. She stopped, sighed again.

This morning had been a Monday. She normally didn't allow herself to have negative thoughts about any day of the week, but it had been a Monday. Her alarm hadn't gone off. Thankfully she hadn't overslept by much, but enough that she had to hit the ground running. This was the first day without Amanda helping in the shop, and she had encountered a particularly testy bag of flour that didn't want to open. Until it did. And it got everywhere. She had cleaned up the floor and the counters, but somehow she had forgotten to clean up herself.

She would just pop back down to the basement and dust herself off. She didn't feel like meeting anyone the way she looked right then. She turned to head back down the stairs when she heard Johnny B say, "There she is now."

"Good. Good," Uriah replied.

Trapped. She was trapped. She dusted herself off as

much as possible, but without changing clothes she felt the effort to be worthless. So she straightened her kerchief on her head and pasted on a smile before moving forward.

"Uriah," she greeted as she walked into the living room. "I wasn't expecting to see you today. I guess you're not here for cookies." She looked to the other two men who had come in with him. One was Thomas Kurtz, the man who had helped get Johnny B into the bonus room for worship, then back down again after church was over. The other, an *Englisch* man, she had never seen before.

"Well, cookies aren't our main reason for being here, but I wouldn't say no," the stranger said. He smiled and took a step forward, extending his hand to Joy. "Simon Wallace. Nice to meet you."

Joy nodded, a bit dumbfounded and a little distracted. "The bakery is down in the basement."

Uriah shot her an indulgent smile. "Later. Simon is a contractor who specializes in renovations to aid the physically handicapped."

"I see." But she didn't.

"After yesterday's problems with getting Johnny B upstairs for church," Uriah said, "I thought it might be a good idea if we came by and looked at the house. Checked out what might need to be adjusted to help y'all in the future."

He hadn't even finished speaking, and she started shaking her head. "I appreciate you thinking of us." And she did, but she would have appreciated it even more if he had told her he was coming. It wasn't like she didn't have a phone in the basement and he didn't have one at the lumberyard. All he had to do was call. Instead he showed up. And as much as she was grateful for his kind thoughts, it wasn't like they were in desperate need. Johnny B was going to walk again. They only had to make do until then. "But all that's not necessary."

Uriah shot a pointed look at Thomas and Simon. She wasn't sure exactly what it meant, but it seemed to say *I told you so*.

"How long has the bed been in the living room?" This from Simon.

"Since we brought Johnny B home from the hospital." That had been March. She had been so grateful at the time that he was alive that having his bed in the living room was nothing. Of course the entire house had shifted and there wasn't as much family space now, but it was worth it, and it wasn't forever. "When he starts walking again—" She had been about to say that he would move back into the room he had shared with Chris. But that wouldn't be possible until he was able to climb the stairs. Still, she told herself, it wasn't forever.

"But no one can tell you when that will be," Simon said. His voice held the hint of a question, so she shook her head.

"No," she replied. "But one day."

The men turned as a snort came from behind them. "That's not what the doctor said." Johnny B was red in the face. His breathing a little heavy. She knew he didn't like to be talked about as if he weren't in the room. "He said this was it. This is as good as it gets."

"You have to remain positive," Joy reminded him. She knew it was hard. It was difficult enough for her to stay upbeat and happy and hopeful and all the other encouraging emotions. By the end of the day she was exhausted from smiling and looking to the bright side. But it was well worth the effort. Still, she understood that Johnny B was having a harder time staying optimistic. That just meant she had to be doubly cheerful and confident enough for the both of them.

Uriah flashed the other two men that same look that he had offered earlier.

Joy wanted to demand to know what it meant. If they had been by themselves, she might have—but he wouldn't have had anyone to share secret looks with if they were alone.

"Sometimes remaining positive isn't enough," Simon gently told her.

"Will someone tell me what this is about?" she asked as calmly as she could. She checked the clock hanging near the kitchen door. She still had a few minutes before she needed to go down and check on the bread.

"It's time," Uriah said.

Not for the bread. "Time for what?"

"We need to make your house wheelchair friendly." Uriah sent her a reassuring smile. Yet she was anything but reassured.

"It doesn't need to be wheelchair friendly. We've only got a few more months before Johnny B will be right as rain."

"Just because you say it doesn't mean it's going to happen." Johnny B's tone was sour.

The men turned to him.

"I know this is a personal question," Simon started, "but are you able to go to the bathroom by yourself?"

He shook his head. "I don't need to," he told Simon, even though his already heightened color rose an extra shade. "I have a . . . bag."

"And you take care of that yourself?"

Johnny B hesitated.

"Son, I work with people who have more tubes and wires coming out of them than you can imagine. I'm not judging. I'm just trying to help."

Joy knew he was trying to help them, but it was all so unnecessary. "I help him."

Simon swung his attention around to her. "Because he is reluctant to take care of it himself?"

"I can't get my chair down any of the hallways. Or into the kitchen."

"That's something we can take care of." Simon spoke with the utmost confidence.

"You can widen the hallway?" Joy shook her head. This conversation was getting a little out there.

"Most times the hallway is wide enough," Simon explained. "It's getting through the doorways that presents the challenge. And we *can* widen those. We can also install toilets that are geared more toward people with limited lower body movement. Add ramps, lower cabinets. But my first suggestion would be to add on a room so this young man here can have some privacy and your family can have their living room back."

Joy opened her mouth to once again say that Johnny B's condition wasn't permanent, but she closed it instead, pressing her lips together before changing her focus. "Uriah, can I see you in the kitchen for a moment please?"

He didn't seem overly surprised by the request. He nodded and followed her into the next room.

"What are you doing?" she asked.

"I came to help." His words were gentle and kind, but she still wanted to scream.

"Johnny B will walk again. I can't see adding on a room and installing special toilets and—and widening doorways—" She stopped to catch her breath. "It's too much. It's too much work. It's too much money." She shook her head. "It's not necessary."

"I came to help," Uriah said again. "Thomas too. I've known Simon a long time. He wants to help as well."

"But he'll want to be paid."

Right after Johnny B had fallen, everyone in Paradise Springs had banded together to help raise money. They even crossed the border and solicited assistance from Paradise Hill. It was safe to say the whole of Paradise Valley got behind them and raised the money they needed to pay hospital bills and continuing medical costs. But it hadn't lasted long. Endless doctors' appointments, trips into Kansas City to specialists, even the very chair he was sitting in. It all cost a small fortune.

"This is not about the money," Uriah told her.

That was easy for him to say; it wasn't his pocketbook.

"I don't have that kind of money. All the funds that were raised are gone." Along with her savings and pretty much everything she had. Not that she was complaining; it was simply the truth.

"Why don't you let me worry about that?"

Was he joking? "I can't do that."

"You can. I can take care of this for you. It's my gift." He shook his head but smiled before continuing. "Did you think I would bring him here for this if I wasn't the one footing the bill?"

She didn't know. She hadn't thought that far. "It's not needed."

"I think Johnny B would disagree with you."

"It's not necessary then. He's going to walk again."

"But that's not what the doctors told you. Am I right?"

"He'll never walk again if we continue to keep our thoughts and prayers closed to the possibility."

He studied her for a moment, and she wondered perhaps if he thought she was losing her sanity. "Okay. So he'll walk again. Maybe tomorrow, maybe next year. If we do all that Simon is suggesting, it's not like you won't be able to use your house in the same way. The doorways will be wider, and you'll have an extra room."

When he put it like that, it seemed silly to not agree.

"He's a good kid," Uriah said. "And he's had a tough turn. The least we can do is make it as comfortable as possible for him."

"I suppose," she said, but her voice didn't sound confident. Not nearly as assured as his did. "It's a lot to take in."

"I haven't done much to help you in the last few years," Uriah said.

"You had just lost Dinah."

"Be that as it may, let me do this for you now."

She sighed, then slowly nodded. She had to relent a little or she would never be able to get back to her day. Then she would call him at the lumberyard tomorrow and tell him thanks but no thanks. "Let me think about it." With any luck he would lose interest in the idea and move on to something else. Though she would only admit to herself that forgetting about things was not something Uriah was known for. No, he was thoughtful, kind, caring, and fair.

He smiled. "Of course." Then his words were punctuated by the shrill blare of the smoke alarm.

"My bread," she cried, and hurried into the basement to rescue whatever she could.

"I can't believe they are going to knock out the living room wall." Jane seemed totally enamored of the idea of destroying their house. She sat at the dinner table, happily swinging her legs as she munched a yeast roll liberally smeared with butter.

"Not the whole wall," Johnny B corrected her. "Just

enough to make a doorway. One wide enough for my
wheelchair to go through."

"And that's going to be your room?" Chris asked. His
tone was disbelief mixed with envy and a dash of anger.
Of all the children, he seemed to be struggling the most.
Or rather, he showed his dissatisfaction. Every day. And
every day there was something new added to the mix.
"So you won't share a room with me anymore?"

"I haven't agreed," Joy said, feeling mean for ruining
the excitement around the dinner table.

After she had run down to the bakery to save the loaves
of bread and turn off the smoke detector, Uriah, Thomas,
and Simon had continued on through the house. The bread
was ruined, her house had been invaded, and she hadn't
agreed to anything. And yet here they all sat talking about
it as if it were a done deal.

"But you will." Johnny B's voice was full of question
and hope. "I mean, Uriah acted like you said it was okay."

Uriah was taking it all for granted that she would give
in. Now she knew what that look meant, the one he shared
with the other two men. He had told them that she was
stubborn and that she wouldn't agree. Well, what of it?
She had been stubborn most of her life. And it was that
stubbornness that had gotten her through. It had carried
her after Rudy died, leaving her with four small children—one not even a year old—and no way to support
herself. That stubbornness had gotten her through her
oldest falling out of the hayloft and fracturing his back.
And when her stubbornness was taking a break, her faith
stepped in. As far as she could see, there was no other way
to be and expect to survive in this hard world.

Some people just seemed to have more trials than
others, for whatever reason. Just look at Job. Abraham
couldn't father a child, Noah's kids were a mess, and Cain

killed his brother. How do you suppose Adam and Eve felt about that?

So there were worse trials than the ones she'd had to endure, and she was grateful that the Lord had gotten her through them. It was His will that she fight, and it was His grace that brought her to the other side.

But this . . . this was something different. It felt like abandoning her faith. Like if she allowed so many changes to her home, she was conceding that Johnny B would never get any better. And that was something she couldn't do.

"It's a lot of money, Johnny, what they're talking about."

"Uriah said he would pay for it."

Joy frowned. "He told you that?"

Johnny B nodded.

Joy bit back a sigh.

"I want my own room too," Chris said.

"You already have your own room, Chris."

"Topher."

She closed her eyes for a moment. Some days it was harder to remain bright than others. "I am not calling you Topher. Your father named you after my father."

"His name is Christian, not Christopher."

"The sentiment is there."

"I don't like it," he said. She had lost count of how many times a day he told her how much he didn't like his name. And she kept telling herself that it was just a phase and he would grow out of it, given enough time. *Lord, give me the patience to handle it until that happens. Amen.*

"I understand. I didn't pick Joy, but here I am making it work for me."

"At school they call me Topher," he grumbled. He was having a tough time these days. It had started after Johnny B's accident, so she could only assume that his brother's health was at the heart of his unease.

Leah scoffed. Up until now she had been quiet, but that was Leah, not willing to jump in and stir up things. "They do not."

"*Jah*," Jane jumped in. "Nancy calls you Rudy's Chris."

"That's because there's another boy named Chris."

"And they call him Danny's Chris," Leah added.

"I don't want to be Rudy's Chris. I want to be Topher."

"If I wanted to call you Topher, I would have named you that."

"Are you really not going to let this happen?" Johnny B asked. His voice was choked with emotions that she couldn't readily identify. He seemed a little embarrassed and a little angry, maybe even a bit resigned.

"I haven't had a chance to sort through it all." She had, but there was no sense completely ruining supper with all that negative talk. She would tell him later. After everything was cleaned up and he was dressed and ready for bed.

"What's there to sort through?"

Everyone stopped eating and waited for her answer. She drew in a deep breath and let it out slowly, being careful not to make it seem like she was sighing. Because she wasn't. She had passed her sigh quotient for the day long ago.

"It's a lot of money to spend on changes that don't necessarily need to happen. Because when you walk again—"

He shook his head and cut her off midsentence. "I'm not. You heard the doctors. This is it; this is as good as I'm ever going to be. Right here. This." He held out his arms as if presenting his case.

He sat there fuming for a moment more before rolling away from the table. But he didn't go far. He couldn't. That was another change they'd had to make. They had to move the dining room table into the living room in order to have meals as a family. Now more than ever she felt it important to nurture those family bonds.

"Johnny, come back and eat." She said the words quietly but tried to make it so they were a command and not a gentle request. She was losing her grip on her family, and she had to get it back. The quicker the better.

They all watched as he sucked in breath after breath. She was grateful for each one he took. She was oh-so aware that he could have easily died those months ago, when he fell. But that wasn't the Lord's will. It was hard to accept as the final truth, but Joy knew that Johnny B's mobility was up to God. But faith, prayer, and hope went a long way.

But then there was the bitterness in his eyes. The anger and resentment for anything and everything that crossed his path. He had done everything that they had asked of him. Exercises and more exercises until he had sweat running down his face and his skin was clammy from the exertion. And still this was as far as they had come.

"Johnny." Leah. She spoke his name in a way that only a sibling can.

He turned and pushed his chair back to the table.

Leah smiled at him and gave an encouraging nod. If Joy had done the same, he would have accused her of patronizing him.

That's not what's important. The important thing is he's here now and eating his supper and calming down. And alive. The important thing was that they were still a family.

"Nancy asked today if you might come back to school after the Christmas break." Leah pinned her brother with a questioning look.

"Why would I want to do that?"

"So you can finish." There was a hard note in her tone.

"I'm behind a year," he said, clearly not willing to discuss it further.

"It's something to think about," Joy said. "If you go back for the last half of seventh grade, then you can finish up the eighth grade right on time."

He shook his head, obviously hating the idea. "A year late," he corrected her. "I'll be fifteen." He said it like it was some sort of disease.

"Actually you'll be sixteen when you graduate." Ever-helpful Jane.

"See?" Johnny B shot Joy a hard stare.

Even as his mother, she didn't have much to say on the subject. Not right now anyway. He needed to go back to school. That much was obvious. It wasn't like the state would allow him not to finish the agreed-upon amount of schooling. Way back before any of them were born, the Amish elders had negotiated with the government in order to be able to carry out their beliefs. It went all the way to the Supreme Court. The Amish could uphold their beliefs that they only needed to go to school until the eighth grade. But they did have to go to the eighth grade.

Joy knew Johnny B would need time to get used to the idea of going back, and of being older than everyone else. And the only one in a wheelchair. She was glad that Leah had brought it up, though she would rather have dealt with it another day. Today had just been a Monday.

"I want to see them knock down the living room walls," Jane said.

And just like that they were back to the original subject.

How would it be if she caved? If she allowed Uriah, Thomas, and this Simon fellow to come in and adjust things? Would it take those bitter lines away from the sides of Johnny B's mouth? Would it soften the edge of hardness in his eyes? Would it give him back his faith? It was all she could hope for, and there were no guarantees. She had learned that one the hard way. And yet it was so worth the chance.

"Okay," she said softly. "They can come in and work on things."

"Mamm, really?"

"One condition: You go back to school in January." She wasn't accustomed to negotiating with her children, but this was important. Plus, somewhere along the way her children had grown up and started thinking for themselves. With Jane and Leah, it was fine. They were both good girls, sweet and accommodating. But the boys . . . *Ach*, the boys. They had grown testy and surly. Joy blamed it on not having their father around. Maybe she had made a mistake in not remarrying, but life was so elusive. How was she to know if her next husband would be around to support her and the children? What if she remarried and had more children to care for when that husband passed?

The thoughts were not comforting to her, so she pushed them aside.

Johnny B all but rolled his eyes at her. But she could see this battle was a tie. He got what he wanted, and she got what she wanted. And in the meantime, she just might get her family back on track. She could hope anyway.

"Fine," he finally said.

"Now pass the rolls," Joy told Chris . . . . Topher. No, she wasn't going there yet. Not yet.

It had certainly turned out to be a Monday. All. Day. Long.

Chapter 3

"You know what?" Leah said the following day as she tied the clean, tan-colored apron around her middle. PARADISE TREATS was embroidered on the bib along with a depiction of a steaming loaf of bread.

"What?" Joy asked as she mentally checked that she had everything she needed. Namely herself and her purse, but this visit to town felt rushed. It shouldn't. She had thought of nothing else since she'd relented the night before and agreed to allow Uriah and his friends to tear her house apart in the name of helping. Except she hadn't relented to Uriah, and now she needed to tell him that she had changed her mind. Or rather, she had decided to allow the changes. That's how she would word it.

She repeated it in her head to make sure she got it right when the time came.

"Mamm, you're not listening." The words were admonishing, but her tone was light, her lips almost curved into a smile.

Joy focused her attention back on Leah. "I'm sorry. What was that?"

Leah's smile grew wider as she shook her head. "I said

you should stop by the inn and visit with the widows group."

The widows group, officially the Paradise Springs Widows Group, unofficially the Whoopie Pie Widows Club, had started meeting exclusively at the Paradise B&B. It was run by Sylvie Yoder and her niece, Millie Bauman. Both were getting married next month. Millie and her husband-to-be, Henry King, were taking over the inn while Sylvie and her new husband, Vern King, were moving out to his farm. Sylvie and Millie wouldn't be widows any longer, and the fate of the group was a little up in the air. Joy had attended for a couple of years, but after Johnny B fell, her time seemed to disappear to appointments and taking care of him and worry. She hadn't been to a meeting in months.

There was a part of her that would love to go to one of the meetings, while another part balked at the idea. It was that part that had her shaking her head. "I don't know, Leah."

"What don't you know?" Leah sounded so much like Joy herself that it took Joy a moment to reply.

"It'll be dark when the meeting is over—"

"That's why we have lights on the buggy."

"I don't have any food to take—"

"These cookies just came out of the oven."

"Cookies?" It was something of a tradition to bring whoopie pies. Usually a special recipe, as the women tried to outdo each other.

"I know for a fact that Sylvie Yoder has barely baked a whoopie pie since her upset at the festival in May, and there's a rumor floating around that Lillian Lambert brought a batch that she had gotten at Buster's."

It was true that Sylvie's upset as champion whoopie pie baker of the valley had hit her hard. After all, she had been reigning queen of the whoopie pie for many years. So many that Joy had lost count. And Joy had actually been at the meeting with the dreaded store-bought pies, but Leah hadn't. "How do you know about the store-bought pies?" she asked.

Leah smiled. "You told me."

That had been the last meeting that she had been to.

"I don't know if my going is such a good idea. There's supper and Johnny B and—"

"I've got this," Leah said. "Go enjoy yourself for once."

The thought was so tempting, to just walk away from her heavy responsibilities.

"Change your dress," Leah instructed. "I'll wrap up the cookies and off you'll go."

In the end the guilt didn't subside, but Joy changed her dress, happy for the excuse to look her best when going in to talk to Uriah. Not that she wanted to impress him or anything, but she didn't want to go in looking as rough around the edges as she normally felt.

Paradise Lumber sat off Main and toward the far edge of town. It was opposite Paradise Stables where most of the Amish who lived in town kept their buggy horses.

Joy pulled her horse to a stop in front of the lumberyard between two others who were already there. Hopefully Uriah wasn't so busy that she couldn't talk to him. She had a few choice things to say before she agreed to the renovations.

She set the brake on the buggy and tied her mare to the hitching post before sucking in a deep breath and marching across the parking lot. *Jah*, she was still a little upset with the way this had been handled. And *jah*, she planned to tell Uriah all about it first, before she actually accepted the offered help. She still didn't think they needed to go through such drastic measures, but if it got Johnny B back in school without a fuss, then it was a sacrifice she was willing to make.

She opened one of the double glass doors and let herself into the shop. The scent of freshly milled wood assaulted her senses, and she stifled a sneeze as she made her way to the counter. There were other smells as well—no doubt whatever they used to treat the lumber and the oil from the machines they used to move it from place to place.

Uriah was standing behind the counter talking with an *Englisch* man she didn't recognize. Christian Beachy who owned the local farm co-op, was waiting on a turn, as was Thomas Kurtz, all-around handyman in the community.

It was going to take forever before she got her chance to talk to Uriah. And who knew who would come in between now and then? Maybe even someone she didn't want to overhear the conversation she needed to have with her brother-in-law.

This was not her finest plan, but it needed to be done. She needed to tell Uriah how she felt about his actions, but she didn't need the entire population of Paradise Springs to know all the details. And they would if Christian Beachy hung around much longer.

Christian lived on a farm with his sister, Malinda, and Malinda was hands down the biggest gossip in Paradise Springs.

Joy was just about to wave to Uriah to silently tell him that she would come back another time, perhaps even call him on the phone and warn him that she needed to talk to him, when a young *Englisch* man came out from between the ceiling-high metal shelves behind him.

"All right, Mr. Beachy. You're ready to go. Just pull

your buggy around the side and the guys back there will load it up for you."

Christian grunted his reply, but that was Christian, always grumping about something or another. Joy couldn't remember the last time she had seen him smile. She did her best to smile every day, all day long. She might have to live up to her name, but she also kept all her blessings in mind. It was far too easy to slip into a dark pit of your own troubles, and she couldn't afford to do that.

Not that Christian had any troubles that she could see. He had a thriving business, a nice home he shared with his sister, and a fine community behind him. No, from where she was standing, Christian Beachy was grumpy because he was grumpy.

He pushed past her and out the door while the young man turned his attention to Thomas. "Mr. Kurtz? You're ready as well. You know the drill." He smiled, showing his perfectly straight teeth. He had probably worn braces on them as a teen, something that the Amish didn't do unless medically necessary. A couple of years back, Lillian Lambert's youngest daughter, Esther, had fallen while swimming in the creek with friends. Somehow she had managed to bang her face on the hard bank, knocking half her teeth loose. The dentist had put braces on then to help them stay in place as the roots grew stronger, but that was the only time that Joy could remember.

"Joy?"

She dragged herself out of her thoughts and turned to Uriah. Thomas Kurtz had concluded his business, and she was alone in the shop with the two men—Uriah and the other man behind the counter.

"I assume you're here to talk to me." The words were a little hesitant, as if Uriah hadn't wanted to say them, or perhaps he wasn't sure how they would be received.

She nodded, mutely, all the words she had practiced on the drive into town disappearing in an instant. She had riled herself up right nice in the buggy, going through the scenario in her head, but now that the time was here, she wasn't sure what she should say about how the situation had been handled. She didn't agree with Uriah coming in and upsetting her household, but admonishing him for that would make her appear ungrateful. And she was grateful. She reminded herself every day of all that she had to be thankful for. Starting, but in no way limited to, her son surviving that nasty fall.

"Can we—?" She gestured weakly toward the door. Whatever she managed to say to him, she didn't want the entire world knowing, and anyone could wander into the lumberyard on a Tuesday late afternoon. With the way her luck seemed to be going, Malinda Beachy herself would breeze in any time now.

No one would think twice about the two of them having a conversation—after all, they were kin by marriage. But the rest she didn't care for anyone else to know.

"Of course." He turned to the young *Englisch* man with the straight, straight teeth. "Frankie, I'll be outside if you need me."

Frankie nodded. "I got it covered."

Just then someone pushed into the shop, and Joy was glad she'd asked if they could talk outside, away from any customers. She didn't know the tall *Englisch* man who came inside, but it could have easily been any other of a number of Amish residents of Paradise Springs whom she *did* know.

The wind tugged at the skirt of her dress as she stopped next to her buggy.

"Are you going to tell me what's put that frown on your face?" he asked a moment or two later.

She had been standing there, mustering up courage and doing her best to remember all the ways she had come up with to tell him what needed to be said without starting an argument. She needed to speak her mind, but she wasn't always good at it.

But if he was in a hurry to find out, he could have it raw, unvarnished.

"I don't appreciate you coming into my home yesterday and riling up my son and getting all his hopes up and talking about knocking out walls and making me burn my last batch of bread—" She didn't have the time nor the extra resources to burn bread all willy-nilly.

He drew back as if she had actually laid her hands on him. "Joy, I . . ." but he didn't seem to have the words.

That was fine with her because she had plenty of them. "I mean, I appreciate it, what you're trying to do, but I don't appreciate being taken off guard."

"Kind of like you did to me today?" he asked.

She gave a shrug, at the same time wondering where her brash attitude had come from. It was wholly unlike her to be this forceful, this in your face, as the *Englisch* say. "How does it feel?"

"Not too good, I suppose."

Joy seemed to run out of steam. "Why did you do that? Why did you think it necessary to come in unannounced and start talking to Johnny B without me in the room?" It was her house after all, left to her by her husband. Bought so they could raise their children in it. Hers. Not Uriah's. And he seemed to act like he could do with it whatever he wanted.

"I suppose it wasn't necessary," he finally said. "It was spur of the moment for me too. I'd been thinking about the problems with Johnny B getting up the stairs at church, so I walked over to the house to see how things were going. I didn't figure church was the only challenge you were facing."

Boy, he had gotten that one right.

"Jane let me in the house during the meal and I saw for myself all the problems you were left with."

"They are not problems," she corrected him. To say having the bed in the living room was a problem was like saying Johnny B was a problem and that was like being ungrateful that the Lord had spared his life. She couldn't have that. Not even for a moment.

"Challenges then. Do you like that word better?" His voice had taken on a slight edge. But Joy wasn't backing down.

"You can call them whatever you want. I see them as steppingstones until Johnny B walks again."

He nodded, frustration hardening his eyes. She couldn't blame him. He had started to do something nice for her family and here she was complaining about *how* he had done it. "Then this is the handrail to help you along the way."

"It's not that I'm not grateful for what you're offering," she started.

His mouth turned down at the corners. "But you're turning me down."

She shook her head. "No. I'm not. I talked it over with Johnny B last night, and we're going to go ahead with the renovations." He didn't need to know the deal she had struck, the one that had her changing her mind. She shouldn't have to negotiate with her child, but desperate times . . .

Confusion wrinkled his brow. "I don't understand. If you want me to come in and do these changes, why are you here—" He brushed a hand through the air as if the gesture was enough to finish the sentence. Or maybe he just didn't want to call her an ungrateful, bullying old harridan to her face.

"I know you meant well." She shook her head. "*Mean* well, but next time you come up with an idea to tear half my house apart, will you come talk to me first before getting my son all riled up?"

Uriah watched the emotions chase each other across her face. She was angry, relieved—whether she knew it or not—and grateful for the offer. And grateful was something that she hadn't been the afternoon before.

He wouldn't call her angry as much as surprised and frustrated with maybe a little bit of aggravation thrown in for interest. Uriah had been about to ask her about her day when the smoke alarm in the basement had gone off. She had hurried away to see to the bread while he, Thomas, and Simon had continued looking at the house. Simon had wanted to take measurements, but Uriah had stopped him. Going that far would no doubt send her straight over the edge, and he couldn't have that. The whole point was to help, not create havoc in the process.

"I'm sorry about upsetting Johnny B."

She dipped her chin in return.

"That was never my intention."

"I know."

If she knew, then why was she here?

"I came to tell you that I agree with the changes you are wanting to make."

"You're going to let us build Johnny B his own room onto the house?"

"*Jah*." It seemed to take everything out of her to say the one word.

Uriah had to bite back his triumphant grin. He was

excited, happy to be giving back. "That's such great news! What made you change your mind?"

She gave another one of those negligent shrugs and shook her head. "No reason." But she didn't meet his gaze when she said the words. Whatever had caused her to relent, she wasn't willing to share it.

"Next week sound okay?" he asked.

She gave a small nod.

"Good. Good," he said, though Joy looked a little like she was heading into the dentist for a root canal. "I'll get with Simon and let him know."

She nodded once more.

"We may need to come by before then and take a few more measurements."

"*Jah*. That's fine," she said, her voice dispirited at best.

He wanted to ask her what was wrong, but he knew. As much as the bishop and the other church leaders talked about the sin of pride, pride was a hard thing to suppress. It was a daily effort to walk the line between pride and being an upstanding and caring parent, sibling, child, and citizen. And Joy King Lehman was a prideful woman. She didn't ask for help. She didn't want outside support. She felt herself capable and able, so why should she accept anyone's assistance when she was doing fine all on her own? But she was too close to the action, as they say, and she couldn't see that help was needed. And needing help wasn't something to be embarrassed about. Not at all.

But one thing to Uriah was plainly certain: He would have to come up with a gentle way to explain to her that he and Simon had talked and come up with a different plan for Johnny B's room. It was a good plan. A freeing plan for Johnny, but an idea that would damage Joy's pride for sure. But only if she would let it.

Chapter 4

"Joy!" The chorus of greeting met Joy as she stepped into the sitting room at the Paradise B&B.

She felt the heat rise into her face and knew she had to be as pink as the tiny *frack* Millie had dressed baby Linda Beth in for the occasion. "Hi," she said in return.

"I am so glad you're here." Sylvie rushed forward as Joy took off her coat and scarf. It had turned off colder in the night and that had carried through to the following day. Old man winter was definitely making a play for control, though she was certain there would be a few more nice days before the season truly set in. She had heard the men talking about having a bad winter this year and just the thought of trudging through all that snow they were predicting made her body tired and her joints ache.

Face it, she told herself. *You're getting old.*

She would be forty this year and had already noticed a few strands of gray in her auburn hair. She had attributed them to Johnny B scaring the life out of her with his terrible fall, but she supposed some of them could be the fault of her upcoming birthday. It was not something she liked to think about. Forty. She supposed to many people that would be considered old, but when compared to Lolly

Metzger and Irene Lapp, who were both in their nineties, she was practically a spring chicken. Yet these days she felt older and older.

"I brought cookies," she told them, handing over the bakery box that Leah had packed. "I know it's not whoopie pies, but I didn't have enough to bring when I was getting ready and the batch in the oven wasn't finished baking and—" Why was she rambling on like a deranged person?

"We don't care what you brought," Hattie Schrock said, patting the empty chair next to her. "Just as long as you're here. Now come sit down and take a load off."

Joy scooted across the room, glad to be able to sit. Not that she was tired; she just didn't like all the attention.

Hattie stood when she got close and went in for a hug. "So good that you're here."

Joy clasped Hattie's hands with her own and leaned toward her longtime friend.

Before she knew it everyone was lining up to give her a physical greeting. Except that Joy really wasn't much of a hugger. Her kids, *jah*, but anyone else and she hesitated at the idea. It was something that had always been a part of her. When she was younger, she had only hugged her parents and her siblings. Then when she got older, her husband and her children. Yet the world, or maybe it was just Paradise Springs, seemed filled with touchy-feely people who always wanted to pull her close. She was certain that her reluctance was noticeable and wondered if the Whoopie Pie Widows showed these acts of greeting just to see who could actually get close to her.

Once everyone had had their chance, they settled back in their seats, and Sylvie brought out the cookies that Joy had brought.

"Joy," Sylvie started, "what are these?"

Joy frowned. "Cookies." Well, she thought they were

cookies. That was what Leah had told her she was packing for the meeting. Maybe she had changed her mind.

Joy stood and went over to the refreshment table. The cookies that she had thought to bring to the meeting were stacked in pairs of two with a decent layer of icing in between. They looked a little like whoopie pies, except in cookie form.

"Cookie . . . sandwiches," she amended. "Leah's idea"—lest Sylvie get upset about the spin on the traditional whoopie pie. She took the practice seriously. Too seriously, and when she was knocked off her throne in May by a brownie disguised as a whoopie pie, her world had shifted. As far as Joy knew, Sylvie still hadn't baked any whoopie pies, much to the chagrin of her fiancé, Vern.

Joy looked over the table, seeing what all was available. Chocolate whoopie pies, raspberry chocolate whoopie pies, peanut butter chocolate whoopie pies, vanilla whoopie pies, her cookie *sandwiches* (she mentally patted herself on the back for her quick thinking), and some desert that she didn't recognize though was familiar all the same.

"They are *baci di dama,*" Sylvie said proudly. "They're Italian."

"Is that Italian for whoopie pie?" Who said that? She hadn't meant to say that, but somehow the words seemed to jump from her before she could stop them. Probably because it was the truth. The little cookies resembled a tiny whoopie pie with chocolate filling.

"They're almond short bread cookies with a dark chocolate center," Sylvie insisted.

And that made a difference? Joy supposed to Sylvie it did. But she could tell on the faces of the other widows that everyone wished Sylvie would get over her crushing defeat and start baking whoopie pies again. It was obvious that was where her heart lay.

"They look marvelous," Joy said, taking two and adding them to her plate. She poured herself a cup of coffee and made her way back to her seat.

The *baca di* whatever were delicious. They fairly melted in her mouth, but the fact still remained that they were as much like a whoopie pie as anything could get without actually being a whoopie pie. Though no one was going to say so.

She looked around the room at these ladies she had become so close to, only to have that bond slip after the accident. Hattie, Katie, Betsy, Elsie, Lillian, Sylvie, and Millie. Well, Millie had never been officially a member but attended at the insistence of her aunt. Millie was the youngest by far, widowed at the tender age of twenty-four.

Only Imogene Yoder was missing, but Joy supposed that should be expected. Rumor had it that Imogene had hired a romance author from Paradise Hill to help her find a daddy for her unruly twins. In the process she fell in love with Jesse Kauffman, the writer's brother. Jesse was a leatherworker who lived in Paradise Hill. Since the pair was planning a wedding for some time in November, it was expected that she wouldn't attend that day's gathering. She was busy moving herself and her boys and their two large, growing puppies to the next town over.

Hattie Schrock was sitting right beside Joy. On the other side of Hattie was Elsie Miller, Hattie's cousin and business partner. The two were co-owners of Poppin' Paradise, the popcorn shop down Main Street a bit from the B&B.

Katie Hostetler was sitting on the other side of Elsie. Katie was the oldest of the bunch, somewhere in her seventies. Joy was fairly certain that of the entire group

Katie (or *Ketty* as it was pronounced) would be the last widow standing.

Besides Joy herself, of course. Joy had no plans to find a man. She had worked too hard to become independent. All the widows surrounding her were likewise. They were all self-sufficient. They had lost their husbands and pulled themselves up by their bootstraps and made something from what remained of their lives. But Hattie was too cheerful not to have some good man try and snatch her up. Elsie was a bit of a worrywart, but she prayed more than anyone Joy had ever seen. And if she turned those prayers into finding a second husband . . .

Then there was Betsy Stoll. Betsy ran the Paradise Apothecary. She saw everyone in Paradise Springs. She was kind and intelligent, and Joy could see some lucky man setting his sights on her as his bride.

And Lillian. Perhaps Lillian Lambert would be among those remaining widows. Not because she wasn't attractive or didn't have a good nature. She had both those traits and more. It was just that Lillian sat firmly under the thumb of her father-in-law, whom she also worked for. Somehow Karl Lambert had squashed the spirit out of Lillian. At least that's what it seemed like to Joy. Even as harsh as it sounded. Lillian couldn't seem to make a move unless Karl deemed it okay. He dictated every piece of Lillian's life and had her kowtowing on a regular basis, though no one said as much. What could be said? It was up to Lillian to change her station or keep living the life Karl had planned for her.

"Joy, we're so glad that you came today," Katie said kindly. "We've all been missing you so." She said it as if she hadn't just seen her at church two days ago, but Joy accepted the compliment in the spirit it had been intended.

"Thank you. I'm so glad to be here." To her dismay

tears rose into her eyes. She had to fake a sneeze and use her napkin to dab her eyes before anyone caught on to her fragile state. She was overly tired, she told herself. This stress of the room for Johnny B and Chris with all his demands. Then she couldn't help but worry about Leah and Jane, who seemed determined to be as happy as two girls could be even if their lives were crumbling around them. That made Joy worry all the more.

"Excuse me," she said and hustled to the table for another napkin.

"There are some tissues on the front counter if you need one," Millie said. She rocked Linda Beth and patted her diapered behind.

Joy shook her head and swiped at her tears, hoping no one noticed.

A part of Joy envied Millie. Newborns were a lot of work, but they were fresh and new. They had the whole world ahead of them.

"I don't know if I'll be able to make it back next week," Joy told them after she had composed herself and returned to her seat.

"Why not?" rang out all around the room.

"I only came today because I needed to talk to Uriah. He and Thomas Kurtz have agreed to build Johnny B a room onto the first floor of the house." She didn't go into all the particulars about widening doorways and lowering sinks and such so he could take care of himself better. No one wanted to hear those parts of a person's trouble. Besides, everyone had some cross to bear. And bear it you must. That didn't mean you should share it as well.

"That's spectacular," Sylvie gushed with a clap of her hands.

Joy didn't think the news deserved that sort of enthusiasm, but that was Sylvie. More joyous than Joy herself.

"He'll be able to take care of himself more until he learns to walk again," Joy said.

A hush fell across the room. Not even a napkin rustled.

"I heard tell that the doctors said he wouldn't walk again," Elsie said slowly. She was the only one who spoke, but Joy knew she had voiced what everyone else was thinking.

Joy sucked in a breath and steadied her nerves. This wouldn't be the last confrontation she had over the doctors versus faith, and she might as well get used to it now. "They did," she said, her tone pert and a little insolent, even if she said so herself. "But doctors have been wrong before, and I have faith that this time they are wrong as well."

Around the room, all the women nodded. Some took a bite of whatever dessert they had on their plates, followed by a sip of their coffee. But no one said anything to refute her claim. How could they?

It was said that faith could move mountains, and if it could do that, surely it could also make one young man walk again.

Chapter 5

"What time do you think we should leave tomorrow?" Rebecca, Uriah's oldest daughter, asked.

Uriah looked up from his meal. Was she talking to him?

Maybe, but it was Rachel who answered. "Early. We're supposed to help get everything ready."

Somewhere along the line he had missed the switch in conversation. They had been talking about the new fabric they had seen through the front window of Paradise Linen and Such, the fabric store down on Main. But this was a new topic.

"Where are you going?" he asked, then shoveled in another bite of tomato pie. It was one of his favorites, and it was a rare treat to have on a random Wednesday evening in November, when all the tomato plants had given up for the season. Ruthie usually saved tomato pie for more special, seasonal occasions. But she had been trying to grow tomatoes in a large planter placed on the closed-in porch. So far it seemed her experiment was a success.

"Dat." Rachel shot him a sad look and shook her head. But that still didn't answer his question.

"Mary's wedding?" Rebecca raised her brows as she talked as if that would—

"That's tomorrow?" He swallowed hard. It was already time?

"I can't believe you forgot." Rachel shook her head at him as if she thought he was sweet and hopeless at the same time. He was neither. Well, he *could be* sweet, but he was far from hopeless. It was just that the days—the months—had passed so quickly. It seemed like his niece Mary and her beau Albie Schrock were just announcing their engagement. How could it be time for them to be having a wedding? It seemed an impossibility.

"I didn't forget," he defended himself. "I just didn't remember."

Ruthie, his youngest, jumped into the conversation. "That's the same thing, Dat."

"Hardly," he drawled, though his mind was scrambling. Had he scheduled someone to cover his shift the next day at the lumberyard? He was normally up front, manning the desk and keeping all the invoices for product—both in and out—in order. The last was something that could be put off until Friday, but he would need someone to hold his place behind the counter and take care of the customers. He'd have to go in early and check. Hopefully he had, otherwise he might end up missing his niece's wedding.

"You can't," Rebecca said.

"I can't what?" he asked.

"You can't miss the wedding."

Could she read his mind?

"I wish I could go," Ruthie lamented. She was only eight but seemed determined to grow up as quickly as possible. Uriah joked that she was eight going on twenty, but the truth of the matter was that sometimes talking to her was like having Dinah back for a moment or two. She was so like her mother. Perhaps more than any of his girls. But she seemed determined to grow up in a third of the time that it naturally took. His daughter Reena seemed equally as committed to staying a little girl. At first after Dinah died, Uriah had allowed it, perhaps even encouraged it a little. But now, four years later, he was starting to get concerned about it. Whereas Ruthie planned the meals, organized the cleanup, and even cooked most of their food, Reena was more content to play with dolls or color in her coloring book or just read. Unlike Ruthie, who had only been four when their mother died, Reena had been eight and could remember Dinah. He wasn't sure if that had anything at all to do with their behavior. He wasn't schooled in that sort of thing, but he suspected.

"All in good time," Uriah told her.

Ruthie sent him a small pout. "That's what you always say."

"And it's what I'm going to keep on saying," he replied with a loving smile.

Everyone always said that children were resilient and could handle more than adults gave them credit for, but in Uriah's case, his two oldest girls had adjusted to their mother's death with a more settled ease. *Jah*, they all missed her in one way or another, and he was sure, like he himself, they missed her every day. But Rebecca and Rachel could better understand their mother's illness, how she had undergone what treatments she could, and when that didn't work to take away the cancer, she had deemed it God's will and waited to be called home. It had eaten him up to see her suffer, but she had suffered in the treatment as well. There was no winning with cancer. It seemed to get a person no matter what they said or did. No matter their faith or their prayers or their worldly efforts. It was a hateful, hateful disease that robbed children of their mothers and fathers, mothers and fathers of their children, and tore families—both *Englisch* and Amish—apart, leaving them bare and shivering. Not that he had given it much thought.

Just like his family. They were getting by—missing Dinah but surviving. Following God, and yet in the back of his mind he was a little resentful, though he would admit that to no one but himself. The thoughts alone were hard enough to deal with. Sharing them was completely out of the question.

"But you'll be there, *jah*?" Rebecca's gaze brooked no argument.

What could he do but say yes? "Of course." And truly he couldn't miss it. If he had to close the yard for a time, he would. His only sister's daughter was getting married, and he needed to be there.

Rebecca seemed to relax a bit, and everyone's attention returned to their food.

"This is good," he told his girls. Tomato pie, green beans, and breaded and fried venison loin with cornbread on the side.

Rachel nodded. "It was Ruthie's idea."

Of course it was. He turned to his youngest, who beamed. He wanted to warn her against pride, but he couldn't bring himself to say the words. She carried out great feats for an eight-year-old, but sometimes he worried that she was missing out on too much of a childhood with all this playing at being grown up.

These days Ruthie planned out all their meals. Instructed them on who should cook what and then orchestrated the cleanup. Most nights she picked out the evening Bible reading.

It was a tradition they had started when Dinah was first diagnosed. They had all gathered in the living room as a family to hear a bit of the word of God. *Jah*, the Bible part of the activity was important. But it was the togetherness that meant so much to Uriah. He could read the Bible on his own anytime he wanted, but being with his girls for a time when no one was squabbling about bobby pins, shoes, or handbags and everyone was sitting in peace and harmony, just being together . . . It was more than a father had the right to ask for, and it was his every night of the week.

As the meal concluded, the girls stood and started clearing the table, Uriah snuck out front for a few puffs on his pipe. He didn't have long before he would gather back inside with his girls and Ruthie would tell them the Bible verse that she had picked out during the day.

Uriah felt a small stab of guilt. He knew the girls didn't mind Ruthie telling them what they were making for supper. As far as they were concerned, it was just one less thing for them to have to do. And Ruthie took her duties very seriously. But he also allowed her to find a Bible reading each day. He wanted to take that responsibility from her, but in doing so he would hurt her feelings, and he wasn't up for that.

He settled down on the old church pew that sat by his front door and lit the bowl. A few good puffs later, the fire was burning, sending the smell of sweet pipe tobacco swirling around him.

Now that he had a moment alone, Joy slipped into his thoughts. He hadn't seen her since the day before, when she had marched into his lumberyard and told him that she would accept his offer of help but the next time he wanted to give something to her family, he should run it by her first.

That was about control. He was smart enough to see that. Joy had lost control over her family. It hadn't been that way before. After Rudy died, they had been as tight as ever. They had banded together and worked as a family.

Joy had opened the bakery to support her family, and that was that. But since the accident, Uriah could see those bonds starting to slip.

He thought of Chris and the demands the boy had made of his mother in front of others, and at worship no less. And then there was Johnny B's sullen and angry attitude. It was understandable to some degree, but Uriah knew for a fact that the boy had been raised to accept God's will. But for some people when faced with trial after trial, they turned and began to question God's will. Not because the person was bad or unholy, but because they were human. Some things took some people more time to process and accept. That was where he saw Johnny B. The boy would come around. He would start to see whatever benefit there was in the accident. And there was. There had to be. Uriah was a firm believer in the idea that everything happened for a reason. That everything was part of God's divine plan. It was something he believed deep in his heart, not something he gave lip service to then lay awake in bed wondering at the mystery of it all.

Yet the tired look in Joy's eyes haunted him, and still she remained as hopeful as ever. He didn't know where all that hope came from. But if she could figure out a way to bottle some of that, she could sell it at the apothecary and her money troubles would be over.

Scatterbrained. It was the only word she could use to describe herself these days. She had always been so organized. A mother of four with a full-time bakery and the youngest in diapers had to be organized. But where had that trait disappeared to? All of a sudden, she felt as if she couldn't remember how to get dressed in the morning.

Stress she told herself. That was what her friends would call it. She could see Sylvie Yoder with one hand propped on an ample hip, the other with a finger pointing, telling her that she had to get ahold of her stress or she could kiss her calm, organized existence goodbye. Except that it had been months since her life had been calm. And she supposed it had been about the same length of time since her life had stopped being organized. Or rather feeling organized.

"Go on," Leah said as she shooed her mother away from the ovens. "If you don't start getting ready, you're going to be late."

Mary's wedding. How had she forgotten that her niece Mary Weaver was getting married today? No one had talked of much else, seeing as how this was the first wedding of the season. And somehow between doctor's appointments and baking and talking of house renovations, she had let it slip her mind.

"But school—" Joy started.

Leah was already tying on a work apron even as she continued to shake her head. "Jane is going to talk to Nancy and ask her to send my work home. Though I don't think that will be necessary. But I won't be behind, and it's not like I'm missing more than a day."

Joy couldn't put her feet into motion to take her upstairs and into a proper dress for a wedding. She hadn't even given any thought to what she might wear. She had been too wrapped up in her own problems to give a thought to the happiness of others.

"Mamm."

Joy looked back to Leah.

"I've got this. Go get ready."

So Joy did.

Joy sniffed and discreetly wiped her eyes as the vows concluded and everyone started milling around, waiting for the food to be served. There were a great many traditional wedding rituals that the couple didn't observe, like the seating of the attendants and the bride wearing blue, but Joy supposed that was the way of it. For so many years, the Amish people had upheld a great number of traditions, but this younger generation seemed determined to change as many of them as possible without giving their parents a heart attack.

Joy had had great fun at her own wedding, suiting up couples and deciding which of her cousins would sit with which of Rudy's brothers and cousins. Now it seemed that the tradition was falling to the wayside. But such was life. Change. There was always change.

Joy looked around at the crowd. The smiling faces and the relieved family members, thankful and happy to see this day come.

"I'm glad to see you here."

Joy turned, a smile readily on her lips, as Uriah came up behind her. "Wouldn't miss it for anything."

He lowered his head just a bit so only she could hear. "I almost didn't make it. I forgot to schedule someone else to work for me today."

A small, nervous laugh escaped her. "Same here. Amanda quit, and I haven't had time to find someone to take her place."

They shared a moment of quiet solidarity, a togetherness brought on by a common problem—too much work, whether self-imposed or naturally occurring.

"Does that mean you're looking for help?"

She nodded. "I really need someone for my baking days."

He frowned. "You only bake on certain days?"

"*Jah*, I bake bread on Monday, Wednesday, and Friday. We bake cookies and cakes every day and when needed, like for special orders."

He seemed to mull that over for a moment. "That's why there's always day-old bread on Saturday."

"Right." And because she didn't want the unsold loaves to go stale on Sunday when she was closed.

"You work six days a week?" he asked, a frown marring his brow.

She shrugged off his obvious concern. "I'm used to it."

He nodded, but the frown remained. "You should talk to Rebecca and see if she knows anyone who's looking for a job." He gestured behind Joy, and she turned to see a beautiful young woman she hardly recognized.

Blond hair from her father's side, smoky gray eyes just like her mother. Rebecca Lehman was all grown up.

When had that happened?

If Joy had seen Rebecca on the street, she might not have immediately known who she was. But she had to have seen her at church and other functions. How had she not noticed that her niece had grown into such a lovely young adult?

She had been busy, that's how. Working those six days a week that Uriah had just been asking about.

"I will," she murmured, still reeling at how grown up Rebecca was now. The other girls, they were probably the same. Though she hadn't really noticed them either.

How terrible that she had been so caught up in her own life's problems and drama that she hadn't given a thought to what was going on in her brother-in-law's family. Rudy would have been so disappointed.

"You should come to supper," she told him. "All five of you."

But he was already shaking his head. "That's a lot of work for you."

She scoffed. It was, but she wasn't going to admit it. She had allowed her life to sort of go on without her, and she needed to reclaim some of that. Her night with the whoopie pie widows had shown her that. She couldn't very well change a great many (truly any) of the issues that brought this about. So the only thing to do was work around it.

She wasn't going to be able to decrease the days that the bakery was open. She needed the income, and her bills weren't about to suddenly decrease, what with all the things that Johnny B needed just to go about his daily life. That wasn't something that could be worked around; it had to be worked through. But if she didn't do something quickly, she would be in her grave wondering where her life had gone. Rudy would be terribly disappointed if he knew. She had to come up with a plan. A good plan. And soon.

"So you'll come?" She fixed Uriah with a look.

He studied her face for a long minute. "Only if we can potluck it."

She opened her mouth to protest, but he cut her off before she could utter even one word.

"I have four capable girls. We can bring our part."

She wanted to tell him no, but there was a piece of her that so needed this interaction. And if this was the only way she would be able to get it . . .

"Okay. I'll cook the meat and potatoes. You can bring the vegetables and the bread."

He smiled at her; the plan made. "As long as you make dessert."

It was decided that Monday would be the day that the Lehmans of both families would get together for the first time in a long while.

And thankfully Monday turned out to be a less stressful day than the previous Monday had been. She had been kneading bread dough when the crew arrived and started planning their moves. What decorations she had on the walls needed to be taken down, and they recommended she pack up her dishes from the hutch just to be on the safe side.

She couldn't very well do that and run her bakery, so Uriah told her that he would make sure her things were safe. It was hard to go back downstairs and leave everything in his capable hands.

And he was capable—it was just that she hadn't had anyone she could depend on in that manner. She could depend on Leah as one would depend on a twelve-year-old girl, but she hadn't had someone there to take care of the things that Rudy would have taken care of for her if he were still alive. It was a strange feeling giving over control to Uriah, whether he was family or not.

But she did it. She managed to go back to the bakery and to the double amount of work she had to do, since she hadn't yet found anyone to help. She had called a couple of businesses and asked around. She had called Poppin' Paradise and asked Elsie if she knew anyone who needed a job. *Englisch* or Amish, it didn't matter to her. She just needed able hands to take some of the load from her on the baking days. She had also called Millie and Sylvie at the B&B and Betsy Stoll at Paradise Apothecary. No one knew anyone off the top of their head, but they would keep a listen out and let her know if they heard anything.

By the time Leah got home from school, Joy was more than ready to pop upstairs and start the roast. She wanted to give it plenty of time to cook so it would be as tender as a mother's love.

Roast and potatoes had been Rudy's favorite meal, and for some reason she thought Uriah might like it too. It might even taste a bit familiar, for she used Rudy's mother's secret ingredients: a can of Dr Pepper and a generous pinch of red pepper flakes.

"How's it going up here?" she asked as she came out of the basement.

Uriah looked up from the papers he held, blueprints of the room they were about to build onto the house. "Good. Good."

Except this was good?

Boxes upon boxes sat around the living room. She hadn't realized she had so much stuff in the room. Lamps and doodads. Samplers on the walls, her memorial shadowbox frame for Rudy that held his Bible and his good church hat. All that stuff was gone, cleared away and stored so that work could begin.

All it did was create more havoc in the room. The room where they would sit down as a dual family and have supper together. In all this chaos.

Well, too bad. It was done. The plans had been made, and the roast was cooking. Supper was still a go. They would just have to work around the mess.

"Hey, listen," Uriah said, his tone immediately making the hairs on the back of her neck rise. Something was up. Or wrong. Or problematic. Though she was pretty sure problematic was already taken.

"What?" She hadn't meant to sound so defensive, but thankfully Uriah didn't seem to notice.

"I talked with Simon this weekend, and we came up with another plan for Johnny B's room."

She didn't like the sound of this. "Why do I feel like I'm not going to like this?"

His smile deepened, but she noticed it strayed away from his eyes. "Just hear me out."

"Oh-kay." She crossed her arms knowing full well that it closed her off from him, but she needed the protection.

From what she wasn't sure, but he was about to deliver a blow of some sort, and she had to be ready. She had to hold herself together even if it was with her own arms.

"I was telling Simon about a *dawdihaus*."

"*Jah*."

"Well, we agreed that a *dawdihaus* is just what Johnny B needs."

"I didn't agree to anything." She would remain calm. Just because he said it didn't mean it was going to happen. A *dawdihaus*! Like the current chaos wasn't sufficient. Like it hadn't been hard enough on her to agree to them building a new room onto the house, now they wanted to build what could essentially be considered an attached apartment.

"It's a wonder that no one has built one on this house before now."

Who said they were building one now? "That's because most of my family moved to Oklahoma so they could use tractors." Actually that hadn't been the only reason, but she had heard that perk tossed around when the decisions were being made.

"Makes sense."

"So see? We don't need a *dawdihaus*." There. Problem solved. She turned to go back into the kitchen.

"I thought you agreed to hear me out."

She stopped. Sucked in a breath and turned back to face him. "Uriah, I barely agreed to a room. A *dawdihaus*?" She shook her head. "That is way more than I planned for."

"You have the room on your property. Your tree is far enough away. Your barn is across the drive. You might have to move your garden next summer, but that shouldn't be a problem. I'll come help you break new ground for it."

"We don't need a *dawdihaus*." She started to leave the

room once again. She needed the sanctuary of her kitchen in order to right her world.

"Stop for a moment and consider this," he said. "What if Johnny B doesn't walk again?"

"But he will."

"You can have all the hope in the world, but you should consider the fact that if he doesn't, he may very well live in this house until he dies. He might not get married. He will certainly need some care from his family.

"Now a *dawdihaus* would add value to your own house, give him some independence as he gets older, and since we're already building this, we can lower the cabinets and counter tops so he can utilize the space."

Forever. Until he dies.

It was a staggering thought, and one she hadn't allowed herself to have. Until now. She was taking it one thing at a time. And first up was getting him to walk again. Once that happened, she could deal with the rest.

Once that happened there would be no "rest." Once that happened everything would go back to how it should be. And he would walk again. She didn't care what the doctors said. She had scanned the shelves of the bookstore in town and seen so many books about people overcoming the incredible odds stacked against them.

There was even one book about a football player who had broken his neck and learned to walk again after the doctors told him he wouldn't. She had almost bought the book to read. To give her hope. But she had hope, and she was a bit afraid that the written experience would taint her own, and she couldn't have that. So she had left it. But the thought had stayed with her.

Every day people overcame insurmountable odds, and they all said it was their faith in God and their prayers for a miracle that had brought them through. She had faith, and she had spent more than a little time on her knees praying for that same miracle.

Matthew was clear. *Ask, and it shall be given you; seek, and ye shall find; knock, and it shall be opened unto you: For every one that asketh receiveth; and he that seeketh findeth; and to him that knocketh it shall be opened.*

She had asked and she had faith that God would deliver. Building an extra room was enough. More than enough. They didn't need to go to all the trouble and expense of a *dawdihaus*. Who would live in it when Johnny B defied the doctors' prognosis? When he walked again, ran around, joined the church, found love, and got married?

What if it doesn't come out that way? What if the doctors are right?

She closed her eyes against the voice of doubt. She had to remain faithful. Hopeful. Vigilant.

"Joy."

She opened her eyes to find Uriah watching her.

"Let me do this for you."

"It's too much."

He nodded as if he understood. "I tell you what. If Johnny B walks again—"

"When," she corrected.

"Okay, *when* Johnny B walks again, you can pay me back. *When* that happens, you won't have as many expenses and doctor bills to worry about. I'll let you cover half of it. But only then. And if he doesn't recover the use of his legs, then this will be my gift to my brother's son."

When he put it like that, how could she refuse?

She hoped she didn't regret this later. "Okay."

A loud *whoop!* rang out.

Joy turned to see Johnny B rolling his chair in through the front door. But how—

"Uriah built me a ramp. A real ramp." He looked like he

had been handed the world. Up until that point, she had taken a piece of roof decking and placed it over the steps up to the porch whenever she needed to get Johnny B out of the house. But it wasn't sturdy enough to leave up all the time, and she and Leah moved it back and forth only when necessary. Building a permanent ramp had never crossed her mind.

"We put it over the stairs, just covered it up. You can take the ramp away if you ever need to. The steps will always be there."

He had thought of everything. All the things that she had not allowed herself to think about in her efforts to keep up her faith that her son would walk again.

She had taken him to countless appointments—doctors, chiropractors, physical therapists, even a holistic healer that Betsy Stoll had recommended. She had cooked his meals, made his bed. Helped him get dressed. Helped him with all the other medical necessities that came with being wheelchair bound. So why did she feel like she had somehow failed him?

"The *dat* always gets the credit, don't you know?" Uriah's words were softly spoken so only Joy could hear them.

Chris and Jane, having heard all the commotion, came rushing down the stairs.

"What's happened?" Chris demanded.

"Are they knocking the wall down?" Jane asked, her eyes alight with expectation. "I haven't missed it, have I?"

"What do you mean?" Joy asked, allowing the children to see the answers for themselves. Looking around them, they chattered.

"Uriah's going to build me a *dawdihaus*," Johnny B said proudly.

Chris frowned. "You're not a *dawdi*."

"Maybe I'll be one day," Johnny B countered.

"The *mamm* does everything for the kids. Takes them any place they need to go, doctors their hurts, feeds them, makes their clothes, all that. Then the *dat* steps in one weekend and takes them to the carnival, and he's the hero. It always works like that."

"You're not his father." The words fairly jumped from her mind straight out into the air. She had no intention of saying any of that and yet she had. Somehow.

Uriah didn't seem to take offense. "I'm the closest thing he has, really."

And she couldn't argue with that.

The children continued to babble on about a *dawdihaus*, who deserved one, and what it meant for there to be, essentially, another house attached to their own.

"Can I have a room in the *dawdihaus*?" Chris asked. He looked expectantly at Uriah, the way *Englisch* children gazed at Santa Claus at Christmas time.

"One bedroom only." Joy wasn't backing down on this one. She had lost too many battles in the last couple of days. She wasn't giving in here.

Just when had her life turned into a war?

She supposed in a certain way it had always been like that. She'd had to fight hard for everything she had.

Why should this be any different?

"Your *mamm* is right," Uriah said. "There will only be one bedroom and that room will be for Johnny B, since he can't get his wheelchair up the stairs."

Chris pouted a bit but let the subject drop. That in itself was a miracle. He was so touchy these days. It wasn't jealousy of Johnny B's injury; Chris saw how hard it was to live in a wheelchair. But he was definitely envious of the attention Johnny B got. And though Chris said that he loved having a bedroom all to himself, he'd always had

Johnny B there sharing with him. Joy knew that Chris missed his brother at night.

"I've got to check my roast." She started toward the kitchen.

"Smells good," Uriah called behind her.

When was the last time someone had complimented her cooking?

A long time ago. Maybe even before Rudy died.

And why was that important?

She didn't know. It just was. It was one thing to know that you were needed and loved, and another to be told so by someone important to you.

Joy had missed that but swore that the pink in her cheeks was caused from the heat of the oven as she basted the meat. And she wasn't backing down on that an inch.

Chapter 6

Rebecca climbed down from the buggy and looked to her sisters sitting in the back seat. "Hand me the food."

Reena handed her the dish of green bean casserole. It was a house favorite, and Rebecca thought it to be a good complement to the roast she was told Joy was cooking. In fact, the delicious aroma of that meat tickled her nose and caused her stomach to growl as she waited for Rachel to climb down and take the corn on the cob from Ruthie. Both were Thanksgiving favorites at their house, but there was a wedding that day, and Rebecca wouldn't be home for it on the holiday.

Most of her friends were starting to get married, as well as family who were a few years older. She hadn't bent her knee and joined the church yet, but she was soon to talk to the bishop about it. The sooner she joined the church, the sooner she and Adam could make their intentions public. She smiled a little at the thought.

"Don't just stand there grinning like a fool," Rachel admonished. "It's cold out here."

Rebecca pretended that she hadn't done anything out of the ordinary and started toward the house.

"I don't know why we had to come here," Reena said.

At twelve Reena was the homiest homebody that Rebecca had ever seen. Sometimes she worried about her sisters. Well, she worried about them a lot. That was what you did when you loved a person, you showed concern for them. But Reena . . . Rebecca worried about her the most. She never went out and played any more. She stayed in the house with her dolls and her books and seemed to build layer upon layer around herself. Rebecca often wondered if it was just a part of her personality or if it had something to do with their mother dying.

Dinah Lehman's cancer had done a number on the family. It was crushing to lose your *mamm* when you're so young. She didn't know how much Reena could remember of their *mamm*. Plenty, she was sure, since she had been eight when Mamm died. But Ruthie had only been four and seemed to make up memories on a whim.

At first she and Rachel had tried to correct her, but soon Rebecca decided that it was a futile attempt at nothing. What did it matter if Ruthie concocted stories that never happened if she found a comfort in them? It wasn't hurting a soul, and she told Rachel as much.

"Joy invited us to come over. She's family. That's why we're here." Rebecca said the words with practiced ease partly because she had said them over and over to herself on the way there. She didn't know why they had to come out on a random Monday night to eat with her kin who were having renovations done on their house. The timing seemed off. But who was she to say? "And when we get in there, be nice."

"When am I ever not nice?" Reena countered.

"You're always not nice to me," Ruthie butted in. "Every day."

"Am not." Reena elbowed her little sister.

"Stop," Rebecca said automatically. One thing was

certain: When she and Adam did get married, she was going to do everything in her power to not have children right away. Once she moved out, she wanted a little bit of a break from being a *mamm*. Since their mother had died those duties had fallen heavily on her shoulders. Rachel too, but not like Rebecca. Their father looked to her to help with the other girls. She didn't mind, of course. She loved her sisters dearly. But sometimes it seemed like too much, too fast, and she just wanted a break from it all.

Lord, forgive me those unkind thoughts, she silently prayed. *And help get us all through the next two hours. Amen.*

They walked side by side, capes flapping around their calves as they headed up the wooden ramp to the porch.

"I don't remember this being here when we had worship last Sunday." Rachel inclined her head toward the new addition to the porch.

"Me either," Rebecca admitted.

"Dat must have built it," Ruthie put in importantly.

Rebecca couldn't argue with that. The ramp surely looked like her father's handiwork. "He's supposed to be getting the house ready for Johnny B and his wheelchair."

"Do you really think he'll never walk again?" Rachel asked, her green eyes wide.

"How would I know?" Rebecca shot back in return.

"But do you think?" Rachel continued.

Rebecca shrugged. "If the doctors don't think he will . . ." She allowed her words to trail off as the front door opened.

Her father stood there, just as you please. "I thought I heard someone out here." He stepped back and allowed them room to enter. "Come in, come in. Joy is just setting the table."

It was weird seeing her father there, like he lived there,

welcoming them to a home that didn't belong to him. Her heart gave a heavy pound.

No. It was nothing. He answered the door because he was the one there. She stepped inside the house, surprised by the chaos that enveloped her.

How long had it been since she had been inside Joy's home? Rebecca couldn't remember. She had so much of her own things to do that she didn't often go visiting. And when she did, it was usually with friends, not family. But she remembered how the room was before. Before Johnny B's accident. It looked nothing like that now.

She remembered a sectional sofa in a soft tan that framed the room to the right. There had been a sizeable square coffee table, just the right size for playing board games. And a large bookcase filled with the family's games and all sorts of good things to read. Only the bookcase remained. In place of the couches was Johnny B's bed. At least she thought it was Johnny B's bed. No wonder her *dat* had volunteered to build an extra room onto the house. (Of course he did. Her father was a good, good man.) But even if Johnny B got back the use of his legs, keeping the room like this for more than a day would have Rebecca *praying* for an extra room. There was no family space at all. Not even on the other side of the area.

For to the left had been two smaller chairs and a grandfather clock. The clock was still in place, though the rectangular dining room table squatted defiantly in front of it. The space that had once been open and inviting was cramped by a long wooden table with a bench on one side and four chairs along the other. Another chair sat at the head of the table with the other end empty. She supposed that was where Johnny B would sit in his wheelchair. Though she sincerely hoped that the extra seats were in place only because they were eating. Otherwise she wasn't sure how anyone got around the large table.

Or maybe it was because of all the boxes stacked everywhere. It looked as if they were moving. She wanted to ask why there was nothing on the walls but decided that had to be what was in the boxes. If they were joining the new room to the house, that would mean demolition, and demolition meant broken things that weren't supposed to be broken if they weren't diligent about it all.

"This is crazy," Rachel whispered to her.

It was true. The whole set up was not user friendly, and yet that's how they were living. Maybe it was better when the boxes weren't sitting around. She was about to say so when Rachel continued.

"I'm glad Dat's building them a room."

Rebecca could only nod. "We brought green bean casserole and corn on the cob." Best to dive right in.

"And my famous cornbread," Ruthie piped up.

Joy stopped arranging silverware on the table and smiled at Ruthie. "Did you now?"

Ruthie nodded.

"Well, I thank you very much," Joy said. "Take off your capes, and we'll eat here in just a bit. Leah is putting the final touches on the mashed potatoes."

"I love mashed potatoes," Reena said beaming at Joy.

"Can I help?" Ruthie asked as Rebecca and Rachel set the warm bowls of food on the table. They pulled off their capes and hung them on hooks on the wall as the conversation continued around them.

"I can always use an extra hand," Joy said with a smile.

Her aunt was pretty, Rebecca decided. It was not anything she had paid attention to before, and she had no idea why it occurred to her now. Yet there it was. Joy had rusty-colored hair that looked as if it might have curl in it if left to its own devices. Her skin was clear, with just a few freckles across her nose, no doubt badges of honor from growing a backyard garden to help feed her family. And Joy had the bluest eyes Rebecca had ever seen. They were the color of the clear Missouri sky on a June day.

Rachel elbowed Rebecca, nodding her head toward Johnny B. He sat in his wheelchair looking sullen and withdrawn. She had the feeling that he really didn't want them there. *That makes two of us, buddy.* Five, in truth. None of her sisters had wanted to come, but their father had insisted, and now there they were.

Rebecca wondered whose idea it was for them to have this family supper. She couldn't imagine her father asking himself to dinner. So it had to have been Joy herself. And with all the turmoil in her house, what made her think a large meal was such a good idea? Not only was she feeding herself and her four children, now she had the five of them to feed. That was a lot of work. Even if Rebecca and her sisters had brought two large sides and a couple of pans of cornbread.

She leaned a little closer to her sister. "We do the clean up tonight. Tell the others." Rachel nodded. She looked a little like she would protest but didn't. Rachel understood. There was too much work left at the end of the day for this family. They shouldn't add to that burden.

Just after they pulled the foil covers from their dishes and Joy oohed and aahed over their contribution, Chris came tromping down the stairs, his sister Jane right behind him.

If Rebecca had thought that Johnny B was sullen, then his younger brother was doubly so. Which didn't make any sense at all. He wasn't the one in a wheelchair.

Leah came out of the kitchen with a large platter of

roast. Joy bustled in behind her and retrieved the huge bowl of mashed potatoes.

Everyone bowed their heads and said their silent prayer.

"Amen." Her father quietly ended the prayer, and everyone started for a seat. It was clear that the Rudy Lehman's children had their own places to sit. As she'd suspected, Johnny B rolled himself around to the end of the table that didn't have a chair. He was seated, of course, but his chair was lower than one of the regular seats and the table hit him mid chest. He would practically have to raise his arms above his head in order to eat. How uncomfortable that must be. And once again Rebecca was grateful that her father was there to help. She hadn't understood his thinking when he had come home to tell them what he was doing and even why. But now she did. The whole family was hurting because one of their own was suffering.

"You don't sleep in your chair, do you?" Reena asked.

"Reena." Rebecca, her father, and Rachel all spoke at the same time.

"What?" She frowned, clearly not understanding that she was being impolite in someone else's home, even if they were family.

"That's not a nice thing to ask," Dat gently explained.

Joy sent her a forgiving smile, but Johnny B's look could have cut glass. He didn't answer, just slunk down further in his seat.

"That's what Danny Esh said at school. That Johnny B never got to leave his wheelchair. So if he's not leaving it, then he sleeps in it, right?"

"Wrong," he said. The one word was short, rude, and to the point.

Rebecca wanted to jump to her sister's defense but thought better of it. No sense in starting something over what was essentially nothing. Just words.

Sticks and stones and all that.

Plus Reena needed to get out more and learn these things for herself. Instead of staying home and playing with her dolls and keeping herself suspended.

"That's enough," Joy said, though her words were kind. "Reena didn't mean any harm." She turned to the little girl. "Johnny B sleeps in that bed right there. That's why your father has come to help me and build us a room."

"Because he can't get his wheelchair up the stairs," Ruthie said as if she had just solved all the world's problems in one stroke of the pen. Or strike of the ax might be a better way to describe it.

Come to think if it, they might need an ax to cut all the tension hanging around the table.

Seriously? Why had her father insisted they come here tonight? To be polite to Joy? Had she asked him to come to supper, and he had refused, stating that he needed to be home with his girls? That sounded like him. And then, naturally, Joy couldn't get around that, so in order to have supper with Uriah, she had gone a step further and told him to bring everyone. So why had Dat caved?

Rebecca looked over at her aunt. Joy was kind. She knew as much. Even now she sent bread and cookies over, occasionally even a pie. Rebecca remembered the time just after her mother had passed that Joy had come over and helped get the house ready for the funeral. She had come with the rest of the Whoopie Pie Widows to clean, dust, and polish. Had that been when she had decided that Uriah would make a good husband?

For surely that was what this was all about. Joy was ready to remarry. And it wasn't like she and Dat were kin through anything other than marriage.

Maybe it had been after Johnny B fell and her workload increased. Rebecca wasn't sure how much more work a sullen boy who couldn't walk was on the household, but she could guess. And in figuring, she decided her guess was probably low. Having a physically handicapped person in a house was most likely double or even triple the extra effort that she imagined.

That had to be it. Johnny B's fall had brought this on.

The rest of the table chatted around her. The conversation was a little stilted, having been bruised by Reena's insensitive question. The atmosphere was wary enough that no one even noticed that she wasn't participating. And for that she was grateful. She had bigger worries on her mind.

Talk turned toward jobs, and Dat mentioned a new worker they had at the mill and how he could do large math sums in his head. Like a human calculator. Joy mentioned that Amanda had quit work in the bakery and if Rebecca or Rachel knew anyone who was looking for a job to send them her way. With Christmas coming on, she needed regular help and holiday help.

Rebecca managed to properly answer the question, saying she would keep an ear out for anyone needing work, but inside she was still doing her best to sort through this new situation that had been handed to her.

What if her father had somehow worked the conversation around to where Joy was forced into a corner and the only way out was to invite him and his family to supper?

That didn't sound like her father at all. Finagling and manipulation weren't part of his makeup. He was fair and honest and open about everything, life. No, this was all Joy. She had set her sights on Uriah as a husband. And to Rebecca's chagrin, she could see the two of them falling in love.

It was subtle, so subtle a person could hardly notice unless they knew to look for it. It was in the smiles they shared. The way Joy asked Uriah to pass the salt. The way he complimented her cooking, making the roast with the same recipe that his own *mamm* used. There were a hundred little signs, and it wouldn't be long before the pair of them were asking the bishop for a spring wedding if she didn't do something. And fast.

The main meal was finished and pie was served. It was delicious. Her aunt was nothing if not a good baker. It wasn't that Rebecca had anything against Joy herself. She was a nice enough person. She was kind and thoughtful, and she cared about her family. She had even defused the whole "do you sleep in your wheelchair?" situation that had arisen. Joy was a good woman. That much was obvious.

Rebecca just didn't want her as a mother. She and her siblings, her father too, had been through too much to get all their happiness and other emotions mixed up with another's. Rebecca wasn't ready to let go of her *mamm*. She knew that, and she would admit it to anyone who asked. *Jah*, her mother had moved on, but Dinah Beachy Lehman was *her mother*. She would always be the woman who had given birth to her, who had raised her, passed down to her gray eyes and a bright smile. And Rebecca wasn't ready to move on from that.

Somehow she managed to move through the rest of the evening with all the proper outward behavior. She and Ruthie helped pack up the leftovers, refusing to take any home. This Lehman family needed them much more than their own. Reena and Rachel washed most of the dishes, while Leah and Jane put them away. Chris had disappeared just after the last piece of pie had been eaten, and her father and Joy went out onto the porch so he could puff a bit on his pipe.

Of course she had mentally scrambled trying to come

up with a reason why Joy and her father shouldn't go out on the porch alone. But barring the cold weather that had recently moved into the area, there was no reason she could give that wouldn't make her seem a little unbalanced.

So she bit back any protest and went about the chores that would bring the evening to an end.

They offered their *danki*s and said their farewells and made their way to their buggies. Dat was leaving at the same time as the girls, and Reena decided she wanted to ride with him. She was certainly what they called a daddy's girl.

That left Ruthie to bear witness to what Rebecca needed to say to Rachel. And it needed to be said.

She switched on the buggy lights and followed behind their *dat* to the main road.

"She wants to marry him," she said quietly, a little hopeful that only Rachel had heard.

"What?" Rachel turned to her, blinking in confusion. "Who she wants to marry whom he?"

"Joy." The one word was explanation enough for Rachel to understand.

"No." She drew back in shock and surprise.

"Think about it. Our *dat* is a catch. And you saw that house. She needs help. She needs a husband." Rebecca bit off her words before she could point out how ill-behaved and angry her children were, how desperate and lonely Joy seemed, and how overly compensating Leah had been. Only Jane had seemed normal, and in that normalcy appeared just as off. She seemed to float around as if nothing were at all wrong. Nothing. Not her brother being in a wheelchair, or her other brother demanding to be called the last part of his given name as a nickname instead of the first part. It had taken Rebeca half their meal to figure out that was where Topher had come from. Chris*topher*.

And the little girl seemed not to notice how bright and forced her sister's smile was. Bright and forced and constant, as if she were afraid to let it drop because if she did, everything would cease to be worth smiling about.

Rebecca felt for them all, just not enough to sacrifice her own family's happy balance to correct it.

"I like Joy," Ruthie put in from the back seat.

So much for only Rachel being able to hear.

"I like her too," Rachel said.

"It's not that I don't like her." And that was true. She loved her aunt. And she wanted to help her in some way. But that way couldn't be allowing her father to marry the woman. That was too big of an ask. "I just like things the way they are."

"Me too," Ruthie chirped from the back.

"Me three," Rachel added, though Rebecca could hear the questions in her tone.

"We can't let them get married." Rebecca lowered her voice a bit more, hoping that Ruthie had lost interest in the conversation.

"Married," Rachel repeated. "You really think that's it?"

"That's the main goal I would imagine." It was every Amish woman's objective.

"What do we do?" Rachel asked.

"I don't know." And how she wished that she did. "I'm going to think of something, and I'll let you know when that happens."

Rachel nodded and pressed her lips together. "*Jah*," she said. "Whatever it is, I'm in."

Chapter 7

Joy brushed the back of one arm across her forehead and hurried over to check the latest batch of cookies. The oven seemed to be cooking a little slower today. The timer had gone off twice and still the edges weren't even set. She hoped the stupid thing wasn't going out. That would be near the top of her list of worst things that could happen. At least in her bakery.

The edges of the cookies had finally turned a beautiful golden color, so she pulled them out and set them aside, replacing the baked ones with the second tray ready to go in to the oven.

She sucked in a deep breath and stretched her back. She had been running nonstop all morning. Of course it didn't help that she had gone to bed a little later than usual last night. Maybe that was the reason she rarely had company these days. On a regular day, she went to bed before the chickens.

She and her children, along with Uriah and his children, had enjoyed a wonderful supper the night before. *Jah*, there had been a couple of times when things got a little rocky, but in the end, everyone had a good time. She thought they had anyway. Sometimes it was hard to tell.

Still, she had enjoyed having company. How long had it been since she'd had friends or family over? Since Johnny B's accident for sure And, *jah*, going to bed a little later was hard on a body, but the supper had fed whatever it was inside her that craved that extra connection with others. She needed to make more time for things like that.

The bell on the bakery door rang, and she turned to greet her customer.

It was a young girl she recognized, though she wasn't a part of Joy's church district. She still had to live fairly close if she was walking into her bakery.

The girl looked around expectantly, then made her way over to the counter, where Joy waited.

"What can I get you?" she asked with a smile.

The girl flashed a nervous smile in return. "I came to apply for the job?" The words came out more question than statement.

"And your name?" Joy asked, thanking the good Lord for small blessings. She wasn't sure what she was going to do if she couldn't find someone.

She quizzed the girl on a couple of matters and had her fill out the necessary paperwork. Evie Brenneman lived in the other Paradise Springs Amish church district but was close enough to the line that she could easily come to the bakery three days a week and help.

Joy released a sigh of relief. Now if she could just get the rest of her life straightened out.

"Two weeks in a row!" Sylvie exclaimed. "Someone write it down in the minutes."

Joy shot her a *pu-lease*! look as she walked into the B&B later that evening. Leah had insisted that she come into town for the meeting. Joy hated to put the dinner on her small shoulders, but Jane had stepped in and promised to help, and Chris and Jonny B agreed to have sandwiches. It was as if they all wanted her out of the house.

Katie Hostetler perked up. "Did we elect a secretary yet?"

Sylvie shook her head. "I was joking."

"We still should take notes," Lillian put in. She was all for recording everything possible. Joy supposed with the way Lillian's family was, taking notes might give her a sense of control over something in her life. If Joy herself thought that might work, she'd write volumes.

"So we didn't elect a secretary?" Katie's expression fell. The old woman had been trying to make them an official club with minutes and records and all sorts of whatnots involved. Most the women—Joy included—just wanted to get out of the house for a bit, have an excuse to eat an extra dessert or two, and be able to help out a community member in need whenever possible. You didn't need a whole bunch of officers for that.

"We didn't choose a secretary," Elsie said a bit louder, patting Katie on the leg.

Katie frowned.

"I can still take notes though," Lillian offered.

Sylvie rolled her eyes as Millie covered her grin with the back of her hand. "It was a joke. We don't need to write anything down tonight." Sylvie turned to Joy once more. "I'm so glad you're here again this week." She smiled, then added, "Even if we're not really writing it down."

Her sincerity brought tears to Joy's eyes. Which was ridiculous. Why was she suddenly so emotional? Perhaps because even though her house was in complete disarray and she had no idea when it might be back in order, her life seemed to be smoothing out a bit.

She blinked back unwanted tears and turned her attention back to Sylvie.

"Next week's meeting has been moved to"—their hostess paused dramatically—"Thursday!"

Everyone clapped as Millie turned as pink as the baby blanket she had wrapped around darling Linda Beth.

"What are we going to do after that?" Katie asked.

"I thought that might be something we should talk about tonight," Sylvie said. "Once Henry moves into the inn and I move out to the farm . . . well, that may change a few things around here."

Millie was already shaking her head. "It doesn't have to."

Sylvie raised an eyebrow and shot her niece a look. "And you're going to host the meeting each week."

Sylvie had sort of commandeered the meetings, having hosted them at the inn for many months now. Not so very long ago, the members had taken turns hosting the meetings, but at some point, it became easier for everyone to just meet at the inn. After a while it simply became understood. Now both she and Millie were getting married, which knocked them out of widowed status and also had them moving. Sylvie was moving out to the farm to live with Vern, and Henry was moving into the inn with Millie. Though other than living arrangements, as far as Joy knew, nothing else was changing. Vern and Henry would continue their farm operation while Millie and Sylvie ran the B&B. But as married women, they would no longer be widowed.

"Why not?" Millie shrugged.

There had been a time when Joy had thought Millie a little reluctant to join in the meetings, but that had been back when she was new to Paradise Springs, back when she was newly widowed, pregnant, and uncertain about the future. These days she seemed much happier and more content by far. She seemed to even enjoy the ladies surrounding her and all the food and chatter that came along with these Tuesday meetings.

"Can she do that?" Katie looked around, seeing if someone was going to protest.

"Why not?" Joy asked.

"Well, once she's married . . ." Lillian started, but broke off expressively.

A collective "hmmm . . ." went up around the room.

"Is this something we have to decide tonight?" Hattie asked. Of all the people Joy knew, Hattie Schrock was by far the most positive. Joy felt certain that Hattie would be crushed to have to exclude someone based on marital status, regardless of the group's official and unofficial monikers, but if they didn't have that parameter, then anyone should be able to join. Was that right? They would no longer be the Paradise Springs Widows Group, or even the Whoopie Pie Widows Club, but perhaps the Whoopie Pie Bakers Some Married Some Not Club. And that surely didn't have the same ring to it.

"Let's wait until the end of the year," Lillian offered. "That way we can all give it some thought and decide after the Christmas gift exchange."

"That's a fine idea." Sylvie beamed at her, but Joy could see a little bit of hurt in her eyes. After all, she had practically started the group, and to no longer be a member was definitely the end of an era for her.

"It's decided then," Millie added.

"If we had a secretary, she could write it down," Katie pointed out.

"I'll remember," Joy told them.

"Does that mean you're going to start coming to the

meetings again?" Lillian asked. "Regular like?" she
qualified.

Why not? She had help at the bakery, and Johnny B was
about to have his own space and be able to care for himself a little more—until he started to walk again. Why
shouldn't she come to visit with friends?

"*Jah*," she said with a confident nod of her head. "I
sure am."

He really needed to be getting back to the lumberyard,
but so far nothing of the morning's plans for the renovation
of Johnny B's personal space was going as planned.

It was pretty simple as far as he could see. The framing
for the space was up and now they needed to cut a hole in
the outside wall. There was no plumbing running through,
no wiring that had to be worried about like when renovat-
ing an *Englisch* home. In fact, they were in a sense just
lengthening a window. And yet . . .

"Mark it off," he told his worker. "Take out the window.
Measure where you want the door to be. Measure it again.
Always measure twice, cut once. Or in this case, swing the
hammer once."

The young man nodded, and Uriah studied his expression to see if he was really understanding what Uriah was
wanting him to do. It wasn't terribly difficult, but he had
to get them rolling before he could go back to work. That
was the trouble with volunteer help: Even if their heart
was in the right place they might not have a head for construction.

"I tell you what," Uriah started again. "You measure,
then come get me. We'll talk it over then."

The young man looked a little bit relieved, and Uriah
supposed that if a person didn't have the vision, it might

be hard to take a sledgehammer to the side of someone's house. And truly that was a good thing. Better than a swing-happy ax man who wanted to destroy it all and see if it would work after the dust had cleared.

Uriah left the young man to his business and went to find Johnny B. He had been wanting to talk to the boy since early that morning. There were several things they needed to discuss, like where he planned on spending his time during the day. Currently he was basically confined to the front room or the front yard. With nothing but the porch in between—literally. But as the weather grew colder, it would be harder and harder for him to spend time outside. In fact, Uriah was reluctant to knock the hole in the wall just yet. He wished he could wait until after the week passed. A cold front was moving in, bringing with it freezing temperatures that would last until Sunday. Not exactly the best time to start tearing out new entrances, but this was something that couldn't wait. They needed that doorway in order to match up the framing. But with the number of volunteers they had, surely it would only be a short time before they had the walls up and would be able to better heat the living space. In the meantime, Uriah needed to tell Joy to pile up the blankets on Johnny B's bed.

"There you are." He found the young man out on the porch, watching with a critical eye as the men toted supplies from the pickup buggies and delivery wagons to the side of the house.

"Here I am." The words were dry and humorless, just like his expression.

"Listen, it's going to get cold tonight. We're going to take out the window and start to knock space for the new entry into your rooms. We'll tape it off with plastic and do what we can to keep the air out, but it might be a little chilly in your room tonight."

He shook his head. "It's not my room." His eyes were somehow cold and blazing all at the same time. He was angry. And it seemed as if he were angry with himself for being angry.

"The living room then," Uriah conceded.

Johnny B nodded, but the hard edge remained in his jaw.

"About the renovations . . ." Uriah started.

"Do whatever," Johnny B said. "I don't care."

But Uriah could tell that he wasn't entirely telling the truth. He figured that most of the huff and puff that Johnny B exhibited was a layer of protection against the world.

But could anyone blame him? Sure the Amish talked all the time about moving forward and accepting God's will, but it didn't come naturally. It wasn't something that just clicked over in a person's heart and all was right with the world again. It took the three Ps: patience, practice, and prayer.

"I'd like to get your input. After all, this room is for you. I want you to be able to enjoy it to the fullest."

Johnny B's eyes narrowed in either resentment or distrust. Maybe both—Uriah couldn't tell. And as much as he knew Rudy would hate to see his son suffering so, Uriah wasn't about to tell Johnny B that. He had enough on his plate right then without having to worry about how his father might view his sullen attitude.

"Because I'm going to live there until I die?"

Uriah managed to keep an even expression as he shrugged. "I don't know. No one knows what's going to happen in the future."

"The doctors say I'll never walk again."

"They might be right. It would be a shame, but it might be the truth."

Johnny eyed him once more. It wasn't the answer he had been expecting. "What if I don't?"

"Then you'll have this place until you get married—"

"I'm never getting married. I have to pee in a bag. What makes you think—" He clamped his mouth shut and shook his head.

"No one knows what the future might bring."

"Is this where you tell me that God has a plan for me?" Johnny B sneered.

"Is that what you want me to tell you?" Uriah kept his tone passive.

Again Johnny B stopped, obviously not expecting such an answer from his uncle.

"Let me ask you this," Uriah started, "do you believe that God has a plan?"

"I dunno."

But those words, like so many before, were a fib to cover up for a scared young man. Not more than a boy really, handed a rough path to walk and then told it was all part of the will of God. No wonder he was so bitter. Who could handle such news all at one time?

"Do you believe that God has a plan for you to walk again?" Uriah pressed.

"I dunno," Johnny B said again.

Another lie. He did know, and the poor boy believed what the doctors were telling him: That he would never walk again.

"I don't pretend to know a lot," Uriah said. "But I know that doctors do the best they can. They go to school and learn everything they can learn, then they come out and practice medicine. You know what practice means, right?"

Johnny B nodded.

"So you know practice means sometimes you get it right and sometimes you get it wrong."

"How am I supposed to know which one it is?" Johnny B whispered, a note of hope creeping into his tone.

"That's where faith comes in."

"So whether I walk again or not depends on faith?" His voice turned cold once more. It had lost its promising ring of hope.

Uriah shook his head. "What you do from there is where the faith comes in."

He wanted to kick something. How many times had he kicked a rock or a log or a can and not thought twice about it? Right now he would give practically anything to be able to take out his frustrations on an unsuspecting soccer ball. But his legs wouldn't cooperate.

It wasn't that he couldn't move them at all. He had a little bit of sensation, but it had stopped increasing weeks ago. That was why the doctors said he had gotten back as much as he would get. He could feel his legs but not control them. The sensation was there, but they would not support his weight. And no matter how hard he worked at the physical therapy classes, his level of improvement had stalled. This was it.

Of course if he could use his legs, he wouldn't have the need to kick something. He wouldn't have the frustration of not being able to walk. Of knowing that his life was over. This was all there was. The rest was just waiting to die.

As terrible as it sounded, that was the long and the short of it. He couldn't do for himself. He couldn't play volleyball or baseball with his friends. He wouldn't date, he wouldn't run around. He supposed he would join the church, but he wouldn't get married. He wouldn't have children. He wouldn't carry on his family.

It was never something that he had thought about before. He had never even imagined what it would be like to be married. He was more interested in getting to sixteen so he could run around and go to singings, meet girls, talk about the girls with other boys. See if he could persuade an *Englisch* girl to kiss him for his first time.

But now . . .

He looked down at his useless legs. Any attention he got would be out of pity. He had seen how the girls looked at him at church. His uncle had said that he would get some credit for going above and beyond in order to be at the service, and he had believed this for a time, but afterward, he had seen the sadness in their eyes. Everyone felt bad for him. Just not bad enough that they would give up their own life to spend a life with him.

He wouldn't even be able to work. Who wanted a husband who couldn't walk, or work, or have kids?

He hadn't asked the doctor about that exactly. He couldn't with his *mamm* standing over him crying like she was. But he was smart enough to figure it out on his own. He knew how most of it worked with men and women and having babies. If he couldn't manage to go to the bathroom on his own, then he surely wouldn't be able to do much else. He might have only finished the sixth grade, but that much was obvious.

He watched his uncle walk away after telling him that he had to have faith. Faith in what? Uriah hadn't said.

But there was one other thing that he hadn't said either. Unlike everyone else around him, his uncle hadn't told him how lucky he was to be alive. And Johnny B was grateful for that. Because from where he was—in a wheel-chair for the remainder of his life—he was finding it hard to be grateful for his life. It had ended when he fell, even though he hadn't died. As far as he was concerned, he might as well have.

Chapter 8

Joy was tired. Truly beyond tired. In fact she couldn't remember a time when she felt so blah and out of energy. And to think she hired someone to help in the bakery so she wouldn't wear herself out every day.

Jah. That was the true problem. Evie was a sweet, sweet girl. She had arrived on time, early even, with a bright smile and a positive attitude. But she was a disaster waiting to happen. What Joy had thought was shyness and perhaps a little bit of lacking confidence turned out to be caution. Evie was prone to trip over her own feet. She spilled everything she touched, she dropped half of the things she picked up, and she was having trouble learning the cash register. Not that it was difficult like the ones at the grocery store. No, it was pretty straight forward. Push in the price for each item and hit total. But even that seemed beyond her.

Joy had even taped a new list of all the prices on the counter at the side of the register. In alphabetical order. As far as she could see it was about as simple as anything. But Evie was having a problem with it. When they got busy just after lunch, Joy was already exhausted, so she

had shooed Evie away from the cash register, telling her
to mix up the latest batch of bread. That was a task even
Jane could accomplish, but apparently, following exact
instructions—or in this case, a written recipe—wasn't in
Evie's wheelhouse either.

As the last customer from the after-lunch rush snatched
up their cookies and happily munched them as they saun-
tered out the door, Joy turned to find . . . disaster.

"How much yeast did you put in there?" she asked, hur-
rying over to the dough mixer. Even as she said the words,
she knew too much yeast wouldn't cause this. This was a
little too much of everything.

"Just what the paper said to." Evie stepped away from
the machine as Joy approached.

There was no way that was all she had put in there. The
dough was growing out of the large mixing bowl like
something from one of those horror films Paradise Movies
Plus played around this time each year. Not that Joy had
been to any of them, mind you. But she had seen the signs
outside the theater.

The dough was a large mound that slowly but steadily
crept over the sides of the bowl, growing and growing and
growing until it looked like it could take over the entire
town. Or at least her basement bakery.

Joy looked over to the empty bag of flour on the counter.
It had been completely full when she had set it there in
preparation for making the next batch of bread.

"Did you put all the flour in there too?"

Evie grimaced and bit her lip. "I thought that maybe if
I made two batches at once it would help."

Joy's anger dissipated. But not entirely. Evie was only
trying to help, but her mistake had cost Joy both time and

money. "The recipe is tailored to the size of the mixer," she patiently explained.

"But there was room for more ingredients," Evie hesitantly protested. "That's what gave me the idea to add extra. There was plenty of space inside."

Joy bit back a sigh. The girl meant well. However . . . "You have to allow for the rising of the yeast. Have you never baked bread? Like with your *mammi* or your *mamm*?"

She shook her head, her *kapp* strings swinging.

That explained a lot.

"My *mamm* died when I was little. The rest of my family lives back in Pennsylvania."

That sounded like it could turn out to be quite a story, but Joy would have to wait to hear it another day. Right now she had to get the mess cleaned up and a new batch of bread started.

She checked the clock. She still had another hour before Leah got home from school. Maybe her daughter could better relate to Evie, since they were closer in age, and Joy was certain that if she had to, Leah could run the bakery single-handedly. She was just that kind of girl.

"I'm sorry," Evie said, her voice trembling. "I didn't mean to mess things up."

This time Joy did sigh, and with it she released her building frustrations. It didn't help that she could hear all sorts of noise coming from upstairs as Uriah and his crew worked on the *dawdihaus* for Johnny B. All sorts of loud noises that sounded like they were tearing her house down. She was afraid to go look. Now she'd had disaster after disaster after craziness in the bakery, and the two weren't mixing well.

"It's all right, Evie. Just don't do it again. Next time follow the recipe just as it's written on the card, *jah*?"

The young girl blinked back tears. She really did mean well. "*Jah.*"

Joy nodded toward the other side of the work space. "If you'll wipe down the counters, I'll clean up this mess."

"I made it. I should be the one to clean it up." Evie rushed forward, stumbling a bit as she stepped on her own shoelaces.

Joy closed her eyes and said a silent prayer that she and Evie would make it through this day. But her eyes startled open as a large crash sounded from above. She and Evie both looked to the ceiling.

"What's going on up there?" Evie asked, her voice filled with questioning awe.

The men had been stomping around and making noise all morning and afternoon long, but this time it was louder than it had ever been.

But how was she supposed to know what was happening?

Johnny B had turned off the baby monitor shortly after he'd gotten up for the day. That was right about the same time that the other kids marched off to school, leaving him alone with the men working on the house. Not that it was a problem. Joy trusted Uriah implicitly. But the noise . . .

"My brother-in-law is building a room onto my house." *I hope.* "Well, a *dawdihaus* I suppose, really." And hopefully *dawdi* houses were noisier to construct. Hopefully.

"For your son?" Evie asked.

Joy turned her gaze from the ceiling back down to Evie standing next to her. "You know about Johnny B?"

Evie's expression turned sad as she slowly nodded. "Everybody knows about it," she said. "And I've seen him around town a couple of times. It must be so hard on your family."

The care and concern in her voice brought a lump to

Joy's throat. So many people cared about her son, and yet all the love in the world couldn't do anything to change his situation.

"I don't know what I would do if I could never walk again."

"*Jah*, well." Joy rubbed her hands down her apron. "Johnny B's going to walk again."

"So the rumors aren't true?" Evie asked.

She didn't even have to ask what those rumors were. "No, they're not true. Johnny B will walk again." And she would do everything in her power to make that statement the rumor that came to be. "Now let's get this cleaned up."

By the time that Leah made it into the bakery, Joy thought her heart might just jump out of her chest. So many bangs, booms, and clatters had come from upstairs, and she could hardly take anymore. Part of her wanted to rush up there and see what all the commotion was about, while another part of her wanted to crawl under her work-table and not come out until Jesus returned.

Jah, her nerves were shot, but when Leah arrived and took one look at the mess in the bakery, Joy knew she had to stay downstairs and explain.

"You must be Evie," Leah said as she tied her apron around her waist.

"Nice to meet you." Evie flashed Leah a huge grin and advanced with her hand out. She tripped over an invisible spot on the floor.

Joy disguised her sigh as a yawn and tried not to shake her head.

Leah's brow wrinkled in concern.

"Evie," Joy started, gently, softly, "Why don't you run upstairs and see if everything's all right?"

Evie's eyes grew wide as she pointed to herself. "Me?"

Joy nodded.

"You don't want to go look for yourself?"

"I trust you to report back," Joy said, but the words held a bitter taste, almost like a lie.

"Okay." Evie started toward the bakery door, the one the customers used. The one she had entered from that very same day.

"This way is easier." Joy pointed up the steps that led from the basement into the kitchen.

"If you're sure," Evie said. She didn't look convinced in the least.

"I'm sure. Then after you come back down you can go home for the day, okay?"

Evie smiled. "Okay," she said, and started up the stairs.

Joy watched her go, saying a little prayer that the girl didn't tumble down the stairs and land in a pitiful heap on the bakery floor. Maybe this wasn't such a good idea, but thankfully Evie made it all the way up without further incident. She looked back once before turning the knob and opening the door that led to the kitchen. The noise grew louder, then muffled again as she closed the door behind her.

"You don't want me to go see?" Leah asked, her brow wrinkled in confusion and concern.

"Evie can tell us what's going on."

"If you're sure," Leah murmured.

Another loud crash rang from upstairs. Truly, it sounded like they were tearing the house down instead of building on.

Joy smiled, but it trembled on her lips. "I'm sure."

* * *

Johnny B winced as the man swung the sledgehammer to take out the exterior wall above the living room window. That's where the doorway would be. The doorway to his new room. Rooms, actually. When Uriah had told him that they were building a *dawdihaus*, he hadn't been kidding. There would be a small living area, something he called a galley kitchen, one decent-sized bedroom, and a private bathroom. And the best part of all? They were making sure that he had everything installed so that he could use it himself. A bar over his bed so he could pull himself in and out of it by himself. A bench surrounding the bathtub with another inside so he could bathe himself without assistance, and lower kitchen cabinets so he could reach everything without help. Alone. The entire set up was contained in only two actual rooms, the main area and the bathroom, which gave him some privacy when he really needed it.

"Is everything okay up here?"

He turned his attention away from the destruction of the wall to look at the newcomer. A girl, maybe sixteen, stood at the entrance to the kitchen. *Must be Mamm's new helper in the bakery*, he thought.

"It's awesome!" Jane was on her feet in a second. She took the girl by the hand and led her deeper into the living room. They'd had strict instructions to not stray past a certain line, and their uncle had given them all safety glasses in case of any flying debris.

When Jane and Chris, er . . . Topher had come home from school, they had immediately plopped down and waited for the show to start—the show being the tearing out of the wall that would be the doorway to Johnny B's new rooms. Then Uriah had given Topher a regular hammer and told him to chip away at the edges of the hole to widen it a bit. Johnny B didn't know if that was because it really needed widening or if Uriah wanted to get Topher involved. Johnny B had a feeling it was the latter.

"Everything's fine," Johnny B said. "Did Mamm send you up?"

The girl nodded.

"Watch this." Chris . . . Topher turned around and grinned at them as he took out another small section of the wall.

"He's having quite a time," the girl said. "Is that your brother?" She hovered near his chair, her hand still in Jane's tiny one.

Johnny B nodded. *She's pretty*, he decided silently. She really was. She had light brown hair and eyes the color of the blue icing his *mamm* mixed up at Easter time and spread on top of the bunny-shaped sugar cookies.

"I want a turn." Jane let go of the girl's hand and raced over to her brother, not giving a single thought to the safety line Uriah had established. "Let me do it."

"You're supposed to be over there." Topher held the hammer high over his head and out of her reach.

Jane jumped for it, missing it by a mile. "Give it."

"No. Girls don't work construction. This is a man's job."

"You're not a man." Jane sprang again, this time with a small grunt that did nothing to help her cause.

"I will be one day."

And it was true. One day he would be more of a man that Johnny B ever would. The thought festered inside him. His brother would be a man, and he would be stuck in this chair, watching, just like he was doing now.

"Don't you think you should do something?" the girl asked.

Topher and Jane were wrestling over the hammer. Jane hadn't managed to reach it, but she had grabbed her brother's arm and was practically swinging from it in an attempt to get him to lower the hammer.

"If he loses his grip on the hammer, it will hit her in the head." The girl nudged him in the shoulder. But Johnny B didn't move.

She let out a sound a little like a sigh but actually more in line with a growl and moved toward the two. "You." She pointed to Topher.

Both children stopped mid whatever they had been doing. Jane was still hanging onto Topher's arm. Topher was still on his tiptoes, holding the hammer out of reach.

"Is this your sister?" she asked pointing to Jane.

Looking a bit stunned, Topher nodded.

"You're lucky to have a sister. You should treat her as such."

"But—" Topher started. "She's a girl and this is construction work."

"And you've never seen a girl working in a construction site?" the stranger asked.

"*Englisch* ones. She's Amish."

The girl from downstairs shook her head sadly, as if there were no hope at all for a stupid boy like Topher. "Girls can work construction. Boys can cook. It's all good."

"You know a boy who cooks?" Topher scoffed, and with good reason, Johnny B thought; they had never seen a man in the kitchen. And up until recently, his *mamm* had been cooking for his great *grossdawdi*. They had *heard* about the man who cooked at the Italian restaurant in town, but he was not only *Englisch*, but Italian as well. And none of them had ever met him.

"My *dat*." She didn't even crack a smile, and Johnny B believed her. "My *mamm* died when I was little, and my *dat* has been cooking for me ever since. Don't tell him I said this, but I think he sort of likes it."

"But you need muscles to work construction."

"*Jah*, you do, but the only way to build up those muscles is to work. And she will never be able to if you don't give her a chance."

Johnny B wasn't sure what Topher heard in the girl's words, but his brother thought about it a moment then thrust the hammer toward his sister. "Here. Try it."

Delighted with the opportunity, Jane swung the hammer and knocked out a small section of the wall before handing it back to her brother.

"I just wanted to give it a try," she told him. "It looks like more fun than it really is."

Topher rolled his eyes at his sister's obvious stupidity and went back to chipping away at the wall.

Jane and the girl came back over to stand next to Johnny B's chair.

"What's your name?" he asked her as she stopped next to him.

"Evie," she said with a smile. "Evie Brenneman."

"Johnny B Lehman."

She continued to grin at him, not dumb-like, but almost shy. "I know who you are."

"You do?" he asked. How did she know who he was?

"I'm Jane," his sister butted in, jumping up and down to gain back the girl's attention.

Evie turned to the young girl. "Nice to meet you, Jane."

"He's Chris," Jane continued, pointing toward their brother. "He wants to be called Topher, but we all think it's a silly name."

"Maybe," Evie said. "But if that's what he wants to be called . . ." She ended with a small shrug.

Johnny B shook his head. "It's not about that. I never

wanted to be called Johnny B, but that's what I got stuck with."

She smiled at him. "Another Johnny in your family?"

He nodded. "My *dawdi*, but the thing is, he doesn't even live here. He lives in Oklahoma."

"But you have family here, *jah*?"

He nodded.

"And Oklahoma is a lot closer than Pennsylvania, *jah*?"

He nodded again.

"Then I would say that it's a good trade-off."

Johnny B had to wonder what she was talking about. A trade-off? "You don't have any family close?" he asked.

She shook her head. "Just me and my *dat*."

There were worse things, he knew. But if that was the problem you had to deal with, it was still your problem. At least that's what he thought, anyway. And at the mention of family, Evie Brenneman got a faraway look in her eyes. She missed them, Johnny B thought. And with as sweet as she was, he supposed they all missed her too.

When closing time for the bakery came around, Joy was almost terrified to go upstairs. Evie had come back down to the basement, talking of them tearing out part of the wall and letting Topher help. That in itself was terrifying. And that had been hours ago. She had no idea what she would find now. But she braced herself for the shock as she opened the door that led to the kitchen and crept toward the living room.

"Mamm." Leah stopped her just short of her goal, placing one hand on her arm. "We should invite Uriah to stay for supper, don't you think?"

"I'm not even sure he's still here," Joy replied. He should have left hours ago. At least that had been the plan.

He and Thomas Kurtz would take turns supervising the volunteers as well as the paid workers. Today was Thomas's day to stay at the house and make sure things went according to plan.

"But if he is," Leah pressed.

Joy nodded, feeling the first pangs of guilt. "If he is, then we'll invite him, But I don't think he will be."

Together the two of them made their way into the mess that had once been her living room.

Someone had moved all the boxes containing the not completely necessary things from the area into the space off the kitchen where the dining table usually sat. And thankfully they had moved the grandfather clock to the same space to protect it from the dust. And there was plenty of that.

"You missed it!" Jane was on her feet when she caught sight of her *mamm*. "They knocked down the wall, and Topher and I helped."

Chris frowned at his sister. "You didn't really do anything."

"*Jah*-huh. I did too. I hit it once and knocked out a big piece of wall." She pointed to the area, which was now covered with plastic.

Joy was grateful for that detail. She wasn't sure how she would have taken it if she had come up to a big hole in the side of her house. Well, she knew they were going to have to knock down part of her house, and she had been living with the sound of it all day long. For two days actually. But to see it was another matter altogether.

The plastic over the hole moved and bulged with the wind. Outside it was already dark, and all the men had gone home for the day, but she could still see a few shadows and lights moving around outside.

"Uriah said he taped the plastic up real good, but I might want to sleep in my long johns and a sock hat tonight."

Joy pulled a worried face. "Maybe you should take my bed tonight."

"What?" Johnny B demanded. "And have you sleep out here? No way. That's a dumb idea, Mamm."

It was an adventure to him. Somehow, through it all, this was the part that he was enjoying. Because he was getting his own space? Because he was trying to move on? She had no idea.

"Fine," she said. "You can sleep in your long johns and a sock hat. But you have to promise to call me if you get too cold."

"I will," he said. And she knew he wouldn't. For some strange reason he seemed to be enjoying this way too much.

"Joy."

She turned toward the door as Uriah came in.

Leah elbowed her in the side, a reminder of her promise to invite him to stay for supper.

"Would you like to stay for supper?" she asked, pondering a bit at the tremble in her voice. "It's the least we can do."

Honestly, she should have invited him every night for all that he had been doing for them, but she knew his answer before he even spoke.

"*Danki*," he said kindly. "But the girls are expecting me."

She nodded, wondering why she was so disappointed.

Because you enjoy having company around.

That was true. It was good to have a friendly face around and not just the worried ones belonging to her children. Truthfully *worried* wasn't right. Johnny B looked bitter.

Chris, er. . . . Topher looked angry. Leah had a perpetually expectant look, while Jane seemed as if nothing at all were out of sorts. That left Joy's face as the one covered in worry. She could feel it like a mask, hiding everything else behind it.

Leah elbowed her again.

"How about tomorrow?" Joy suggested. "Or the next day. That way you could give your daughters a fair warning and they wouldn't be worried about you."

"We won't take no for an answer," Leah chimed in.

Uriah chuckled. "I would like that very much."

"The day after tomorrow then," Leah confirmed.

Joy's tongue seemed to be welded to the roof of her mouth.

"Day after tomorrow."

Uriah opened the front door of his house just as the exhaustion set in. He must be getting old. He didn't used to get this tired over nothing. *Jah*, he had started his morning out at five a.m. at the lumberyard only to finish it up at six p.m. at Joy's house.

The renovations were coming along nicely. A couple more weeks and they should have most of it completed. It wasn't a complicated build, the biggest hurdle being the plumbing for the new bathroom and kitchen they were installing. But he had a connection with someone over in Paradise Hill who could help out, and was willing to do so at a reduced rate in order to help a needy family.

Everything else should come together just fine. As long as the weather held out.

For now, it was good to be home. He felt a little guilty walking into this neat-as-a-pin house. Rebecca and Rachel kept everything tidy, and the mess he had left at Joy's made him shiver.

What was the saying? *You can't make an omelet without breaking eggs?* The only problem was, Joy had never asked for anything to eat at all, and he was shoving an omelet at her with everything he had. Why?

He had no idea.

He took off his coat and hat and hung them next to the door. The house was warm, dinner smelled delicious, and the air buzzed with the camaraderie of his girls. He could hear them chattering away in the kitchen about this, that, and the other as they prepared the evening meal.

"Dat! You're home." Ruthie raced from where she was setting the table to launch herself into his arms. She was getting almost too big to do that, and he was dreading the day when that happened. He wasn't sure which of them would be the saddest to see the greeting go. Probably him, for she was his last. And she was so much like Dinah that it sometimes made his heart hurt just to look at her. In a good way, of course. He wished his wife were here to see herself in miniature.

Of all his girls, Ruthie was the one who took after their mother. All of them had one thing or another from their *mamm*. Rebecca got her clear gray eyes, Rachel got her dark hair, and Reena had the same single slashing dimple in her right cheek. But Ruthie . . . Ruthie was Dinah straight over again. Dark hair, gray eyes, pert nose, and a mouth that couldn't stop smiling. Not even if she tried. Of course, with that smile came the dimple that matched Reena's.

"Supper's almost ready," she said importantly as she slid to the ground once more.

"Smells *gut*,'" he told her. And it did.

That was another thing Ruthie had inherited from her

mamm: the ability to whip up a fantastic meal from nothing special at all.

Of course, Ruthie did more bossing around of her sisters than actual cooking. For some strange reason, they didn't mind. They did as she instructed and the meals came out great. As long as it was working for them . . .

But sometimes he worried about Ruthie. She seemed to be growing up too fast. And not just from a *vatter*'s perspective. She fretted over meals and the Bible reading they held each night—something they had started to do when Dinah was ill. Ruthie had been so small then, but somehow she remembered that time and was determined to keep it going. She was a little woman, commanding her sisters and making sure the house ran to her mother's standards.

And yet he didn't worry about her near as much as he did Reena.

Speaking of . . . she came down the stairs, her American Girl doll clasped in one hand. Today she had dressed her in a blue *frack*, cape, and apron the same color as the one that Reena was wearing, without a cape of course. A white prayer *kapp* was pinned to the golden blond hair that matched Reena's own.

Somehow Reena had managed to talk Rachel into sewing her doll a new dress from the scraps of material left over from when she made a dress for Reena. He supposed it was a good thing that Rachel liked to sew. She had been trying to teach Reena, but her sister was reluctant to give up her dolls in exchange for a sewing machine.

He sighed to himself. He was going to have to address the issue soon, but no one was getting hurt, and right then he simply didn't have the energy.

"What's for supper?" Reena asked, lifting her doll to cradle it next to her chest.

"Oven-roasted chicken and potatoes, green beans, and deviled eggs."

That was another thing. Ruthie loved deviled eggs and had to have them at least twice a week. She would prefer to have them more often, but her sisters put their foot down and limited it to twice.

"I like roasted chicken," Reena said.

"Me too," Uriah added. "Let's go wash up."

Reena deposited her doll in the chair next to the fireplace and together the three of them went to the kitchen to wash their hands and see if the other girls needed any help.

Rachel and Rebecca both fell strangely quiet. Like they had been discussing something they didn't want him to know about. Or maybe they didn't want their sisters to know. No, it was most likely him that they wanted to keep out of the loop. Which meant they were probably talking about boys, the singing coming up this weekend, and anything else dealing with friends, meetings, and the other fun times that teenagers lived for.

"How was your day, Rebecca?" he asked as he dried his hands.

"Fine," she replied.

He turned his attention to Rachel.

"I had a good day," she dutifully said.

Slowly the conversation started back up, mainly because Ruthie was a chatterbox and could carry on an entire discussion all by herself.

Together they carried the platters and bowls of food to the table. They sat, prayed, and started to fill their plates.

"This is really good, girls," he told them, taking another bite of the chicken.

"*Danki*," Ruthie said, with a small nod.

Rebecca playfully rolled her eyes. Uriah knew what it meant. Like Ruthie had done it all by herself.

Rachel chuckled and shook her head.

"It's nice to come home to a warm meal," he told them, thinking of Joy. She had Leah there to help, but they would be doing the cooking for their family after working all day and going to school. It was a hard life, he was sure, and he was truly blessed with kind and loving daughters.

"Speaking of which," he continued, "Friday night, I'm staying over at Joy's for supper."

All four of the girls stared at him in shock and disbelief. A person would have thought he had declared that they were leaving the Amish and moving to Alaska.

"We were just over there," Rachel said.

"I have plans," Rebecca said.

"It's crowded over there," Reena said.

"Do we have to?" Ruthie asked.

Uriah looked at them all for a moment, then decided to address them together, since one answer would take care of them all. He cleared his throat. Got a drink of water. "I don't believe that the invitation was for everyone."

"Just you?" Rebecca waited, open mouthed, for him to answer.

"I suppose so." He shrugged as if it was no big deal. "I mean, I can ask, if you want to come too."

"I don't want to," Ruthie said. "I like eating here."

"Me too," Reena added, though Uriah thought her desires had more to do with being close to her dolls than the food she was taking in.

"So you're going to be eating there?" Rachel asked.

"*Jah*," he said.

"Why?" Rebecca asked.

"I suppose she just wants to thank me for helping out at the house. You know, with all the renovations and things."

"I suppose," Rachel muttered darkly, though for the life

of him he couldn't figure out what they were so upset about.

"You shouldn't go," Rebecca told him sternly. "She has so much to do that she doesn't need to be feeding an extra mouth. It's not necessary."

"You're right," he told her, and for a moment he thought he saw her shoulders drop with . . . relief? "But she is insisting, and I have to allow her this." It was important to Joy, and he needed to give her the opportunity to express her gratitude. Whether it was necessary or not.

"I still think it's a bad idea," Rachel said.

"So you won't be here for supper?" Reena looked as if her entire world were caving in.

When was the last time he hadn't eaten supper with them? A while ago—a year, maybe two, and that time had been because of work. Sometimes the girls stayed with a friend and ate supper at the friend's house, but their father had always been a constant in their lives. He had designed it that way. Everything had turned upside down when Dinah had passed. For all the time they'd had to get used to the idea that she was dying, despite all the talk of God's will and accepting it with grace and a happy heart, the time had been hard for them all. Back then they had needed to know that he was there for them. And he had been. But now they were growing up. It wouldn't be long before Rebecca joined the church and got engaged. He didn't know of any boys who she had an interest in, but it was coming, he was sure. And Rachel was right behind her. The years would slip by quickly. And then what?

He didn't know.

"I won't be here for supper," he said, though his voice had a strange, strangled quality to it. "But your sisters will, *jah*?" He looked from Rebecca to Rachel.

"*Jah*," Rebecca said, albeit reluctantly.

"*Jah*," Rachel echoed.

"I thought you had plans." Rebecca pressed her sister with a sharp look.

Rachel shook her head. "I'm not going."

"Because I'm not going to be here?" he asked.

She shook her head and somehow looked close to tears. What was going on here? "I forgot it was cancelled."

He wasn't sure how much of that he believed, but he couldn't exactly call her out on it. So he nodded and turned back to the youngest two. "See?" he said, pasting on a smile that didn't quite fit. "Everyone will be here except me. And I bet y'all don't miss me at all."

Chapter 9

The unusual dinner conversation stayed with Uriah from the time they got up from the table until the time he actually pulled his buggy into the drive at the other Lehman house.

Things were really shaping up. Despite the colder-than-normal weather, they were making progress. It was cold, *jah*, but the sun was shining and the sky was clear. Not the best working-outside conditions, but not the worst either.

He swung down from his carriage and went over to the room to see what the others had gotten accomplished while he was working the previous day. Thursday had been Thomas's turn to supervise so that Uriah could be at the lumberyard, where he was needed. That way neither man had to take too much time off from their regular work, though things really slowed down for the both of them as the winter months settled in. And winter was definitely settling in he thought as he pulled his collar a little higher around his ears.

The frame was up and the decking on the roof. Tomorrow maybe they would be able to start on the walls. Today was all about plumbing and gas lines. But he had men coming out to help with that. Still, he would be around to make sure it all went according to plan.

"You're here."

He turned as Johnny B pushed his wheelchair through the front door. It was a close fit, and he had to propel himself forward using the sides of the doorframe as leverage. But he was getting around and that was good. At least now he could come out into the yard whenever he chose to. Might not make much difference now, but any freedom was better than none at all. Or so Uriah supposed. He had never been trapped inside a house. Unless you counted the time the valley flooded. Anyone who had a house on high ground had been spared the water damage, but that didn't mean they were able to go anywhere. If *Englisch* thought flooded streets were hazardous to a car, try driving a horse and buggy in three inches of standing rainwater.

But even that was nothing like what Johnny B was facing.

"You make it okay in the nights?" he asked the young man.

"Mamm dressed me in my long handles and let me sleep in my stocking cap. I was plenty warm." He grinned. "It felt a little like the time Dat took us camping."

Rudy had loved to go camping. Uriah had misplaced that memory of his brother. Not forgotten, just not brought forth in a long, long time.

"Maybe when the weather is a little warmer we can go again."

Johnny B's eyes lit up like the stars in the sky. "You mean that?"

Uriah nodded but backpedaled. "As long as your *mamm* says it's okay. I can't have her worrying about you."

Johnny B flicked one hand in Uriah's direction as if to

disperse the notion. "She's going to worry. We can't let that stop us."

"I suppose you're right about that. But we should at least ask her before we start making too many plans."

"Okay," Johnny B agreed.

It was the only thing Uriah missed, having only girls. He loved his ladies. They were everything to him. His world. But it would have been fun to have a little boy to roughhouse with, play ball, go fishing and camping. He had tried to take Rebecca fishing when she was little, but she was having none of it. She was a girly-girl through and through. Rachel had been the same, and Reena even a bit worse. Ruthie had been his one hope, but then Dinah had gotten sick, and he hadn't had the time or the heart in him to be away from her for too long when he didn't have to.

Perhaps he would wait until spring and see if Ruthie wanted to give fishing a try.

Or you can always take Johnny B and Chris . . . Topher.

And he could, he thought. It was just another way to honor his brother's memory. He made a mental note to take them fishing or camping or whatever else it was they wanted to do. He owed them that much.

"Is your *mamm* inside?" he asked Johnny B.

"She's down in the basement." He pointed to the ground as if that were accurate.

"Already?"

Johnny B nodded. "She's down there by four every morning."

Four. And he thought he got up early.

"Want me to call her?" Johnny B held up the baby monitor he had hidden at his side, between his leg and the chair.

"No, that's fine. I'll go down and see her in a bit."

"Okay, just don't tell her I have it with me, okay? She'll start thinking that she can call me all the time."

Uriah shook his head, hiding a smile as he did. "I won't say a word. Your secret's safe with me."

"Are you staying for supper tonight?" Johnny B asked.

Uriah nodded. "I had planned on it."

"Good," Johnny B said.

Uriah didn't ask him what he meant by that. He had something more pressing to ask. "I had thought that we might have pizza. That's what I was going to suggest to your *mamm*. Do you think she'll go for it?"

"I don't know what she'll think, but it sounds delicious to me."

Uriah couldn't help but grin at the boy's enthusiasm. "Okay then," he said. "We'll make it our mission to convince her."

Chapter 10

"Why does it seem so quiet?" Ruthie mumbled as she set the table for supper that Friday evening.

Rebecca shook her head. "It's not any quieter tonight than it is any other day." But it seemed that way to her as well. Because their *dat* wasn't home with his booming yet gentle voice and his big smile.

Reena sat down in her seat, still holding her American Girl doll as if it were a lifeline.

"Go put your baby doll in the living room," Rachel instructed as she placed the last dish on the table.

"It's not a baby doll," Reena shot back.

"Well, put it in the living room anyway," Rebecca countered. "It's time to eat."

Reena pouted a bit but did as she was told.

Rebecca couldn't hide her frown as she watched her sister take the doll into the other room. It was her constant companion, like a security blanket for a baby. Was that normal for a young girl to tote around a toy like that? She was twelve, almost a teenager, and yet she was acting younger than Ruthie.

Biting back a sigh, Rebecca lowered her head to indicate it was time to pray. But even as she closed her eyes, the words weren't there for her. It was usually easy to thank the Lord for blessings and food and all the good things that surrounded her. She was blessed; she knew that. But this time it was harder to find the gratitude. She missed her father. She missed him being there with them for their evening meal. He was always there. Always.

Except for tonight. Tonight he was over with Joy and her cousins. Rebecca understood that they wanted to thank him for everything he was doing for them. It was just the way things were done. But they had already had a meal together. Why did they need to do it again tonight? And why did they feel the need to only invite their father? Not that she wanted to go over to the chaos that was her aunt's house. Everyone was tense and angry. On edge. It was much more pleasant to be right where she was. But she wanted her father there with her as well.

The minute the thought jumped into her head, she wanted to destroy it. It was childish and mean. She shouldn't feel that way. But she did. She wanted—

A sharp pain seared through her lower leg. It came from her left. She peeked over and Rachel, hands folded on the table, gave her an expectant look.

It was long past time for the prayer to be over.

She cleared her throat and rustled around so the younger girls would know it was time to lift their heads.

Rachel's steady, probing gaze bore into her as she started dishing food onto her plate.

"Bec?" Her sister's tone was full of questions.

Rebecca shook her head. "I'm fine." But somehow she knew her sister didn't buy it, and that there would be more inquiries to come.

"I wonder what they're having at Joy's," Ruthie mused.

Rachel nodded toward the creamy beef casserole that

Ruthie had decided was that night's supper. "Probably nothing as good as this."

Ruthie beamed, which was just what Rachel had wanted.

"It's good," Reena agreed, taking a bite and nodding in satisfaction.

Everyone filled their plates and buttered their rolls and complimented Ruthie on a supper well done.

It was good to keep the child happy with praise. It kept her diligently helping in the kitchen so all the work didn't fall on the older girls. In truth, Rebecca thought that Ruthie actually liked to cook and boss them around. It didn't bother her as long as they all worked together, without her exclusively having to fill the position of *mudder*.

Of course she wasn't the only Amish girl in their district who had had to take on a mother's role early in life, but she had plans, and she didn't want to be worn out with the novelty of being grown up before she even got married. It could happen. It might happen. She just wasn't willing to take the chance. Not when they could all play a part in running the household.

But what of poor Ruthie? her conscience asked. She was eight going on twenty. How was she going to feel in another ten years? The chores had only fallen to Rebecca four years ago, and even then, her father took care of a lot of things. They had a great deal of practice; adjustments had occurred when their mother got sick. They'd had time to prepare, to reach a new, altered normal.

But she liked that normal. And it included having her father at home each night, sitting in his place opposite her at the rectangular table. Now all she saw was an empty seat, further reminding her that he was gone.

"You like him," Reena teased, bringing her out of her thoughts.

Rachel's face filled with color. She ducked her head, but not before her sisters saw.

"You do," Ruthie hooted. "But he's not cute."

"There's more to life than cute," Rachel muttered, but Rebecca was fairly certain she was the only one who heard.

"Who?" she asked, looking from Ruthie to Reena.

"Daniel Esh." Reena grinned as if she had revealed the world's best-kept secret.

"Of course she likes him; he's nice. Everybody likes him," Rebecca pointed out.

Ruthie shook her head at her sister's foolishness. "She likes him likes him."

"So what if I do?" Rachel raised her head. Her chin lifted and her brows raised as if asking what Ruthie was going to do about it.

Ruthie shrugged, possibly realizing that she had pushed her sister too far. "I don't care if you like him. But are you going to get married?"

Rachel rolled her eyes and turned her attention to Rebecca. The reprieve was just enough for her to regain her footing. "Sisters," she drawled, and then turned back to her two younger siblings. "We can't get married until we date, and we can't date until we join the church, and we can't join the church until we go through baptism classes. I just started running around." She shrugged, having recovered herself. She took a bite of roll and silently dared any of them to say anything else on the matter.

Reena watched the change in her sister and switched her attention to Rebecca. "And what about Adam?"

"What about him?" Rebecca tried her best to play it off. She hadn't been through classes yet either, so she and

Adam were not officially a couple. But unofficially . . . He was the sweetest, most handsome boy, and she couldn't wait to marry him, move out, and eventually start a family.

Then all this will be gone.

The little voice was sobering. It was what she wanted. She wanted to be free from some of the responsibility that dogged her. But then she wouldn't be sitting around the table talking about boys and teasing her sisters until they turned pink.

All in good time, she told herself. And when the time came for her and Adam to get married, which would be ages from now, she would have gotten all this out of her system. She would be ready to move on. Ready to start a new life.

It was weird to think about that, and in the next second dislike that her father wasn't there for their meal. Things were going to change, that was inevitable. But that didn't mean she had to let it all go now. Nope. For now she would do what she could to keep it all together.

"What's the plan?" Rachel sidled up next to Rebecca as she started filling the sink with water to wash the evening's dishes.

"I don't have a plan," Rebecca admitted. She had been trying to think of one for over a week, but nothing would come to her. Only that she needed to do something to stop whatever it was that was happening between her father and her aunt.

That sounded strange. Even though the two weren't related by blood, she had a hard time trying to wrap her mind around the fact that there could be a romance between the two of them. And it was so obvious that something was happening. All of a sudden there were new rooms being built and dinner invitations. How long would it be before Joy sank her claws into their father and claimed him as her own? What would happen to their family then?

Rachel looked at the clock hanging to the side of the refrigerator. It was almost eight. Eight o'clock! *It's eight o'clock; do you know where your* vatter *is?*

"I'll think of something," Rebecca promised.

Rachel nodded. "*Gut.* Just do it quickly."

"That was good. Right, Mamm?" Johnny B looked expectantly at her.

Joy stood and started gathering up their paper plates to take to the trash. That had been Uriah's idea. In fact, he had thought of everything. From pizza and breadsticks to paper plates and napkins for easier cleanup. "It was very good," she agreed, and it was.

Dinner had gone smoothly. Better than any dinner she could remember for a long time. Why was that?

Because she was less stressed because someone else had brought their food to them, and she and Leah weren't in the kitchen working away after baking and serving customers for hours downstairs? Or was it merely Uriah's calming presence?

Then that begged the question: Was it Uriah himself or just the fact that there was a man in the house?

Joy had no idea.

"I say we make Friday night pizza night," Johnny B proclaimed.

"I'll second that," Chris put in. He was the most content that Joy had seen him in months. He had eaten without fuss, had added to the conversation at the table, and not once had he corrected anyone over his name. At least not that she could recall. Truth was, she couldn't remember if anyone had actually spoken his name while they were eating, but the rest was there.

"We'll see." Joy nodded toward the pizza boxes. "Would you like to take any of that home?" she asked Uriah.

He patted his firm middle. Unlike most men nearing fifty, he wasn't growing overly thick around the waist. Probably because he was still so active. Yet some she had seen grew fat even with all the farm work and chores they performed each day. "I don't think so. You keep it."

"Too bad there's not enough to have for breakfast in the morning," Johnny B lamented.

Leah made a face. "Cold pizza? First thing in the morning?" She shuddered as she scooped up the boxes, stacking the one with slices still left inside on the top of the pile.

"You should try it," he said with a laugh.

"I think I would like pizza at any temperature and any time of day," Jane said. She bobbed back and forth in her chair, and Joy could tell she was swinging her legs, a sure sign that she was happy and content.

That had been the only thing missing from Jane's behavior since Johnny B's accident. In other ways she appeared as if everything was perfectly the same, but tonight she appeared happy. Truly cheerful. And for that Joy was grateful.

"Me too." She smiled as she agreed with her youngest.

"So what about it?" Chris asked. "Can Friday night be pizza night?"

"*Jah*," Jane chimed in. "And Uriah can come eat with us."

Joy sent her an apologetic smile. "I'm not sure Uriah wants to eat pizza every week."

Jane's sweet little face crumpled into a frown. "Why not?" She turned to her uncle. "Don't you like pizza?"

He nodded, his expression serious. "Of course I do."

"Then you'll come." This from Johnny B.

"Hold your horses a second here," Joy cut in. She kept her tone light, but she had to put the brakes on this conversation before it completely got out of hand. "I'm sure Uriah appreciates your generous offer, but he has his own family that might want to have him for their own pizza night on Fridays."

"But Mamm," Jane cut in. "This allows us to thank him every week."

"And we don't always have to have pizza," Chris added. "I like takeout Chinese too."

Joy looked to Uriah for help. It was kind of her children to want to spend time with their uncle. It was sweet of them to invite him to a weekly supper. And she liked the idea of a Takeout Friday, when she could rest up a little for the busy Saturday that loomed ahead. But every protest she could come up with, one of her four children seemed able to deftly counter . She needed backup, and fast.

Uriah cleared his throat and sat up a little straighter in his seat. "I wouldn't mind a Friday night supper. We might need to invite the girls, though. If that's all right. My treat."

But Joy was already shaking her head. "You can't buy supper for ten people every week."

"I can if I want to."

"Uriah," she breathed his name, somewhere between a sigh and a plead for sanity. For him to show sanity.

"Yes!" Chris pulled a fist pump and then gave a high five to his brother. She couldn't remember the last time she had seen them this excited. And with all the heartache that they had all been faced with, she wasn't able to squash it.

"I suppose," she relented.

"Awesome," Leah said, giving a knowing nod to her

sister. Then she took the empty pizza boxes into the kitchen to the trash. Joy finished gathering up the paper plates and carted them off to the kitchen as well.

She started to get out a baggie to store the leftover pizza, but Leah shooed her away. "Go visit with Uriah," she told her mother.

Joy wasn't sure she liked the spark she saw in her daughter's eyes.

"You know he's just being kind to us because your father was his brother."

"I know." But that gleam said otherwise.

"Leah . . ."

Her daughter shrugged as if it were no big thing. "It's just nice, you know? The boys seem to really like him. Johnny B almost looks happy. Sometimes, anyway, and—"

"And he's their uncle and will always be. Uriah will always be a part of their lives. That doesn't mean there needs to be any more to it than that."

"*Jah*, Mamm." But her posture slumped as she said the words.

Joy patted her on the shoulder and went back to the table. She had worked hard for her independence. When Rudy had died, she could have remarried. She loved her husband, and she missed him. However she wouldn't say that they were meant only for each other. So *jah*, she could have remarried and found a man that could take care of her and the children. But she hadn't wanted that. She had loved her husband and lost him. She wasn't up for that kind of loss again. So she worked hard to find her way.

Uriah was a good man, but that didn't mean any more than that. Paradise Springs—in fact all of Paradise Valley— was full of good men. But she was an independent Amish woman, and she planned to stay that way.

"Where's your uncle?" she asked as she entered the living room once more. A fire blazed in the fireplace, but still there was a chill in the air. Uriah had told them at supper that he hoped that by the end of next week they would have the room closed off enough that the living room wouldn't be so cold. She hoped he was right about that. Of course, it didn't help at all that the weather had turned so cold this week. The frigid air seemed to slow everything down. Fewer people came to help, and everything that did get accomplished seemed to take twice as long as usual. Such was life. As soon as you got going good—road block, speed bump, curve in the road.

"Out on the front porch having a smoke," Johnny B said.

"In this weather?" Joy asked, though she really didn't expect him to answer.

Johnny B just shrugged.

Joy grabbed her shawl off the back of her dining chair and wrapped it around herself. "Chris, go take a bath."

"Topher," he corrected.

So they were back to that.

"Go on with you." She shooed him toward the stairs and made her way out onto the porch.

The warm scent of pipe tobacco colored the cold night air.

"It's a bad habit, I know," he intoned before she could say a word.

"I'm not going to fuss about it." She wrapped her shawl a little tighter around herself and stopped next to him. She had forgotten that Uriah smoked a pipe. There weren't many opportunities these days to witness it. She supposed that he had waited for the drive home to light up last week. But she liked the sweet scent. Somehow it was comforting and familiar. Rudy had never indulged, but she could remember being out with Uriah and Dinah and his smoking back then. Perhaps that was where the warm fuzzies were coming from.

"I don't know if it was the fact that I didn't have to cook after being on my feet all day long or if it was the wonderful company, but that was the best meal I've had in a long time."

He chuckled as the gray smoke circled around his head, partially hiding his expression, or at the very least disguising it. "The company was good for sure, but I'm fairly certain it had more to do with the not having to cook it yourself that made it so tasty."

"Hm-mm . . ." She wasn't sure she one hundred percent agreed with him on that one. "*Danki* for having supper with us," she said. "And buying pizza and agreeing to come back on Friday." *And making my children smile again.*

"You're welcome. I'm happy to do it."

A mantle of comfortable silence settled around them as they stared out in the direction of the darkened barn. The wind rustled the leaves on her big tree at the side of the house. What leaves were left on it anyway, dried and brown. The only other sounds were the low murmur coming from the house and the crackle of fire and tobacco from his pipe bowl.

It was nice—beyond nice to stand there with him, connected but separate. Familiar and comfortable.

But it was cold. If she'd donned her coat instead of her thin, crocheted shawl, she could have stayed with him like that forever. Well, a long time at least. But as it was, her teeth started to chatter as the wind picked up.

"You should go back inside where it's warm," he told her.

She needed to, but she didn't really want to. She nodded. "You coming?"

"I'll be there in a minute," he told her.

"How about a couple of hands of Rook?" she invited.

"I should be getting home," he protested.

"It's not going to get any darker," she told him. "Even if you stay for another hour."

He grinned at her, and she felt the action to the tips of her toes. "Well, when you put it like that . . ."

Chapter 11

"I should be going," Uriah told Joy, nodding toward his buggy.

It was getting late. Well, late for Joy. And most likely late for him as well. They were both early birds.

But she had talked him into a hand of Rook that turned into three games, and now it really was getting late. Still, it was hard to walk away and abandon the success that the night had been. She wanted to keep it forever. At least until tomorrow. Her children had all been happier than she had seen them in a long time, and she wanted to hold that as long as she could.

"You have to get up early in the morning," he continued.

"As do you," she said in return.

But still neither of them made a move.

"How are you doing, Joy?" he asked quietly. "And I don't want the answer you give when someone else is listening. This is me and you. I've known you most of my life."

They had known each other forever. They had gone on double dates together—her with Rudy and he with Dinah. They had shared family meals, weddings, births, deaths, and a whole lot more.

She looked into his green eyes and the caring she saw there nearly took her breath away.

"My life is just a series of events known as God's will. But I'm all right. Hanging in there."

"It'll be better soon," he promised. "When we get the *dawdihaus* finished. And not just because we'll be out of your way, but because Johnny B will have freedom of movement. He'll be able to care for himself. That will take so much from your shoulders. That's why I'm doing this, you know. To help with the burden."

She had been doing and caring and running everything by herself for so long that she had forgotten what it felt like to have someone there other than her daughters to lend a hand.

Joy's palm itched to touch his face, run her fingers down his rusty blond beard. But that action was too familiar. It was the touch of a wife to a husband when they were alone. Not that of a sister-in-law to her brother-in-law. Not at all.

She pulled her shawl a little tighter around her to keep her hands busy with something other than reaching for him like some love-starved newlywed.

He took a step away from her.

Could he feel her emotions? Her thoughts? She had to get a handle on herself. She couldn't go around like this. What was wrong with her today?

She missed it, she realized. She missed the companionship of a husband and helpmate. She missed having someone to share her day with, to talk to when the lights were out. To sleep next to and take comfort in their steady breathing all through the night. She didn't just miss Rudy; she missed all that he gave her as well.

"Good night, Joy." Uriah took another step away, then turned and made his way down the ramp.

"Good night," she said after she finally found her voice, but he was already striding away toward the barn to retrieve his horse.

She didn't wait for him to hitch up his buggy and leave. For some reason she couldn't stand the thought of watching him go. She told herself it was the cold that chased her inside, but it was something else. Something more.

Her hands shook as she turned off all the lights. Johnny B was already in bed, his body facing the wall with the large cutout sealed with a thick plastic sheet.

She moved quietly through the house. It was quiet and dark and lonely. That last word nearly stopped her feet. When had it turned lonely? She couldn't pinpoint the exact time. Maybe around the time that Jane had started school. Definitely after Johnny B had come home from the hospital. Somewhere in there, the house had grown lonely. Even with four children underfoot.

She brushed her teeth and brushed her hair, putting it into a ponytail for the night. She donned her pajamas and crawled into bed. Then Joy Lehman, for the first night in a long time, cried herself to sleep.

Rebecca looked at the clock for the umpteenth time since the kitchen cleanup. She couldn't even pay attention to the Bible reading. She would need to be extra diligent tomorrow in both her prayer and her study. Thank goodness Sunday was a church day. She really needed to get herself back on track.

"What do you suppose he could be doing?" Rachel muttered where only Rebecca could hear.

At least Rebecca thought she was the only one who heard Rachel's question. She hoped she was anyway. She didn't want the younger girls to get into a tizzy over whatever was happening between their father and their aunt.

"He's just being kind," she murmured in return, trying to convince herself as well. Their father was a very kind man. It was his nature to care for others. For him to change would alter who he was at his center, and they couldn't ask him to go against that.

"I thought you were worried about her trying to marry him," Rachel shot back.

"Who's getting married?" Ruthie asked.

That girl had ears like a . . . like a . . . well, like something that could hear really well. With all these other thoughts running around in her head, Rebecca couldn't think of one creature with that ability. That was how badly this whole thing was affecting her.

"Henry King and Millie Bauman, for one," Rebecca managed to shoot back.

"I so love little Linda Beth," Reena cooed. "She's like a living breathing doll."

She was cute and sweet and babbling and fun, and Rebecca was glad that talk of the baby was keeping her sisters from asking more questions about her almost-private conversation with Rachel.

"Where's Dat?" Reena asked. "He's coming home tonight, right?"

Spoke too soon.

"He's coming home," Rachel said, then added for Rebecca's ears only, "I hope."

"Will he be here before bedtime?" Reena looked at the clock doubtfully.

"I think so, *jah*." Rebecca said the words, then her confidence plummeted. "But if he's not, I'll tuck you in, okay?"

Reena slightly pouted but gave a small nod. "I guess so."

"Now," Rebecca stood and clapped her hands together. "The two of you need to go get ready for bed."

"And then Dat will be home?" Ruthie asked hopefully.

All Rebecca could do was cross her fingers and wave them both up the stairs. It was getting late, and though tomorrow was a Saturday, they would have to get up and go into the lumberyard. Rebecca logged all the week's orders, and Rachel filed all the invoices while their *dat* worked the front counter. When the town library opened, Reena and Ruthie walked down to look at books and whatever exhibits were on display for the week. There were even art classes and other activities that they could do. But the two hours between the time they got to the lumberyard and when the library doors were unlocked were some of the longest that Rebecca had ever lived through. The empty time left too much room for sisterly squabbles and hurt feelings. It wasn't always like that though.

Only since their mother died had they been pressed into going with their father and helping out. It wasn't that they minded the work or assisting in any way possible. Their father was a *gut* man, and they both loved helping him. It just would have been a lot easier if he hired someone to do this during the week and left the girls at home to clean and get ready for church the following day.

"Now what?" Rachel asked once the younger girls disappeared upstairs to get ready for bed.

"Shhh . . ." Rebecca cocked her head to one side and listened once more. "I think he's home." She nearly sighed with relief. But she couldn't let herself get too far ahead of where she was. Not until he walked in the front door. It was ten minutes before that happened, and this time Rebecca did sigh. He was home.

"Dat." Rachel was on her feet in an instance. "Did you have a good time?"

He smiled, and Rebecca wasn't sure she liked the look of it. It was too . . . content. Too happy. Too much like a man who was falling in love. She wondered if Rachel saw it as well. "We had a great time. And guess what? We've decided to make Friday nights family takeout night at their house."

Rebecca blinked. "At Joy's house?"

"Every Friday?" Rachel seemed to be having just as much trouble processing it.

"*Jah*. It'll be fun. Everyone's invited. We'll use paper plates and cups so there's no cleanup. And then we can play games afterward. As a family."

Rebecca swallowed the lump that was quickly forming in her throat. As a family? Just what had happened tonight? "Is that what y'all did?" she asked. "Play games and eat takeout?"

He nodded. "It was great fun. I think all y'all are going to love it."

"What if . . ." Rachel stopped. Rebecca was certain her sister had been about to say, *What if we don't want to go?* but stopped herself just in time. "What if we get invited to go somewhere else? I mean, it's a Friday night. In the spring my youth group will be going overnight camping and stuff."

"We can cross that bridge when we get there. But for now, every Friday night, okay? You're going to have such a great time."

* * *

"You have to do something," Rachel said as they lay in their beds that night.

Rebecca turned over in the darkness to face her sister. "What do you expect me to do?"

"I don't know. You said you would come up with a plan."

That was turning out to be harder than she had anticipated. "Well, I haven't yet."

"Obviously," Rachel grumbled.

"Why don't you come up with a plan?" Rebecca punched back.

"You're the oldest."

"Like that matters."

In the darkness she heard her sister harrumph in reply.

They fell silent for a moment.

"Maybe we should warn him that she's out to get him," Rebecca finally said.

"For a husband?"

"It's obvious, isn't it?"

"I don't think she wants him for support. You know, money," Rachel said in the darkness.

Rebecca silently agreed. Joy Lehman's bakery was very successful. She didn't need their father's support, at least not financially. Not as far as Rebecca could see. So she was after him for something else.

"She needs him for a father." The words almost surprised Rebecca, even though she was the one who said them.

"A father? Doesn't she have a father? He lives in Oklahoma."

"Not for herself," Rebecca retorted. "For her children. You saw how they were at supper. Chris kept arguing to be called a different name, and Johnny B is . . ." Well, Johnny B was obviously angry. Understandably so, but still. They were Amish. They pulled themselves up and moved forward. They had been doing that for hundreds of years.

"The other two seemed okay," Rachel said.

"The youngest kept acting like nothing was wrong, and Leah, the oldest, she kept running back and forth to the kitchen like she was the *mamm*. I don't think that's good, do you?"

"I suppose not."

"Then Joy herself," Rebecca added.

"What about her?"

"She was practically dead on her feet. You didn't see how tired she looked?"

Across the room the covers rustled, and Rebecca knew that her sister had shrugged, even if she couldn't see her. "I guess so."

"She's exhausted," Rebecca said. "It's no wonder, really, what with all she has to face in a day." Rebecca turned it all over in her head. Johnny B so sullen and mad. Chris also sullen, also mad. Leah running around like a little *mamm*, trying her best to make everyone happy. And Jane, the little one, acting as if nothing at all were out of place.

"I guess that makes sense," Rachel replied.

Then the awful truth struck her. "Dat's building a room onto their house."

"I thought it was a *dawdihaus*," her sister countered.

"That's even worse."

"What do you mean?"

"That room—*dawdihaus*—is where Johnny B will stay, right? Because he needs all the special things that Dat is installing. And the doctors say he won't walk again."

"Joy seems to think that he will."

"Joy is kidding herself," Rebecca said crossly. "It's been a long time since the accident, and if he hasn't gotten the feeling back in his legs already, then it's a fair possibility that he never will. He'll probably live at home for the rest of his life. And do you know what that means?"

"No."

"It means that if the two of them get married, we'll all be moving in there."

Uriah got ready for bed, a mysterious smile twitching on his lips. Why did he suddenly feel like smiling? Maybe because he was doing things that were making a difference in Joy's life. He needed this. He needed to help her. It was good for his soul to offer something to her without asking for anything in return.

But somehow he knew it was more than that.

Standing there on the porch with her, he'd had the strangest urge to lean in and kiss her. Which was beyond crazy. It was plain unacceptable. A man didn't just go around kissing women all willy-nilly. Most couples had rarely even kissed before they got married. And he certainly wasn't marrying his brother's widow.

So why the desire to reach out and touch her?

They had a connection, *jah*. But it wasn't that kind of connection. Maybe he had been alone too long. Paul was clear in Corinthians I when he said it was better to marry than to burn with passion. Was he burning with passion?

Burn was a strong word. And passion was too. Uriah enjoyed spending time with Joy and her kids. He felt he made a difference there.

And what of your own children?

True, his children were still adjusting to the loss of their mother. He supposed that was life—one big adjustment. But he thought they were doing well. They were surviving and carrying on. Better than Joy's kids for sure.

That wasn't to say that he didn't worry about Ruthie trying to mother everyone and Reena's insistence on playing with toys that weren't exactly for her age group. Rebecca and Rachel still had their American Girl dolls in their rooms, but they didn't dress them every day. At least not any longer. There had been a time when they had, but they had grown out of it. Reena would too, he was sure. And those dolls were expensive. So it was good that she was getting his money's worth from it, *jah*?

He undressed and pulled on the cotton knit shirt and drawstring pants that he slept in. The house was quiet. The girls had all gone to bed just after he arrived back at the house. He had gotten a drink of water and taken his blood pressure medicine, then brushed his teeth. He was getting old. Blood pressure medicine. Who knew that was going to strike? It was all under control now, but taking a daily pill made him feel decrepit. Even when he told himself that growing old was a privilege, and he believed it, that little white pill taunted him every day. It served to remind him of the fragility of life and the certainty of death. Not that he needed any reminders, but there it was, waiting for him each night before bed.

Uriah pulled back the covers and slid into bed, settling the quilt high on his neck and shoulders. It was a cold night, and it was only going to get colder. He hoped Johnny B had enough blankets to combat that big hole in the wall. Next week they would install the door to the room, and that would help. Then soon, he hoped, they would be able to move him into the space.

The next day was Saturday, and he wouldn't be going over to Joy's to work. He had to catch up things at the lumberyard. He had a few workers going to Joy's house, and Thomas said he would stop by for a bit just to make sure everything was going smoothly.

It was kind of sobering to think that he wouldn't see Joy tomorrow. He had seen her every day that week. He had gone downstairs one day and sat with her while he ate his lunch. She was taking bites between customers and the constant in and out of the oven with cookies. He didn't know how she managed to get a bite in with everything she did.

He meant what he'd told her this evening about helping her, needing to take some of the weight from her shoulders. He meant every word.

But he wouldn't see her tomorrow. He wouldn't get to see her again until Sunday. At church. Now that thought brought the smile directly to his lips. And he fell asleep thinking about Sunday.

Chapter 12

"He's been over there every day this week," Rachel reminded Rebecca the following Friday as they headed to their aunt's house.

"Shhh." Rebecca tossed a look over her shoulder, then turned back to Rachel. "Don't be loud." But the horse hooves clopped as they rode along and thankfully that noise mixed with the whir of the steel-rimmed wheels on the pavement and the chatter about the upcoming Christmas pageant floating in from the back seat, she knew her two younger sisters weren't paying them any mind.

She also knew that the current state of listening and not listening could change in a second.

"Every day," Rachel repeated.

Rebecca didn't need reminding. She had lived it right alongside her sisters. For the past four days, their father had not only been to Joy's house working on the new addition to the home each day, but he had stayed for supper as well.

Now it was Friday, and they all were headed over for the takeout and game night.

Rebecca was aggravated over having to go. Why should she give up her Friday night to a family dinner when half the family wasn't like family-family? Or maybe she just resented being eighteen and having to do this instead of something she wanted to do. But she had no plans, and that had been the agreement with her father. Still.

"I know, Rachel," she huffed in return.

"And we're going to play board games?" Rachel shuddered. "I don't even play board games with my own siblings."

That was because no one in the house played them at home. Rebecca played them when she was out with her friends, but not the kind she would have played with her siblings. If they played at all. As it was, Reena was more interested in her dolls and Ruthie was more into bossing everyone around.

"We have to do this for Dat," Rebecca told her sister.

It was what she kept telling herself. Somehow coming over here helped their *dat*. Even though it seemed he was working twice as hard because he was going to the lumber-yard during the day then working in whatever daylight was left after that. Not that there was much. And then he stayed for supper and came home smiling. Smiling!

Though it was *gut* to see him smiling about anything, it was troublesome to see him smiling over that. He was being manipulated, though he couldn't see it. And Rebecca worried that eventually he would be trapped and unhappy when the truth finally came out. That Joy just wanted him for a father to her children.

"Pay attention tonight," Rebecca told Rachel.

"To what?" her sister asked.

"Everything. Anything. We have to find something about her that will show him her true colors. Once we have that, we can make sure it doesn't go any further than him building this addition onto her house."

* * *

Something was up.

Joy could almost sense it in the air.

On the surface everything seemed just like it should. Uriah's girls had arrived just in time to settle in and play a hand of Dutch Blitz with Jane. Actually it was Ruthie, Reena, and Rebecca who got down on the floor in front of the fireplace and waited for their hand to be dealt.

"Where's Dat?" Rachel asked, looking around the crowded front room as if he were lurking in a corner, ready to spring out and surprise everyone.

"He's gone to get the food."

Joy had called from the bakery phone to place an order with Paradise Chinese Buffet for takeout. Thankfully they were more than just a buffet and also offered New York–style menu options. Joy wasn't entirely sure what New York had to do with it, but she did love General Tso's chicken and fried rice. But she had ordered more than that. Uriah was picking up several entrees along with fried rice, steamed rice, and lo mein. She'd also ordered spring rolls, wontons, and steamed dumplings. She had no idea what anyone would want to eat. This way they got a little bit of several things. That was the other problem: She had to make sure she had at least ten of those single items. Ten dumplings, ten spring rolls, ten wontons, and so forth. She just hoped that she had ordered enough of the entrees to satisfy all tastes. It was a challenge to feed so many, especially when she didn't know what half of them even liked to eat. But who didn't like sweet and sour chicken?

She pulled in a deep breath and held it for a moment to keep her swirling thoughts from completely getting out of hand. She was nervous about tonight.

Why? Because she wanted Uriah and his children to have a good time at this first Friday night get-together? *Jah*, she wanted everyone to have a good time.

Even though she had bought an extra deck of Dutch Blitz, it remained unopened. Chris held back, determined to be above all the fun. Leah, of course, was in the kitchen making drinks for everyone. If she kept this up, she could go to work at one of those *Englisch* party planners in town. She would be an expert by age thirteen. And Johnny B couldn't very well climb out of his chair and sit on the floor like the other children. Not yet anyway. So he watched from his perch in his wheelchair, slowly getting into the game as Jane quickly took the lead.

What Joy really wanted to know was Rachel's reason for remaining aloof. She stood over the others, watching the game closely. At least she looked like she was watching; she had her head down as if studying what was going on at her feet, but Joy could see her eyes dart around from time to time as if she were trying to gauge her surroundings and not let anyone know. Had Rachel been reluctant to come? She was sixteen and running around. Joy hoped that her father hadn't made her miss some big something by coming here tonight. It was a little early for Christmas parties, but Joy had been hearing talk of something new called Friendsgiving, where friends got together to celebrate Thanksgiving like a family would. Truthfully, it sounded like great fun, and with the real Thanksgiving coming up the following week, it was possible that Rachel's youth group might have hosted some event tonight.

Joy should talk to the girls the first chance she got and make sure they knew: This Friday supper was all about fun and family and not about missing things that were important to the people who were invited.

Leah bustled out of the kitchen carrying a tray of drinks. Joy had picked up a few two liters of flavored soda at Buster's the last time she'd been in town. They didn't normally serve such sweet drinks, and especially not with a meal, but this was a special occasion, like a party, and they should have something special to go along with it.

Everyone cheered as Jane took a bow. Apparently she had won the first round of Blitz. Perhaps Joy should turn this into a fun competition with little prizes for the winner and an overall prize each week. Just something more to add to the party atmosphere.

You're just trying to get all the children involved, a little voice inside her chided. *Leave them alone and let them come when they are willing.*

Good advice. She just had to heed it.

"Anybody hungry?" Uriah came in through the front door, a large, full sack in each hand. The plastic over the new doorway billowed as he nudged the door behind him closed with his foot.

"Chris, go take care of your uncle's horse real quick. Then come back in and eat." Joy nodded toward the front door.

"Topher." She knew he said the word automatically these days, but still it bothered her. She had named him Chris after her father. Why couldn't he just accept the name she had given him and live life? Chris wasn't a bad name.

"Chris, please." She wasn't up for arguments tonight.

He raised his chin.

She sighed. "Topher, go take care of your uncle's horse."

For a moment she thought Chris was going to protest, even though she had caved to his demand.

Then Uriah stepped in, setting the food on the table and catching Joy's eye. "Let's eat first. I put the food in the cooler for the trip back here, but it's only just over thirty degrees out there. We need to eat before it gets too cold to enjoy."

Joy nodded, secretly thankful that the crisis was averted.

Yet that's what her life seemed to consist of those days, one crisis after another. Small, large, medium. Every day. Drama, drama, drama. It was wearing her down, despite all her prayer and positive thoughts. And she was very thankful to have Uriah there to help her untangle some of the little snarls.

If only she could figure out the rest.

"I thought you were going to do something to try and break this up," Rachel said into the darkness.

Rebecca sighed. She had known this was coming. She had been expecting it ever since she had knelt down on the floor and started playing cards with her sisters and her cousin Jane. She could almost feel Rachel's eyes boring a hole in her back as she stood over them and pretended to watch the play.

Rebecca didn't know for a fact that Rachel had been pretending, but she didn't need to see it for it to be true. Her sister was even more worried about their father than she herself was. But only by a small measure.

"I'm thinking."

Rachel let out a small unladylike growl. "Think harder. Did you see him at supper?"

She had seen him. How could she have missed him? Showing their cousins how to hold chopsticks and eat with them. Rebecca hadn't even known that her father knew how to eat with chopsticks. Okay, so he had been showing all of them, but she couldn't help but notice how Joy's children reacted to her father. The same way the other children did. Everyone laughed as he worked the sticks like the mouth of an alligator.

Well, everyone but Rachel. Her sister had merely smiled just a bit, but Rebecca caught sight of it. It was forced, wobbly, and fragile. Rachel was upset. And Rebecca supposed she had a reason to be. Her sister had looked hurt. Not in her smile, but in her green eyes, so like their father's. She was hurt by the fact that he was sharing something with Joy's children at the same time as he was sharing with his own. That meant he'd had the knowledge all the while. So why hadn't he shared it with Rachel and her sisters long before now?

Why did they have to share that experience with their cousins? Somehow it made the whole night seem watered down.

"He's falling in love with her," Rachel said into the darkness.

"He's just being kind," Rebecca countered. But she had seen the way her father's eyes had lit up when he came in with the food. He was falling in love. And not just with Joy, but with her entire family as well.

Rebecca knew her father. She was old enough to see the writing on the wall, as they say. He had strong familial ties and wholly embraced the Amish beliefs of family and community. He hadn't done much for Joy and her brood in the past few years. She could remember some of the things that he had done back when her uncle had died. She remembered her mother telling someone that her father was going over to help turn Joy's basement into a bakery.

But she couldn't remember any of the particulars. Just that it was. And it is.

The bakery.

"Rachel," she breathed quietly in the darkness. "I know what we're going to do."

"Joy?"

She whirled around, a little stunned to be caught lurking in her own thoughts when she had a business to run.

"Hi, Rachel." She pressed a hand to her heart as she greeted Uriah's second oldest daughter. "Rebecca. I didn't expect to see you here today."

The girls shared a look. They were so close in age, a fact that made Joy a little sad for her own daughters. Her girls and her boys were split in ages, with larger gaps between them. These girls were just a couple of years apart. Each one most probably couldn't remember life without the other. To have that closeness . . .

"We came to ask if you were still looking for help here in the bakery."

"I've hired one person." Evie. Who was never around when the baking began. The young girl seemed to disappear upstairs for long periods of time. Joy had no idea what she was doing up there. Unfortunately Joy had a lot on her mind these days and seemed to lose track of her part-timer every shift.

"Oh." Rachel and Rebecca shared another look.

"What about just for the holidays?" Rebecca asked. "Are you looking for seasonal help?"

That wasn't a half bad idea. At least she would have someone in the bakery when she needed them. "Do you know someone who needs a job?"

Another look passed between the two girls.

"*Jah*," Rebecca said. "Us."

It might have been the last thing Joy had expected for them to say. Her brows raised. Were they serious?

"You're serious?" She looked from one of them to the other.

They nodded solemnly. Then both turned to the other and smiled. "*Jah*. We'd love to work here."

"What about the lumberyard?" Joy asked. The girls usually worked at the lumberyard, in the office. At least that's what Joy had always believed.

"Well," Rebecca started with a shrug, "it's not a straight-paying job, if you know what I mean."

Joy did. She didn't always give Leah a set salary but made sure her daughter had whatever money she might need for anything that cropped up.

"There's something that we want to buy for Dat," Rachel chimed in. "And if we ask him for money . . ." She trailed off expressively.

"You want to keep it a surprise," Joy guessed.

Rebecca smiled in apparent relief. "*Jah*. For Christmas."

Christmas was just around the corner. Another reason why Joy needed more help. Special orders were already coming in. Plus the fact that she had her own shopping to do. Without extra help there wouldn't be a holiday to speak of in their house. Having not one but two ready helpers—plus Evie—was more than she would have dared asked for herself.

She looked at both girls in turn. "When can you start?"

"Good news," Joy said over supper that night. Her attention was trained on Leah, so the boys paid no mind.

"What's that?" her oldest daughter asked.

"I hired two more helpers for the bakery. That should get us through Christmas just fine."

"Good, good," Leah said. She smiled and took another bite of her peas.

Joy could only thank the good Lord for watching out for her and sending Rebecca and Rachel to help. After the holiday was over, she wasn't certain she could use both of them, but she was open to considering the option. After all, that would take a little bit from Leah's shoulders as well as her own.

"Who is it?" Leah continued, turning most of her attention to slathering butter on a piece of bread—some of the same bread that Joy had baked that afternoon while Evie was out running around doing only heaven knew what instead of working.

"Rebecca and Rachel Lehman."

Leah's gaze immediately raised to hers. "Our cousins?"

"That would be them." Joy stopped, considered it all for a moment. "They're going to work Tuesdays and Thursdays," she explained. "So after the holidays I may just let Evie go and keep on one of them."

"No!"

Joy's attention swung to her oldest.

Johnny B was slouched down in his chair earlier but now was sitting up straight, leaning toward her with an urgent look on his face. "You can't let her go."

She smiled at her son. "Actually I can. Every time I need her, it seems like she's never in the bakery. I don't know where she gets off to." It wasn't like the bakery basement was that big, but somehow between customers and checking timers, Evie just managed to disappear.

"You shouldn't let her go," Johnny B said. "She's a sweet girl."

"That she is." Joy turned back to her meal, though she had a feeling now where Evie was getting off to, and it had nothing to do with baking.

* * *

Uriah raised his head after the prayer and immediately reached for the pork chops. Around him the girls started chattering away as they always did. It was good to be home.

Joy had invited him to supper again tonight, but he had to turn her down. As much as he enjoyed spending time with her and her children and as much as he knew he needed to spend the little more time with them than he had in the past years, he also had his own family to think about. He had been away far too much lately.

"Guess what," Rebecca said. She leaned forward, her eyes bright.

His heart gave a hard pound in his chest. This was it. She was going to tell him that she and Adam were getting married. Not that they could be official yet since neither had joined the church. But they could speak for one another, announce their intentions before actually becoming engaged. "What?" he managed to say.

"Tomorrow Rachel and I start at the bakery."

It took him a second to assimilate those words and turn into something that made proper sense. Not that her words themselves were confusing. His head had just been in a totally different place and now he had to get his thoughts on a different track to figure out exactly what she was telling him.

"Bakery?" he asked. "What bakery?" Not that there were so many in Paradise Springs, mind. But he still had to ask.

"Joy Lehman's bakery," Rachel said.

That was what he thought she was going to say. "That's a lot of work for you two."

Rebecca shook her head, and Rachel followed suit. "Not so much," Rebecca replied. "We are only going to be there on Tuesdays and Thursdays. That leaves plenty of time to do your books on Saturday morning."

He couldn't argue with that. "If this is about money, I can give you some." He set down his fork and started to reach for his wallet.

Rachel and Rebecca shared a look that he had no idea how to decipher.

Rebecca turned back to him. "It's not about money."

"Then what's it about?"

Rebecca gave a loose shoulder shrug. "Well, I guess it's about the money, a little. I mean, I'd like to have the money. But I want to earn it." She scrunched up her face into a sort of confused scowl. "Does that make sense?"

Hardly. But who was he to argue with the minds of women? "If you're sure," he said. "I don't want you guys to get worn out."

They both shot him matching sweet smiles. "We won't," Rachel assured him.

Uriah nodded, not entirely certain. But they were young, and they would bounce back if they got too tired over the next few weeks. Instead of protesting further, he turned to Reena and Ruthie. "You girls need to come straight home from school on Tuesdays and Thursdays."

"We will," Reena said.

"We promise," Ruthie added.

It would be okay, he told himself. Reena and Ruthie would only be alone for a couple of hours, and they were trustworthy enough to spend the afternoon alone. Still he was a little shocked that Rebecca and Rachel wanted to find jobs.

"It's just until Christmas," Rebecca reassured him.

"Somebody wants to buy somebody a special gift." Rachel cut her eyes to Rebecca and then back at him, a smug grin on her face.

"I can give you the money," Uriah protested once more.

Rebecca rolled her eyes at him, albeit a little playfully. "Dat."

"It's Adam," Ruthie said. "Adam Yoder."

"Like it's any of your business," Rebecca said.

"Just saying," Ruthie said.

"Girls," Uriah interrupted their back and forth.

Thankfully Ruthie shoved a big bite of bread into her mouth, effectively cutting off anything else she would say.

Rebecca pressed her lips together and cut her eyes back toward Rachel. She wasn't mad, Uriah could see that much, but it had him mentally scratching his head. Something was going on. He could press and find out what it was, or he could let it go. That was what he decided to do: He would let it go for now.

"How are we gonna get upstairs and check on Dat?" Rachel asked Rebecca quietly as they tied their bakery aprons around their waists. Joy was just a few feet away talking to a customer.

"I haven't figured that out yet," Rebecca whispered back.

"I don't think I told you this, but I'm not really excited to be working here," Rachel said.

"It doesn't matter if you're excited or not," Rebecca returned. "This is about saving our family."

And it was. This was for all of them: Dat, Reena and Ruthie, plus the two of them. They had to find out something adverse about Joy before their *dat* fell completely in love with her.

"Are you ready to bake?"

Rebecca and Rachel turned to Joy. Her eyes were

sparkling, her mouth curved into a smile. She clapped her hands together and rubbed them in excitement

"I've never really baked anything before," Rebecca said. "Besides chicken, that is."

"*Jah*, and Ruthie usually oversees that," Rachel said jokingly. But she was serious at the same time. Ruthie oversaw all the kitchen chores.

"But Ruthie is . . ."

"A tyrant," Rebecca supplied.

"I was going to say eight," Joy said in return.

"That too," Rachel said.

Joy studied them for a moment, as if trying to determine whether or not they were serious.

Finally Rebecca shrugged. "Ruthie likes to run the kitchen," she said. "Sometimes it's easier to just let her."

Joy nodded her head slowly, as if trying to absorb the words, take them all in and make sense of them. But there was no making sense of any of it. Ruthie just liked to boss everyone around. And they didn't care much. They loved her, and what difference did it make if they were cooking dinner anyway?

"Well, we're not making any chicken," Joy said. "But we are baking cookies, cupcakes, and strawberry scones."

Rachel's forehead crumpled into a confused frown. "What's a scone?"

Joy's eyes widened in surprise. "You've never had a scone?"

Rachel turned to Rebecca. Rebecca shrugged then looked back at Joy. "No. Never."

"Oh, boy," Joy trilled. "Are you in for a treat."

It turned out that a scone was a lot like a biscuit with fruit in it. Rebecca learned that the British like to eat them with something called clotted cream. Clotted cream, she discovered, was a little like high-quality butter—unsalted, of course. And the other thing she learned was that they tasted amazing.

"How much butter are in these?" she asked Joy.

The baker gave her a sly smile. "A lot."

Rebecca cast a sad glance at the tray of strawberry scones she had just pulled from the oven. They were perfect, just barely golden brown around the edges and on the peaks on the top. They smelled like heaven, and after having one taste she knew she could eat the whole tray of them in one sitting. But not with that much butter in them. If she did, she would outgrow all of her clothes in a blink.

"I know," Joy said, without Rebecca having to say anything at all. "I limit myself to one a week."

"They are delicious," Rachel agreed. She threw a longing glance at the scones as well.

"I'm just surprised you've never had one," Joy said.

"I've been thinking about that," Rebecca said. "We were kind of young when Mamm got sick. When she didn't feel well, baking was the last thing anyone worried about. In fact, we all kind of learned to cook by trial and error."

Joy smiled. The action lit up her face and made her look years younger. Remorse zinged through Rebecca over her deceit. Joy seemed so happy to have them there that Rebecca felt guilty at her deception. No, that wasn't right. She couldn't feel guilty. She was there to save her family, and she steeled her heart against Joy's obvious happiness.

"I'm delighted to be able to teach you," Joy said. "In fact, I'm sorry I never thought to do it before now."

Rebecca didn't know what to say to that, and thankfully

Rachel waved a hand in the air as if that dispelled any notion that Joy owed them a thing.

The upstairs door opened, and Leah came tripping down the stairs. She was a cute girl, Rebecca thought. She favored her mother. Rusty-colored hair and blue, blue eyes. Unlike her *mamm*, whose face showed the stress of her life, Leah was perpetually happy. Bright and happy. Rebecca had to wonder what went on inside her brain. No one was that happy all the time.

Leah stopped when she caught sight of them. "Hey. What are you doing here?"

"I told you," Joy said. "I hired Rebecca and Rachel to work with us up until Christmas, so we can get through the rush."

"*Jah.* I just didn't think they would start so soon." That brightness on her face dimmed considerably. Then as quickly as it changed, it went back to its former illumination. "But that's *gut*," she said.

She was threatened, perhaps even a little bit jealous, Rebecca thought. That was further solidified when Leah smiled and said, "Just through Christmas though, right?"

Joy didn't seem to notice her oldest daughter's uncomfortable manner. That was something Rebecca hadn't counted on. But how was she supposed to know that Leah would feel like she and Rachel were somehow trying to take her place? Or maybe she just thought they were horning in on the attention she received from her mother. It was hard to say.

Rebecca hadn't spent enough time with them to know. But she had the feeling that Leah overcompensated due to the death of her father and her brother's accident. She was all smiles, smiles, smiles, and Rebecca questioned if that feigned happiness didn't worry Joy from time to time. Or perhaps her aunt was just too busy to see it.

The bell over the door rang, and several Amish young people walked in. No doubt they were classmates of Leah's, just out of school and looking for a snack.

"That's what happens," Joy said. "Leah comes in, and the after-school rush starts."

Joy had Leah work the front counter while Rebecca and Rachel helped her with another batch of cookies. To Rebecca it seemed like Leah was not very happy with the arrangement, and she wondered if that was jealousy again. She really hadn't meant to upset Leah, and she hoped she wasn't too crushed over the change. At least it wouldn't be for very long.

"When do we get to decorate them?" Rebecca asked. She could feel Rachel's gaze on her, in a *who are you and what have you done with my sister?* kind of way. But Rebecca was a little excited at the thought of making beautiful icing designs like the cookies that were already in the case.

Joy shook her head. "I wasn't going to have you learn to do that, but if you want to . . ." She trailed off with a slight rise of her shoulders, almost a shrug.

"I want to." Who said that? Rebecca almost didn't believe it was her voice. But it was. This wasn't part of the plan. The plan had been to get a job at the bakery, so they could spy on their father during the day—at least on Tuesdays and Thursdays—and hopefully find out some sort of bad habit that Joy had that would send their father running away as fast as he could.

Was it really a problem if she learned how to bake in the process, and possibly even decorate cookies?

"I'll teach you then." Joy's voice was full of happiness.

Rebecca could feel Leah's gaze on her, questioning, suspicious. Really, she had nothing against the young girl, and she hoped her cousin didn't get too upset over the whole ordeal. They would be gone after Christmas. Or at least as soon as they got their *dat* to realize that Joy wasn't the woman for him.

"And cakes?" Really? Who was doing all this talking? Rebecca was even surprising herself.

Joy blinked at her in amazement. "I'm not sure we'll have time for that, but we'll see."

Rebecca could tell that her aunt didn't want to tell her no, but she was right. There wouldn't be time to learn how to decorate cakes. But standing in the bakery, with the smell of sugar and vanilla in the air, just made her want to create . . . something. It was a strange feeling.

They finished up the rest of their shift with a few more batches of cookies and a beginner lesson in decorating. Then they all tromped upstairs to see what was happening with Johnny B's rooms.

Their father's eyes lit up when he saw them come through the kitchen. "How was your first day?" he asked.

"Very good," Rebecca didn't even have to fib on that one. She had truly enjoyed herself in the bakery. She couldn't say the same for her sister; Rachel seemed to tolerate the work. No, that word seemed all wrong. Rachel simply didn't *enjoy* it. She did it because it was what needed to be done. She did it, but not with the same smile that Rebecca had seen on Joy's face and felt reflected on her own. Who knew she would love to bake? The idea surprised even her.

"Are you headed home?" Dat asked.

"Going now," Rachel said.

"You're coming too?" Rebecca's words were more statement than question, though she did let her voice rise on the end, so he knew she wanted an answer.

"I'll be home soon," their *dat* said.

"So you'll be home for supper?" Rachel pressed.

Dat nodded. "I'll be home for supper." Then he paused for a moment. "Promise," he said when neither girl moved toward the door to leave.

"We'll see you there," Rebecca said. Then she turned to Joy. "Thanks for a great first day."

Her aunt smiled. "Thanks for all the help."

"That goes for me too," Rachel said, but not with the same enthusiasm that Rebecca's voice held. Kitchen work was obviously not Rachel's favorite, though the girl could sew.

Joy nodded at Rachel. "See you Thursday," she said, her look encompassing both girls.

"See you Thursday," Rebecca echoed, and she started for the door. "And I'll see you at home."

"See you at home," Dat said.

The girls made their way out the front door and over to their buggy. Neither one said a word as they hitched up their horse and started for home.

"I think we won round one," Rachel said.

And she was right. Their *dat* would be home for supper that night. It was a twofold win. He wouldn't be spending any extra time with Joy, and he would be spending the time he usually did with his daughters. So why didn't she feel as triumphant as she should over the whole situation?

Chapter 13

"Hey."

Johnny B straightened at the sound of her voice. Evie.

He resisted the urge to run his fingers through his hair and make sure it wasn't sticking up in all directions. He hadn't been paying that much attention to it that day. But he hadn't thought she would come up.

"Aren't you supposed to be working in the bakery?"

"Your *mamm* sent me up to check on you. She said you turned off the baby monitor again."

Johnny B willed himself not to turn pink even as he felt the heat rising into his face. How embarrassing. To have your *mamm* make you keep a baby monitor close so she could check on you. He wasn't a baby. He might be a cripple, but he wasn't a baby.

"I'm okay." He pushed himself up a little straighter in his wheelchair, chagrined to see a smear of mustard on his light-blue shirt.

Great. The prettiest girl he'd ever seen was standing before him, and he had a stain on his shirt.

Like it mattered. She could think him all kinds of messy or all kinds of fantastic, but it wouldn't change the fact that he was never going to walk again. Things would never be the same for him.

It wasn't like she was without stains of her own. She had flour and what looked to be blue food coloring all down the front of her tan-colored apron. He bet his *mamm* was unhappy about that food coloring. Or maybe it was ink. Possibly even worse.

"So," she started, slowly tracing the seam on her apron as she talked, "are you going to go back to school in January?"

School. That was all anybody ever wanted to talk about. What did school matter? Sure, he promised his *mamm* he'd go back if she let his uncle build him a room on the house. But ever since then, he had been thinking of ways to get out of it. There were so many reasons why he didn't want to go back to school. *What was an education to him now?* topped the list. And then there was the fact that he would be the only one there in a wheelchair. And the fact that he would be the oldest there. And the fact that he didn't want to go and have everybody staring at him. It was bad enough in church, but at least that was only two days a month. School would be forever and forever and another whole year.

"Why do you care?" he asked her, his voice holding a sullen note even as he tried to stop it. Maybe she didn't notice. "You don't even go to school."

She looked up and met his eyes. Hers were such a pale baby-blue that they almost looked translucent. "That's because I've graduated."

Johnny B pushed himself around in his chair a bit, just from side to side. He might not have a lot of feeling in his lower body, but there were times when he had prickly pains that felt a little like someone was sticking him with a pin. His mother thought that was good. He just found it annoying. "Good on you." What else was he supposed to say? She had graduated, but he had fallen out of the barn loft. What difference did it all make anyway?

"Baby monitor?" She held out a hand toward him.

If it wasn't school, it was the baby monitor. He reached behind him in his chair and pulled out the small white device. He placed it in her hand and gave her a look as she turned it on. "He's fine," she said into the microphone piece.

"Good." His *mamm*'s voice crackled through from the other side. "Leave it on and get yourself back down here. We've got customers waiting."

Evie handed the device back to him. "You heard her," she said, though he thought he could detect a note of apology in her tone.

"*Jah.*" It was all he could say.

"So I guess I'll see you around," Evie said. She backed slowly toward the kitchen door, then finally turned and made her way out of sight. A moment later he heard the basement door open and close. She was gone.

"She's a cutie." Uriah couldn't help teasing Johnny B just a bit. He had watched as Evie glanced at Johnny B one last time before heading back down into the basement. She was flirting. Definitely flirting.

The boy merely grunted in return.

"I think she likes you," Uriah pressed.

The boy was far too serious for someone his age. Not that Uriah blamed his nephew for his sometimes down-right surly attitude. He'd had to deal with a lot in the past few years.

But it was good to see him take an interest in a girl.

Even if it was his mother's three-day-a-week help in the bakery.

Uriah had come inside to talk to Johnny B about the bathtub they were installing. He wanted him to see it before they actually put it in. But when he came into the house he found Evie, obviously interested in Johnny B. And Johnny B trying his best not to show that he was interested in Evie. Despite all his big talk about never getting married, Johnny B was interested in the pretty girl.

The boy shook his head. "It doesn't matter whether she likes me or not. I told you: I'm never getting married." He looked down at the baby monitor sitting in his lap, then flicked the switch to *off*. "Why does everybody insist that I'm gonna get married someday?" He shifted in his chair, using his armrests to pull his body around, and Uriah got the feeling he was gearing up for rant. He was right.

"You know what really makes me angry?" Uriah waited for him to continue. "It's not my *mamm*'s tireless hopeful attitude, though that grates on my nerves so much. She means well, you know?" Johnny B sucked in a deep breath and plowed on. "What makes me really mad is when people tell me that I'm lucky to be alive. How so? Tell me one thing about being alive and not able to walk that's lucky." His voice changed as he mimicked someone else speaking. "'You could be dead.' *Jah*, I could be dead. And if I were dead, I'd probably be with Jesus. Most likely anyway. So I'd be in heaven. And I'd be able to walk. So tell me what's lucky about being alive? Down here my life is over."

Uriah had no idea how to respond to that. Johnny B was right, but it wasn't something Uriah could agree with. "But Evie . . ."

Johnny B shook his head. He turned a violent shade of pink as he started again. "Things don't work anymore." He didn't have to explain further. Uriah knew what he was referring to. It was something that Johnny B might have talked to his father about. Or a doctor if he were allowed to go to appointments alone. But Uriah had a feeling that Joy hovered around Johnny B at every doctor's appointment, soaking in all the words the doctor was saying and all the hope that she could glean from those words. And his father was long dead.

Things don't work anymore. That must be the reason why Johnny B didn't believe he could have a normal life in a wheelchair. And as far as Uriah knew, there was not one thing anybody could do about it.

"Johnny B," he started slowly trying to find the words to continue, "you're not going to . . . do anything . . . drastic?"

"No." Johnny B shook his head, his eyes closed in what Uriah considered to be disgust. "I'm not going to kill myself or anything stupid like that. I just wish people would stop talking out of both sides of their mouth. Death equals heaven. For me life equals stuck in a chair. Besides," he continued. "I know what it would do to my *mamm*, but if I had the choice . . ." He paused, his eyes boring into Uriah's, his gaze blazing. "If I had the choice, I couldn't say that life in a wheelchair would offer anything over death. But I understand. It's God's will and that's all there is to it."

"See you." Joy waved to Sylvie and rushed down the porch steps. She had to hustle over to the stable, get her horse and buggy, hitch everything up, and get back to the bakery. And as quickly as she could.

She had left Leah, Rebecca, and Rachel in charge of the bakery. With the three of them there she was certain that everything would be okay, but she couldn't help worrying a bit. It was a Thursday, and currently Thursdays were a bit slower, since they were in the middle of wedding season. Everything would be fine, she told herself.

It was just that Joy had wanted to come to Henry and Millie's wedding. She knew she wouldn't be able to stay long. There might be three of them at the bakery, but it was Rebecca and Rachel's second day at work. It just wasn't fair to leave Leah alone and have her be in charge of baking, running the cash register, and training two new, green recruits. So Joy was rushing around, scurrying home to make sure she got there in plenty of time to help clean up whatever disaster had occurred while she was gone.

She was definitely prepared for a disaster, a huge mess to clean up. You know, *when the cat is away* and all that. Flour everywhere. Napkins and other trash scattered about. Dirty towels and aprons to wash. Burnt cookies. The whole nine yards. It was what she was expecting, even as she told herself that everything was going to be all right.

She rushed through the house and down the stairs to find . . .

Everything in perfect order.

She looked around, then looked around again to make sure she was in the right place. "Everything . . . looks . . . great," she said.

"Hi, Mamm." Leah beamed. She was standing by the cash register showing something to Rebecca. "I've had good help."

"*I've* had good help." Rebecca playfully elbowed her cousin in the side.

Rachel was standing behind them. She made a face that only Joy could see. Apparently these mice had had a pretty productive time while the cat was away.

"And look at this." Leah led her over to a new batch of Christmas cookies. The designs were intricate, beautiful. Bells, wrapped presents, stockings, and crosses. There was even a batch of light-blue snowflakes with tiny pearl accents.

"They're gorgeous," Joy breathed. And they were, but they must've taken forever to complete.

"Rebecca did them while I cleaned," Rachel said. No doubt the girl wanted Joy to know her part in the day's activities. It might not be quite as smart as decorating cookies, but the place was spotless.

"It looks great in here," Joy said, then she turned her attention back to Rebecca. "How long did it take you to do these?"

"A long time," her niece admitted. "But it was lots of fun. I was thinking maybe we could do these for special events. We could charge a little more?" She made a face, part apology part question. "I mean, that would only be to recoup the time it took, since we wouldn't be able to do other things while we were decorating these."

Rachel raised her eyebrows at her sister. "You mean while you decorate those."

Leah laughed.

A warm feeling came over Joy, one that had nothing to do with the commercial ovens behind them. It was one thing to teach someone how to do something, and another one altogether when they enjoyed that something, loved it as much as you did. And that was Rebecca. Not even her own daughter seemed to love baking as much as Rebecca did. Joy knew that hiring her to work in the bakery was perhaps the best decision she had made in a long, long time.

Chapter 14

"What's up?" Leah slid into the chair next to Johnny B in the dining room. Chris was already on the other side, slouched in his chair like he had someplace else to be.

"Family meeting," Johnny B said.

Leah looked around. "Where's Jane?"

Johnny B shrugged. "I don't know."

"Shouldn't she be here?" Leah asked. "She is part of the family. And what about Mamm?"

"This is just a family *kids* meeting," Johnny B said. He wished his sister would stop asking stupid questions.

"Then Jane should definitely be here." Leah started to rise, as if going to find her sister.

"Jane's too young. Plus she's a girl."

Leah rolled her eyes. "If it's a family kids meeting and she's a family kid, then she should be here." She pushed her way out of the dining room and left Chris and Johnny B waiting for her to return.

Thankfully it wasn't too long before she came back downstairs with their youngest sister.

Jane shot Johnny B a scowl, and he wondered if Leah had told her what he'd said. He hadn't really meant anything by it. But she was so little. And girls tended to be . . .

not logical sometimes. Still he supposed Leah was right; Jane was part of the family.

"Are you gonna tell us why we're here?" Leah asked.

"I want to talk about Uriah." Johnny B looked around the table. No one seemed surprised at their topic of conversation.

"I like him." Chris nodded. These days Chris saying he liked anything was surely a good sign.

"What about him?" Leah sat back in her chair and crossed her arms. The pose looked defensive, but Johnny B couldn't tell from her expression if she was upset or just trying to get more comfortable.

"I like him too," Jane added, unwilling to be left out again.

"Do you think things are . . . better since he's been hanging around?"

Leah gave a small shrug. "I guess. I never really thought about it."

"Well, think about it now," Johnny B instructed. He thought of nothing else. Of all the people he had encountered, from the bishop straight down to his own family, Uriah was the one who treated him with the most dignity. He knew his Mamm meant well, and his siblings did their best, but Uriah was different. He didn't pretend to have all the answers, he didn't fret over him and treat him like a baby. But it was more than that. So much more.

"I suppose you're right," Leah agreed. "Mamm seems a bit happier, maybe not as stressed out. But at first . . ."

At first when they had started the demolition in the house, their *mamm* had been more stressed than normal. But as the room had come together and the mess had been cleaned up from the widening of the doorways, his mother's anxiety lessened a little more each day. Johnny B had protested that it should be just the one doorway.

Now that he would have his own quarters, he only needed to be able to get into the dining room for supper at night. But Uriah had insisted that all were widened, in the off chance that something happened and he needed to get down the hallway to his mother's room, or into the kitchen for some reason or another. So he had relented. It had made an even bigger mess, but now that it was done, everyone was relieved that they had gone ahead with that part of the plan.

"I think she seems a lot happier." Johnny B looked around to see if anyone was going to agree with him. No one nodded, but he could see they were mulling over everything that had happened in the last couple of weeks.

"He calls me Topher," Chris mumbled. All eyes swung to him. He looked up startled to find everyone staring at him. "I like him because he calls me Topher."

"I've just been thinking . . ." Johnny B started again. This was a delicate conversation, and he wasn't sure exactly how to proceed. He knew what needed to be said, but he needed to say it in a way so his brother and sisters would agree.

They patiently waited for him to get his words in order. He had to do this. He had to get it right. He would never walk again. Although he would most likely live at home for the rest of his life, he couldn't be the man of the house in a wheelchair. Chris was too young, and Johnny B hadn't realized it up until now, but they needed help. And his *mamm*, she needed help as well. Being widowed, he supposed, she needed a lot of things.

He felt the heat of a blush rising into his cheeks, but there was nothing he could do to stop it. He looked down at his lap before continuing.

"I've been thinking about what it might be like if

maybe Mamm fell in love with Uriah and the two of them got married."

He expected outbursts, even soft cries of *no*, but only silence met his ears. He looked up, glanced around the table at their faces.

Leah was biting her lip, obviously in deep thought over what he'd just revealed. Jane had one elbow propped on the table, her head balanced in that hand and a far-off, dreamy look on her face. Who knew what she was thinking? And Chris . . . Topher . . . was still slouched back in his seat, though now he was nibbling on his thumbnail as if somehow that would help him think more clearly.

Johnny B leaned forward, his gaze traveling around to each of their faces once more. "No one has anything to say?"

"I like him," Topher said.

"You've already said that," Jane admonished.

"But it's true. I really do like him." Topher nodded with each word he spoke. "I really do."

"I really do too," Jane said.

Johnny B swung his attention over to Leah.

"He's a good man," Leah said, acting like she was all grown up. "But what if Mamm doesn't want to get married again? Or what if she doesn't want to get married to him?"

"But we like him," Jane reminded her.

"This has nothing to do with our feelings. This is about her. She's the one who has to marry him."

Johnny B turned to Leah. "You just had to go get her."

Leah shrugged.

"I think it's a good idea," Johnny B said.

"I like that he likes pizza," Jane said. "I like that he played cards with us the other night. That was fun."

For the first time since they'd sat down at the table,

Chris actually smiled. "I like that he likes Chinese food, and he knows how to eat with chopsticks."

Johnny B liked that he talked to him as a man. He liked that he didn't coddle him. And he liked that the fact that his uncle seemed honest and true. Those were all good traits, weren't they? Still he didn't want to say that to his siblings. "We all have a lot of reasons to like him. Does anybody have a reason not to?" He looked around the table.

Jane started to swing her legs, but otherwise no one moved.

"I don't know, Johnny B," Leah said. "Is it really a good idea to mess in this?"

Johnny B bit back a snort. It was always the girls. "We're not gonna *make* them get married," he said. "Just maybe give them more opportunities to be together. More opportunities to maybe fall in love. And to see that they need each other." He knew he would feel better if his *mamm* had someone she could depend on. She needed someone until Chris got old enough to step in. It would be a few years before that was possible and a few years was a long time when you were having to do everything yourself.

Leah worried her bottom lip a bit more with her teeth, then finally let out a sigh. "Okay. I guess."

Relief flooded Johnny B. This was going to work. This was perfect. He glanced around the table once more. "So we're all in agreement?"

They all nodded.

"Okay, just do everything you can to try to get the two of them to fall in love."

"How do we do that?" Chris asked.

"*Jah*," Jane added. "I don't know what to do."

"Just be good," he told them. "Help Mamm and don't cause any trouble. Leah and I will do the rest."

"Are we done?" Chris asked.

Johnny B nodded. "We're done."

Chris hopped up from his seat and headed for the door, Jane hot on his heels.

Leah looked to Johnny B. "What are we supposed to do to make them fall in love?"

That was a good question. "I don't know yet," Johnny B told his sister. "When I think of something, I'll let you know."

But by the time that evening had rolled around Johnny B hadn't come up with one single plan. You would think a guy who couldn't do anything but sit and think would be able to come up with some sort of idea. But he was at a loss. He wished he had one of those romance novels they sold at the grocery store. Maybe he could get some ideas from that. But there was nothing like that around this house. Their books all consisted of encyclopedias, dictionaries, and volumes on animals. Not that they weren't interesting, but there was nothing about falling in love in any of those.

"Stay for supper," Jane's voice floated into the dining room to Johnny B's ears. He hadn't even left that room when his siblings had all gone about their business. And still he hadn't thought of one single thing.

"*Jah*," Chris joined in. "Stay for supper. Eat with us."

Johnny B rolled through the dining room door back into the living room in time to see Uriah set Jane on her feet. It was possible that when she issued her command she had thrown herself into his arms. She could be that way. He hoped Uriah didn't mind.

He didn't seem to. He was smiling when he turned her

loose. "I would love to, but I've got to get home and make sure my girls eat."

"Isn't Rebecca there?" Jane questioned.

Johnny knew that Rebecca had already left to go home. She had gone early to help with a wedding. That was Thursdays in the Amish community, especially in November and December. Everything got put on hold for the weddings.

In fact, today was even Thanksgiving and no one was doing anything special because weddings were all over the place. Not that Johnny B cared much for Thanksgiving. It wasn't like there were gifts involved or anything. They were thankful at every meal, praying before and after they ate. But it would've been nice to spend Thanksgiving with Uriah. It might've meant something to him to be with them. But Johnny B hadn't thought that out beforehand. He was new at this matchmaking stuff.

"*Jah*," Uriah said with a small nod. "Rebecca's there, but I still need to go home."

Jane gave a small pout. "You don't want to eat with us."

Uriah shook his head. "You know better than that. Besides tomorrow is Friday and family dinner night, right?"

Jane nodded, but she didn't look any happier. And speaking of unhappy . . .

Rachel looked downright stormy. What was her problem? Johnny B had no idea. Rachel was not as warm and fuzzy as Rebecca. Ruthie and Reena were little girls, like Jane. But Rachel was harder to read.

"Do you want Chinese tomorrow?" Uriah said. "Or maybe barbecue . . ." He raised his eyebrows. "We could call Hannibal's."

Hannibal's barbecue was about the best thing to eat in the Valley.

"I could go for some Hannibal's," Johnny B put in.

Uriah looked at him and smiled. "Hannibal's it is."

"Mamm likes the chicken," Johnny B told him. "And that chocolate pecan cobbler they have."

"I'll keep that in mind," Uriah said with a nod. He clapped Chris on the shoulder and rubbed one hand against the side of Jane's face. "I'll see you both tomorrow."

He left with Rachel trailing sullenly behind him.

Johnny B felt satisfied with that exchange. He'd always heard people say that the way to a man's heart was through his stomach. He could only hope that the same thing went for women too, and that chocolate pecan cobbler would work its magic on his *mamm* tomorrow night. Because despite all his bluster, Johnny B had no idea how to make two people fall in love.

It was a feast. Four kinds of meat, two kinds of potatoes, mac and cheese, baked beans, coleslaw, and Texas toast. And, of course, chocolate pecan cobbler.

"This is too much food," Joy said, looking at the spread. There was so much on the table, there was hardly room for anybody to sit and eat.

Uriah shrugged, but she thought she saw the ghost of a smile. "I just thought it would be fun."

"Fun, *jah*. Plus ten pounds of chocolate pecan cobbler."

"A family-sized portion is not ten pounds."

Joy shook her head. "No, that's what I'll gain if I eat all I want of it."

Uriah laughed. "Johnny B told me you liked it."

"He did?"

It shouldn't have felt a little thrilling that Johnny B and Uriah were planning things behind her back, but it was. Or maybe it was that Uriah had done that to please her.

"Come on, everyone," Joy said. "Gather round and grab a plate."

They did as she asked, the younger kids running and the older kids coming at a more leisurely pace, with Johnny B wheeling himself in after.

Somehow everyone managed to find a seat and a space for their plate. There were oohs and ahhs as everyone gazed at the spread before them. It was about as big as the Thanksgiving meal they had missed this year.

"That looks fantastic," Rebecca said.

They all agreed.

Joy caught a grin and a satisfied nod between Uriah and Johnny B. They were proud of themselves for coming up with the idea, and that little thrill came back to her.

"It's time to pray," Uriah said.

Everyone bowed their heads and said their silent prayer of thanks for the food. When prayer was complete, something near controlled chaos reigned. Plates were passed, scoops of this and that were added. In general, the air of happiness and contentment seemed to settle around them all.

It was good, Joy decided. It was all so good. And she was happy that they had decided to have these dinners. It was wonderful to get the family together, but somehow tonight felt different. More cohesive. Not as if they were two families getting together but one. Yet why?

She looked around the table. What was so special about tonight? She couldn't credit the chocolate pecan cobbler, though as far as she was concerned, that was complete magic. No, something seemed to have shifted tonight. The kids were all getting along. There was no bickering or arguing like often happened when you have eight children in a contained space. It was just an overall feeling of happiness. It was as simple as that. Just. Happy.

She looked up to find Uriah watching her. Could he feel

it too? This bond that seem to have formed between them all? Was she just imagining things? Or maybe she was just engaging in some very wishful thinking.

Her family had been broken for so long. Somehow she had kept it all together. She and the kids were fine. They were good, even, and they were happy. They had family dinners. They had times where they went and visited. But something about this was different. Something about this was special.

Uriah gave her a knowing smile.

She had a feeling he had noticed it, that he could sense the joining of the families. What was that all about?

Maybe it was just about good food, enjoyable company, something nice to do in the winter months when it was too cold to do much else but stay inside and eat. Maybe that enjoyable company was just what had been lacking in their lives. All their lives. That had to be it. Companionship and fellowship and the whole loving your neighbor thing.

But part of her wanted it to be about something more. Part of her wanted it to be about a new life. A new start. That was what it felt like. Johnny B was getting his room, though she still fully believed with all of her heart that he would walk again someday. She could see the change in him almost by the hour as the room was being built. Rooms, she corrected herself. The addition was a complete *dawdihaus*, with a small galley kitchen, a private bed and bath, and a small sitting area.

When they'd started building it, Joy felt as if she was giving up all hope. But the hope that she saw it bring to Johnny B was bigger than her fears. He needed that space, and she hadn't realized it until now. She only had one person to thank for it: Uriah.

She looked up at him again only to find him watching her once more. There was a wistful look in his eyes, as if he was missing the same things that she had just been thinking about. Family, companionship, all the rest that one person missed when another was gone from their lives. She shouldn't be surprised by that look. She had a feeling her own mirrored it perfectly.

"Mamm." Jane pulled on her sleeve.

Joy turned toward her youngest. "What's the matter?"

"I asked you three times," Jane grumbled.

"Asked me what?" She hadn't heard her, having been a little lost in her own thoughts.

"I asked you to pass me the potato salad," Jane said. "But you weren't listening. You were too busy staring at Uriah."

Joy felt the flush of red heat her cheeks. Everyone was talking and laughing, but Jane's voice carried, and Joy was certain they'd all heard that she'd been staring at Uriah and not paying attention to her daughter.

Staring was such a strong word. She was just looking at him. She had simply looked up and caught his gaze as she thought about things and . . . well, that was all.

She grabbed the spoon resting in the potato salad and scooped up some for Jane, plopping it onto her plate. "There," she said. "Is that enough?"

"*Jah,*" Jane replied. She started swinging her feet as she dug her fork into the tangy treat.

With Jane taken care of, Joy found her gaze straying back to Uriah's.

He hid his smile behind his napkin, but his green eyes were twinkling above the white paper. It was strange, like they had been caught doing something they weren't supposed to be doing. Which wasn't the case at all. She could look at him anytime she wanted. But maybe it was because the look had lasted longer than it should have. Or maybe because it had looked like something more than what it really was. Like maybe she liked Uriah. Well, she did like him. But this would be more. Like maybe something was going on between the two of them. Which it was not. Not at all. And it would be downright strange if it did. As much as she appreciated Uriah, he was her late husband's brother. Which meant he was a brother to her as well. Yet there were times like this when things didn't really feel brotherly at all. And each day that they spent together, the relationship felt less and less brotherly.

Stop it, she silently admonished herself. *You are making up things where there's nothing to be made up. Uriah was being kind, and you were staring off into space, and you got busted by your daughter. End of story. Let it go and go on.*

She turned her attention back to her meal and was careful not to let her gaze stray to Uriah anymore while they ate.

"Better eat fast," Chris said, looking around at the other Lehman children. "You girls don't know this, but Mamm loves chocolate pecan cobbler. If you want some, you have to hurry, finish your plate of food, then get your cobbler before she gets to it. Otherwise there won't be any left."

"Hey," Joy said with a mock pout and hurt expression. "That's not fair."

"It might not be fair," Johnny B said with a laugh, "but it's true."

Jane and Leah nodded to back up Chris and Johnny B's teasing.

Everyone at the table laughed. At least now they were thinking about her eating habits and not whether or not she and Uriah had anything going.

She was grateful for the distraction. She might not be able to figure out the specialness of the evening, but one thing was certain: There was nothing going on between her and Uriah and there never would be.

* * *

"*Danki* for getting Hannibal's tonight," Joy said.

Uriah nodded, glad that the barbecue had been a hit.

It was almost time to hitch up his carriage and head home. Maybe it was time. Or past time.

But still he lingered. He was on the porch with the pretense of smoking his pipe before he left for home. Joy stood next to him, wrapped in her cloak to ward off the winter chill.

"I still think you should take some of the leftovers home," Joy told him.

Uriah shook his head. "The girls take care of my supper every night. I know Leah helps you, but both of you work so hard in the bakery, it'll be good to have some leftovers you don't have to cook."

"I appreciate that."

From the sweet smile she gave him he knew those words to be true. And he meant what he said. He had help at home that she didn't have. He didn't have to come in and cook after spending a long day at the lumberyard, but Joy worked in the bakery all day and then had to turn around and cook for her family. Leah went to school all day and came to the bakery and finished off the shift there. Then she went upstairs to help her *mamm*. *Jah*, it was the Amish way to work hard, but these girls worked *hard*. They deserved any break that he could afford them.

"I can't talk you into taking the rest of chocolate cobbler, can I?"

He turned and shot her a playful frown. "There's some left? I thought you had finished it off ages ago."

"Ha, very funny. But there's half a pan left. Someone ordered two family-sized servings and an apple pie."

"That's because I thought it was your favorite."

"It is." She laughed. "But if you leave it here, I'll probably have it finished off before I go to bed."

He returned her smile. "Good, then. You deserve it."

"I deserve to be big as a house?"

Uriah shook his head. "You're not big as a house. And one extra helping of pecan cobbler is not gonna do that much damage. You'll still be able to wear all your clothes come tomorrow."

She scoffed. "That's easy for you to say. You work in the lumberyard and run around all day. I get to smell baking cookies and baking bread and baking scones, tarts, pies, and cakes. Sometimes it's hard."

"I would think that after a while you might get tired of it."

She shot him a look with an arched brow and a devious light in her eyes. "Get tired of bread and cookies?"

Uriah laughed. "I guess you're right. Forget I said anything."

He took a puff off his pipe and gazed out at the night. It was really too cold to stand on the porch and smoke for a long time. But it became easier, maybe even a bit warmer, to stand there with Joy.

The look she had given him at supper tonight . . . there was just something about it. He couldn't quite name the emotion, the feeling, the energy, or whatever that surrounded them, but it was there, nearly tangible, like a connection between the two of them that had never existed before. Or maybe it had existed and he just hadn't noticed it. He had no idea which.

"I really do enjoy the suppers," Uriah said quietly into the chilly darkness.

"*Jah.*" She spoke from beside him, but he was staring out at the night still, almost afraid to turn his full attention to her.

Afraid? What was he afraid of? This was Joy. He'd known her most all his life. He appreciated her resilience, her ability to bend and not break. He even appreciated her stubbornness, for he knew that was what got her through the trials she had suffered these last few years, ever since Rudy died.

She was his brother's widow, mother to his nieces and nephews, aunt to his own children, a good friend.

And yet he could feel the stirrings of something more.

Or was that just the wind and the night talking?

"I really can't believe Rebecca is gone again today."

Joy turned and smiled at Rachel. "It's okay. I understand. And I have you here to help."

"*Jah.*" But Rachel didn't look convinced. In fact, she had been sort of hovering around all day. She did anything and everything that Joy asked her to, yet Joy still got the feeling that the girl was a little uncomfortable around her, like she expected Joy to be angry with her for something.

You're just being silly.

And she wasn't being fair. Rebecca had fallen into bakery work, loving everything from getting flour all down the front of her apron to decorating cookies. Joy couldn't expect both of them to embrace the job quite so enthusiastically. She just wished Rachel would loosen up a bit. She wished she would be herself. Joy had a feeling that Rachel was holding a piece of herself back, but she had no idea why.

"Is there something you would like to bake today?"

Rebecca had enjoyed baking anything and everything, from scones and pastries clear down to cupcakes.

Rachel shrugged. "I don't know much about baking."

Joy nodded. "That's what you said. Then check this

out." She reached to a nearby shelf and pulled out an old cookbook. "Look through here, see if maybe there's something that catches your eye."

Rachel took the book over to a nearby worktable and set it down. She opened it, flipping through with half-hearted interest.

Joy turned back to the cookies she was dishing out on one of the large cookie sheets she used. Crunchy peanut butter with mini chocolate chips. They were Johnny B's favorite, and since she had fresh ones, she thought she might take one up to him in a bit. Anything to keep the peace. He seemed to be a little bit happier these days, and his room was almost done. Thank the good Lord for that.

Yet there was still chaos upstairs. *Jah*, the dining room table had been moved back into the dining room, but in the living room things were still in boxes. The couch was still out on the back porch. Johnny B's bed was still smack-dab in the middle of everything. But soon . . .

"What about bread?" Rachel asked.

Joy slid the cookies into the oven and turned back to her niece. "You want to bake bread?" Bread was perhaps the hardest thing to bake when you started comparing it to biscuits, scones, and cookies, but she wanted Rachel to have at least a smidge of the same love for baking as her sister had. "I usually bake bread on Monday, Wednesday, and Friday, but we can make a couple of loaves today if you really want to."

Rachel gave a small frown. "I would. I would like to bake some French bread. You know, that crusty stuff like they have at the Italian restaurant."

Joy managed to stifle her small laugh. "I believe that's Italian bread. But we can make some." She went over to where Rachel stood at the work counter and flipped through the book until she found the page where the breads were listed.

"Look though here and see what you can find. There should be a couple for us to choose from. Find the one you like the best."

"How do I know it's the right one?" Rachel asked.

"It'll say Italian bread for one. Then read through the recipe and see if there's anything about the process that intrigues you."

"Intrigues me?" Rachel shot her a dubious look. "I can't say that I've ever been intrigued by a recipe—for bread or anything else, for that matter."

Joy just smiled. "There's a first time for everything."

While Rachel read and studied the recipes, Joy went back to set the timer on her cookies and help the couple of customers who had wandered in. She could hear Rachel behind her reading the names of the recipes just barely under her breath.

"Brioche? What in the world is that? Ciabatta. Focaccia. There's French bread. Garlic, cheese, and onion. Garlic and cheese. Herb. I think I found one," she called to Joy. "What's a sourdough starter?"

"You've had sourdough bread?"

Rachel nodded.

"Well, you can't have sourdough bread without sourdough starter. It's the base for the bread. It's what gives it that that special taste."

"Like Amish Friendship Bread?"

"Just like that."

"Do you have any?" Rachel asked, almost excitedly.

This time Joy couldn't hide her smile. "I do. Do you want to make sourdough bread or Italian?"

"Sourdough," Rachel said with a definite nod. And Joy

wondered what had changed her mind from Italian. Then Rachel smiled at her. "It's Dat's favorite."

They went about measuring out the starter and adding the proper amount of flour. Joy explained that sourdough bread, unlike most other breads, contained no yeast.

"It rises because of the fermentation in the starter."

Rachel nodded, and Joy tried to temper herself. She didn't want to overwhelm the poor girl. For the first time Rachel seemed to be enjoying herself in the bakery.

"Do you make Amish Friendship Bread too?" Rachel asked.

"I do. I sell the starter as well."

Rachel shook her head. "That seems weird. Selling a starter for Friendship Bread."

"It's a business," Joy reminded her.

"I suppose."

"Besides," Joy continued, "it's the *Englisch* who buy the starter. And I'm sure they pass it on to their friends. It all works, see?"

A smile fluttered on Rachel's lips as if she wasn't sure if she should laugh or not. "You're quite a business-woman."

Joy shrugged off the compliment, but in truth it warmed her inside. She had worked hard on her bakery. She had worked hard building her reputation, making the best pies in both Paradise Springs and Paradise Hill. She offered pastries that other bakeries in the area didn't, like scones of various flavors with clotted cream, and Mexican sopapillas made with sugar and cinnamon and topped off with a spoonful of Rufus Metzger's local honey.

"I do what I can."

Rachel tilted her head to one side and studied Joy. The

look made Joy slightly uncomfortable. "I think you do more than that."

The pair fell quiet as they worked on the sourdough bread. Then they slid it into the oven, and Rachel leaned her hip against the worktable and crossed her arms. "Do you ever think about getting married again?"

Joy shut the oven door and whirled around to face her niece.

"Sorry," Rachel backpedaled. "That's a really personal question, but you just have such great things going on here. Do you not miss being married?"

"No," Joy said. "But it's okay. Being here. Sometimes I think about it, but not often." She remembered that wave of loneliness that had washed over her just a few days ago, when she had been standing on the porch talking to Uriah. *Jah*, there were times when she got a bit lonely, but she had worked very hard for what she had. She had worked very hard for her independence. What would happen if she gave her heart to another and lost it all? It was possible. She'd heard terrible talk of people who changed after the wedding and decided they didn't want their spouse to do this or that or the other. It didn't happen often, but it did happen. What if she fell in love with a man who didn't want her to run the bakery? What if he said the hours were too long? There were a hundred reasons why she should stay single. But none that she wanted to share with Rachel.

Still, she knew her pauses were very telling of her feelings on getting married again.

"Being married is wonderful," Joy finally answered. "When you love someone, it's amazing. It's truly a gift from God. Some people get that more than once and some people don't." Joy didn't want this young girl to be tainted against marriage because of her own fears.

"And you think you're one of those people who only gets the gift once?" Rachel asked.

"I don't know," Joy said honestly. "I suppose anything could happen." Though she seriously doubted she would ever fall in love again. She'd had one good love with Rudy. And now her love was baking. It wasn't such a bad deal.

But then she thought about the previous Friday night and standing on the porch with Uriah. She felt the pull toward him. At supper, she could feel them all, connected, together, living life like a family. Even though they weren't. Even though they never would be. Not like that anyway.

The thought was sobering, and yet she couldn't help but daydream a little about her and Uriah and what it might be like.

"A penny for them." Rachel held up the copper coin, a teasing smile on her face.

Joy gave her a wistful look and a small laugh. "I'm not sure they're even worth that."

"Surely they are." But Rachel tossed the coin into the little dish at one side of the cash register, the one they had placed for people to share their spare change with others.

Her thoughts might be worth something, given time and the inclination to share, but right now, Joy had neither. She had a business to run, a family to raise and support, a son to get back on his feet again, literally. She had no room in her life for romance or love or trying to please another person. There was too much on her plate already.

But Uriah's smile . . .

That was something not so easily dismissed.

* * *

"So?" Rebecca asked Rachel as they got ready for bed that evening. They hadn't had a chance to talk until now. Everyone wanted to hear about the wedding over their meal, and she certainly couldn't ask Rachel what happened at the bakery in front of their *dat*. But now that she had her alone, she wanted all the details she could get. She had to know everything in order to foil any plan that Joy might have concocted to get her *dat* to propose.

"We made sourdough bread."

"I know that." Rebecca rolled her eyes at her sister. "We ate some at supper, remember?" This was not the sort of information she needed.

"*Jah*," Rachel mumbled, but she continued to brush her hair, staring off into space without saying anything more.

"Joy?" Rebecca prodded her. She started removing the pins that held her bob in place, releasing the ponytail that was wound around itself. "Do you think she's trying to get Dat to marry her?"

"I don't know." Rachel's voice was filled with something akin to torment. "I've been trying to figure it out all night. The afternoon was sort of strange."

"Strange how?"

"She's different one-on-one."

Rebecca let out a sigh that was two steps down from a growl. Trying to get information from Rachel tonight was like pulling teeth. "Different how?"

Rachel shook her head. "I don't know. Just different. I think she really wanted me to like baking."

Rebecca slipped her nightgown over her head pulled her ponytail free. "And you don't like it."

Rachel shrugged, then laid down her brush and donned her own night clothes. "I don't hate it," she finally said. "But it's not the same for me as it is for you. But she really tried today to make me enjoy myself there."

Rebecca undid her ponytail holder and released her long, dark hair. She grabbed a brush and waited for her sister to continue. "So what did you talk about?"

"I asked her if she wanted to get married again."

"You did not." Rebecca whirled away from the mirror and faced her sister once more.

"I did." Rachel gathered her hair and secured it into a low ponytail for the night.

"And she said?" Rebecca waited—mouth slightly open, brush suspended —for her sister to continue.

"She didn't really answer me. But I kind of feel like that *was* the answer, you know?"

"How so?"

Rachel gave her another of those loose shoulder shrugs. "Just that she didn't answer said that she didn't want to tell me. I don't think she wants to get married again. Because right after that she started telling me how wonderful it was to be married but that some people only get the gift of love one time."

Rebecca tapped the flat end of the brush against her chin and thought about this a moment. "That's good though, right?"

"Not if she ends up breaking Dat's heart."

Rebecca turned to her sister and made sure she had her full attention. "We just have to make sure that doesn't happen."

Chapter 15

As far as Johnny B was concerned Friday was a great day. It was cold outside, but the sun was shining and that was great for the end of November. His room was almost ready for him to move in. And that was great. Plus, Evie had managed to sneak out and come see him once again. And that was great. Sort of.

He still wasn't sure if he wanted her to, when at the same time he looked forward to her visits. Yet what could become of a relationship between the two of them? Nothing.

You could be friends. He already had friends he told himself, then he did his best to quiet that little voice. The thing was, he didn't have a friend like her. She understood him. She didn't avoid him because of his wheelchair. In fact, she'd been seeking him out. *And* she didn't act all awkward around him.

He had tried to figure that one out last night as he lay awake in bed, covers, piled high to ward off the chill. He had decided that perhaps she didn't feel uncomfortable because she had always known him in a wheelchair. He was fairly certain he'd seen her around from time to time, but it wasn't like they hung out or knew each other. They weren't in the same church district. They didn't go to the same school. But now that she worked for his *mamm*, their paths were suddenly crossing. To her, he's always been this way. He's not different. He hadn't changed. That was what all his friends said now: that he had changed. Of course he had changed! He was never going to walk again. He was dealing with some serious stuff. He *had* changed, to be sure, but Evie didn't see it that way.

"So I guess I'll see you later," Evie said. She played with one of her *kapp* strings as she talked to him. Was she flirting? It felt like it, but he wasn't quite sure. He wasn't sure how he felt about that either. What could he offer her above friendship? Not one thing.

"*Jah*," he said. "I'll see you later."

Johnny B watched her walk back through the living room and head for the kitchen. She stopped at the threshold, then turned and looked at him once again. She gave him one more little smile, then she disappeared from view.

"I think she likes you."

Johnny B nearly jumped out of his skin as the voice sounded behind him.

"Uriah!" He hadn't meant to yell. "You scared the life out of me."

"Sorry about that." His uncle gave him an apologetic smile.

"Why are you sneaking up on people?"

"I wasn't," he said slowly. "I guess you were just so busy talking to Evie that you didn't hear me come in."

Johnny B supposed that *could* be the problem if he had been that into talking to Evie. Which he hadn't been. Which meant Uriah had been sneaking up on him. But arguing with his uncle would do no good. "What's going on?" he asked him.

"I was thinking about what you said the other day."

Johnny B watched as his uncle shifted in place. Johnny noticed then that Uriah held several sheets of white paper, stapled together and folded in half.

"About?" Johnny B asked.

He and Uriah talked about a lot of things. It seemed like they had managed to have a conversation pretty much every day. Uriah was good company. When the room was finished and his uncle wasn't hanging around all the time, Johnny B would surely miss him. All the more reason to figure out a way to get his *mamm* to fall in love with his *onkle* so they could all be one big happy family.

"About the personal stuff that you were talking about." The pink started at the collar of Uriah's dark blue shirt and worked its way up to his hairline. Johnny B had never seen a grown man blush, but he supposed the subject matter was enough to make anyone a little flustered.

"Okay," Johnny B replied. He could feel the heat of his own rising color leech into his cheeks. What a pair they made.

Uriah thrust the papers toward him. "I looked up things at the library about life after a spinal injury. There's some—" He cleared his throat and started again. "There's some pretty personal stuff in there, so don't leave it around for your sisters or your *mamm* to find. But I wanted you to see that maybe there's some hope."

Johnny B's hands started to tremble. He wanted to look at it but wanted to wait. Needed to wait, if it was that intimate.

"There's a lot in there that suggests you might be able to have a normal-ish life, even if you never walk again. There would be some . . . adjustments, but it might just be possible."

Johnny B felt the warm hope rising within him, and he squashed it back down. "It's not possible. How can I hold down a job if I can't walk? And how can I be married if I can't hold down a job?"

"Not true," Uriah said. "You can hold a job. I tell you what, you come down to the lumberyard tomorrow morning. I usually have Rebecca doing the books. She can show you what to do, and you can have a job with me. You'll see that you can hold down a job, even if you are in a wheelchair."

"One day a week, and I'm gonna be able to support a wife and children?"

"If you do a good job for me, there may be other people who want you to keep their books. But you'll never be able to do it if you don't finish school and you don't give it a try."

His uncle gave a curt nod in his direction, then spun on his heel and went back outside. The door closed behind him with a definite click, as if underlining what he had said. As much as Johnny B didn't want to admit it, he knew his uncle was right. He would never be able to do anything if he didn't give it a try.

After barbecue from Hannibal's the week before, the family dinner takeout rotation swung back to pizza. But who didn't love pizza? They got several different kinds of crust and toppings, so that everyone would have at least one piece of their favorite.

Uriah looked around at all the happy faces. Well, most were happy. He'd been so excited when he found that information on life after a spinal cord injury with options for family life, with emphasis on men in wheelchairs. The only problem was he was giving it to a boy. He was mostly "boy" anyway, but Johnny B was growing up. And he needed to know that he had hope for a future. Still, it had been hard to hand him those papers. They were so very personal. But Johnny B didn't have a father to talk to about that sort of thing, and he surely couldn't talk to his *mamm*. That left only Uriah to pick up the slack.

He leaned one elbow on the table and idly munched on the crust of the last piece he'd eaten. He dipped it in the garlic butter sauce which of course dripped down his chin and into his beard. He wiped it with a napkin and continued to watch the game of Dutch Blitz that was underway on the floor just outside the dining room. Soon they would have all the living room stuff back in place and these family dinners would be much more relaxed. As it was, everybody sat around on the kitchen chairs, played cards on the floor, and otherwise hovered around as they tried to enjoy themselves. Despite these challenges, it seemed everyone had a good time.

"Chris," Reena said. "Pay attention. It's your turn."

"Topher," he said. He made his play as Reena rolled her eyes at him.

"That's a really dumb nickname," she said.

"Reena," Uriah and Joy spoke at the same time. Joy turned to look at him then nodded, allowing him to take the lead. "That was rude. Apologize to him at once."

"I'm sorry I said your nickname was dumb, even if it is."

Uriah shook his head. "Not exactly what I was going for. Try again."

Reena let out an exasperated sigh. "I'm sorry, Chris."

Uriah closed his eyes briefly said a quick prayer for guidance on this one. This age was so hard. No one told you that when you had babies.

"Topher," Chris corrected again. "Why won't anybody call me Topher?" He jumped to his feet and flung his cards down, then spun on his heel and ran for the front door.

As it slammed behind him, Uriah turned to looked at Joy. She started to her feet, but he shook his head. "Let me." For a moment he thought she might protest, say no and tell him that Chris wasn't his responsibility, but she nodded and eased back into place.

"I'll play his hand." Rebecca hopped up from her chair and knelt down on the floor with the others. They couldn't play Dutch blitz with only three players. Well, they could, but they started with four and they should end that way too.

The game continued, a little more quietly now. Uriah snatched his coat off the hook by the door. He put it on, then grabbed Chris's coat and headed outside. At least he thought he had Chris's coat. It was a coat and a boy had left without one, so any should do.

He looked around to see where Chris might've gone, but he was at something of a loss.

The door opened behind him, and he turned to see Jane standing there. Apparently the game had been put on hold once again, so she could come talk to him.

"He's probably in the barn," she said. "We have some new kittens out there."

"*Danki*." Uriah nodded to the little girl, and she shut the door on the cold.

He made his way down the ramp and toward the barn. True to her word, he saw Chris kneeling in the hay by the empty stall. A brindle-and-white cat lay there, snugly nursing five baby kittens. Three looked just like their mother, one was orange tabby, and the last was solid black.

Jane wasn't kidding: They were new. Barely had their little eyes open.

Chris didn't look up as Uriah approached. The boy just stared at the cats, his face still red with anger. "Are black cats really unlucky?" he asked.

Uriah knelt down in the hay next to him. The mother cat stretched out a paw toward him, letting him know she knew he was there. She was a good mother it seemed. Purring as she nursed her babies.

"God made all creatures, right?" Uriah asked Chris.

"*Jah.*"

"And cats are creatures, *jah*?"

Chris merely nodded.

"How could any of God's creatures be unlucky?"

Chris seemed to think about it a minute and finally nodded. "I guess you're right."

Uriah dipped his chin in return. "I like to think I am."

They sat there in silence for a moment.

"What about snakes?" Chris asked.

"All the creatures have a purpose." It was something he'd been taught his entire life.

"Even skunks?" Chris wrinkled his nose in distaste.

"Even skunks," Uriah confirmed.

"Johnny B got sprayed by a skunk once. Mamm had to give him three baths in tomato juice before he stopped stinking."

Uriah couldn't help but chuckle. "It must have been bad then. I only had to take one tomato juice bath."

Chris had turned his attention back to the kitten but swung to face Uriah once more when he heard this. "You got sprayed by a skunk?"

"Long time ago." Uriah nodded.

"I don't guess Johnny B has to worry about that anymore."

He shrugged. "Maybe. Maybe not. Who knows what God's plan is for your brother?"

"God," Chris said quickly—almost too quickly, as if he had been waiting for someone to ask that very question.

The boy was nothing if not smart.

Silence fell between them once again as Chris reached out and stroked the purring mama cat.

Finally Uriah asked the question that had been burning in everyone's mind since all of this nickname stuff started. "Why Topher?"

Chris sighed. He drew circles in the cat's fur, staring down his finger as if he took his eyes off it something terrible would happen. "There's another boy named Chris at school," he started.

"It happens," Uriah replied.

"So you know how they do," Chris said. "They call me by my father's name and Chris, and they call him by his father's name and then say Chris."

"*Jah*," Uriah agreed. "You would be Rudy's Chris."

Chris looked up his eyes blazing. "I don't want to be Rudy's Chris."

Uriah knew immediately that he had to proceed carefully here. There was so much anger in the little boy—so much that it was spilling out everywhere. And the question, he supposed, was where all that fury was coming from. "Whether they call you that are not, you'll always be Rudy's Chris."

"But I hate it." Venom dripped from each word he spoke.

It was heartbreaking, Uriah decided. Now that he had the boy away from everyone else and there were no distractions or siblings cutting in, he was able to see it for what it was. As plain as day, he could see the heartbreak in the child's eyes. "Tell me why," Uriah softly demanded. He knew the answer. At least he thought he did. He just needed Chris to say it out loud. Then they could find a way to make it right. As right as it could be anyway.

But Chris didn't answer. He simply continued to draw

those little circles in the mama kitty's fur as she continued to nurse her babies and purr out her contentedness.

"It's hard for people to change," Uriah tried again. "It's not that no one wants to call you Topher; it's just we've all called you Chris for so long it's hard to change. No one is trying to be mean or disrespectful to you. It's just not easy to switch."

"Mamm says she named me after her *dat*."

Uriah could only nod. "And there's that."

"I don't remember my *dat*," Chris finally said.

"I don't suppose you do," Uriah agreed. "You were what? Three when he died?"

Chris nodded sadly. "I don't remember him at all. I don't remember anything about him. And yet they call me by his name. And every time . . . It makes my stomach hurt," Chris admitted.

"That's understandable," Uriah said as evenly as possible, though his heart was breaking for this little boy. His brother's boy. Who never got to meet his *dat,* not really. Who could remember things from when they were three years old? Not many people, if any.

"You know what," Uriah continued. "I have all sorts of memories about your *dat*."

Chris dropped his gaze back to the cat and continued to pet her and her babies. She swung her head up and licked his hand.

Uriah tucked his legs under him and sat down fully in the hay, right there in the stall next to the nursing cat and the heartbroken boy. "One time," Uriah started, "our *dat*, your *dawdi*, brought home this horse." He smiled with the memory. "He was a beautiful animal. Slick, black, so shiny in the sun he shone blue. With just a little touch of white on all four hooves. But the rest of him . . . black as the night.

"Anyway, he was a wild beast. I don't know where *dat* got him, and your *dat* got it in his head that he was going to break him and ride that horse all over creation."

Chris looked up from the cat and stared at him, wide eyed. "What happened?"

"I stayed up with him all night because he had such a concussion the doctor said not to let him go to sleep. Of course, they've changed that now, so who knows what you really should do, but I stayed up with him. Woke him up every hour to make sure he was okay."

"So the horse threw him?"

Uriah made an arcing semi-circle in the air. "Thirty feet if it was an inch."

He hadn't thought it possible, but Chris's eyes grew even wider. "Whoa."

"He was lucky he didn't break his neck."

"Like Johnny B," Chris said.

Uriah nodded solemnly, not realizing until that moment the different effects that common phrase might have on people who knew someone who had broken their neck. "But a concussion couldn't keep your *dat* down," Uriah said.

"What happened then?"

Uriah was pleased that Chris was getting into the story. Maybe that was just what the boy needed: someone to tell him about his father. Someone to talk about Rudy. Joy hardly ever mentioned his name. And Uriah just figured that she had been so in love with Rudy that she didn't want to talk about him because it made her miss him more.

Or maybe he was just a romantic old fool.

"He had to heal from that first concussion. Your *mammi* wouldn't let him on that horse at all until the doctor said it was okay. That was about a week. Then it took three more tries, but he broke that horse."

"Did he ride him all over creation?" Chris asked.

Uriah smiled. "He sure did. And it was a sight to see. He zoomed across the pasture. His hat came flying off. He was whoopin' and hollerin', and that horse was galloping so fast you could barely see his feet move."

They sat in silence for a moment. Chris had gone back to drawing circles in cat's fur. The only sound was the purring of the mama cat, who was kneading in the air stretching her claws without disturbing her babies.

"I think we should go in," Uriah said. He pushed to his feet and held a hand out to help Chris up as well. The boy accepted, and Uriah pulled him to his feet.

"Uriah," Chris said softly. "Will you tell me another story about my *dat*?" He looked up and shook his head. "Not now. But someday. Will you tell me other stories about him?"

"You got it, pal. Any time you want."

Chapter 16

"I told you we should have brought another blanket," Reena groused from the back seat.

"And I told you to bring gloves," Rebecca reminded her as gently as possible. "Put your hands in your cloak pockets and stop complaining."

"It is cold out tonight," Rachel agreed.

"It's winter," Rebecca said, her tone incredulous. "It gets cold in the winter. You should know this by now."

"I don't like winter clothes," Ruthie said. "I don't like wearing stockings. I don't like wearing scarves. And I don't like wearing shoes."

"Who said I like wearing stockings?" Rebecca asked over her shoulder. "But I can tell you this: If you don't wear stockings your legs are going to freeze, and frostbite is a lot more inconvenient than having to wear stockings."

"If you say so," Ruthie grumbled, then snuggled further down into her cloak, pulling the blanket up nearly to her eyes.

"Why do you suppose Chris wants to be called Topher?" Rachel asked.

She didn't say more, but Rebecca could hear those words despite the fact that they weren't spoken. It was a weird nickname, highly unusual for them. And just because there were two kids in school with the same first name didn't mean you had to go completely off the rails and pick some random nickname—okay, so it wasn't that random. It was the last part of his name. But no one in Amish country that she knew of used the last part of Christopher as a nickname. They were more apt to call a guy Chrissy than Topher.

"I still think it's dumb," Reena said.

Rebecca used the rearview mirror to glance back at her sister. "Please don't say that anymore. Especially in front of him." She didn't continue. She didn't say that she worried about Chris—he seemed so mad at everything.

He was ten years old. What did he have to be mad about other than he lost his *dat* and his *brudder* was gravely injured? They had lost their *mamm*. And even though you suffered those losses, that didn't mean you just gave up on life. You had to keep going.

"I think I'm gonna try to start calling him Topher," Rachel said. "I mean, it obviously means a lot to him."

"*Jah*," Rebecca said. "It just wears Joy out though."

"Calling him by different name?" Rachel asked.

Rebecca shook her head. "Just all that contention all the time. You just see it in her face. In her eyes. The poor woman needs a break."

Her sister turned in her seat and looked at her. "You like her."

"Of course I like her. She's our aunt."

"No, you really like her."

"Whatever," Rebecca said, though in her heart she knew what Rachel was saying was true. She had grown quite fond of Joy these last few days. Especially working in the bakery side-by-side with her and learning all the fun tips and tricks that professional bakers knew.

"I like her." Ruthie raised her head out from under her blanket to chime in.

"I like her too," Reena said.

"And I think Dat likes her," Ruthie continued.

Jah, they had all seen it before. It was the exact reason why they were trying to find something bad about Joy. So they could convince him not to fall for her. But that had been back when they thought she was perhaps trying to trick him. Yet if what Rachel said was true, and Joy didn't want to get married again . . .

"Do you think Dat will propose?" Reena asked.

Rebecca looked back just as Ruthie wrinkled up her nose. "They can't get married."

Rachel turned in her seat to stare at her younger sisters. "Actually, they can. They're not related by blood."

Ruthie seemed to think about that for a moment. "So she would be our *mudder* and our *aenti*?" There went that nose wrinkling again. "That sounds weird."

"You say weird; I say awesome," Reena said.

"I guess it might be awesome," Ruthie mused.

Would it be?

"She said she didn't want to get married again, but maybe we can get Dat to propose," Rachel said.

Rebecca shot her a sideways glance. "You sure switch sides awfully fast."

Rachel shrugged. "I like her too."

"Great," Rebecca said. "It's agreed. We all like her. But other than that, we need to stay out of it." Yet for the rest of the way home all she could think about were ways to bring the two of them together. It seemed she had switched sides as well.

* * *

"You should go back in." Uriah had just finished hitching up his horse to his buggy while Joy stood on the porch and watched. She supposed he didn't need a spectator, but she wanted to see him off. The kids were all upstairs getting ready for bed. His girls had already headed home. And she just wanted a minute to tell him good-bye.

"I'm going to," Joy said. "It's cold out here." But she made no move to go into the house.

Uriah came back up the ramp and stood next to her on the porch. "It was a fun night."

"What did you say to Chris after he ran out of the house?"

Uriah shook his head. "That's between the two of us."

"But I'm his *mamm*," she said.

He gave her a brief nod. "That you are. But when men talk, it's between the men."

She shot him a wry grin. "Is that so? He's a man now?"

"He will be soon enough."

How true it was. They were growing up so fast. And this year . . . This year had been so tough on them all. But they were getting through it. And that was the most important part.

"*Danki* for trying to help him," she said.

"Of course," he replied. He stood close to her. Perhaps a little too close. And she could almost feel the heat coming off him, his warmth fading in the cold night air. But it was there all the same, almost beckoning her. She could step a little closer. And then what?

Nothing.

For as much as she enjoyed Uriah, he couldn't take Rudy's place. She didn't want him to take Rudy's place. She loved Uriah's company. She loved his children. But after talking to Rachel this week, she understood more and more that she also loved and cherished all that she had built. *Jah,* pride was a sin. And she was prideful of all that she had accomplished.

But Uriah . . . If it was anyone, maybe it would be him. That was just because she had been a tad lonely lately. The change might be on the way. It was hard to say. But melancholy did not a marriage make.

For a moment she thought he might take a step closer, but he didn't. He took a step back, and then another. "Good night, Joy."

She swallowed hard around the lump that suddenly formed in her throat. "Good night, Uriah." Then she let herself into the house feeling more melancholy than ever.

"I don't get it," Johnny B said, staring at the green paper ledger in front of him.

"There's not much to get," his cousin told him.

As promised, Johnny B had come into the lumberyard to help with the books. And as promised, Rebecca was showing him how. But it seemed as if everything she was telling him was bouncing straight off his head. "This is the inventory ledger. Any orders in or out are tallied here."

"Then what's this?" He tapped a random number in the ledger, a subtraction out that made no sense at all to him.

"Every three weeks or so they take out two percent for a remnant charge," his cousin explained.

"That's what I don't get."

Rebecca closed her eyes and breathed through her nose. He could tell she was doing everything in her power to remain calm and patient with him, but it just wasn't making sense.

"When you're doing business, you expect a certain

amount of loss," she said. "People measure wrong, people count wrong, boards get cut wrong. Boards get lost. Boards move. All sorts of things can go wrong when you're dealing with lumber. So we subtract two percent as a loss each month from our anticipated, so we don't go over."

"Go over what?"

Rebecca gave him a tight smile. "Our anticipated income from the inventory."

"But if you have less inventory than you think, how could you go over?"

Her smile widened and turned a bit icy around the edges. He was bothering her, he could tell. But how was he supposed to do this correctly if he didn't understand?

"I tell you what, do this: Take these invoices and write them in the first column. List the vendor and the amount, then go to the next one. We'll worry about percentages and things later."

"I'm sorry," he said. "I'm trying."

Rebecca nodded understandingly. He knew she was being as patient as she possibly could. And he hoped she knew he was trying with all his brainpower.

"Did I hear Joy say you were going back to school in January?" Rachel asked. She was filing papers on the other side of the small office.

"I'm supposed to," he said.

"That didn't sound very positive." Rebecca turned her attention to him once again.

It wasn't positive. Not at all. Ever since he had promised that he would go back to school if she allowed Uriah to build a *dawdihaus* for him to live in, he had been trying to think of a way to wheedle out of it. It was just so embarrassing. Being a year and a half behind, having to deal with little kids. Everyone knowing that he fell out of the hayloft. Being the only one in a wheelchair. There were a hundred things that were just not okay. A hundred things he didn't want to deal with on top of the hundred things he was already dealing with.

"You need to go back," Rachel said. Her voice was sweet and encouraging, almost a plea for him to listen.

But he didn't want to. He didn't want to have to go through all that embarrassment. All that embarrassment for a long time.

But now . . . He looked down at the ledger before him. He couldn't do this, and he couldn't farm, and he couldn't run a dairy, and he couldn't deliver pizza. . . what was he going to do?

"I hope I can say this without making you upset," Rebecca started. She had lowered her voice so it was soft and matched Rachel's. "But if you are going to be unable to use your body, your legs, to make a living, you are going to have to be able to use your brain."

She didn't need to say the rest. That if he didn't go back to school his brain was practically worthless.

But the thought made him feel like crying. Blubbering like a baby. And what good would that do? He still wouldn't be able to walk. He would still need to go back to school. And he would still have to find a way to earn a living sitting down. Not impossible, he supposed, but he sure wasn't fighting his *mamm* about school anymore.

"Everything looks delicious," Joy said Saturday night at supper. It'd been a frantic day. Now that Thanksgiving was over, everyone had decided that Christmas was coming. They had known before, but all of a sudden it came. The great demand for Christmas cookies, Christmas cakes, peppermint cupcakes, fruitcake, friendship bread, and a hundred other desserts that everyone needed for parties and dinners. She was glad to be able to sit down to this nice meal with her family, even if they were still all crammed up with the construction mess. That would soon be over. The next day was Sunday. And an off Sunday. No church. Which meant rest and relaxation.

Most people in their community went to visit others they hadn't seen in a while, or maybe just someone they wanted to spend more time with. But after working a six-day week of twelve-hour days, Joy was ready to drop by the time Saturday night came. This week was a little bit better. Probably because Rebecca had taken so much from her shoulders. Still, with the Christmas rush, things were hectic.

"*Danki*," Leah said. "Jane did the potatoes."

Jane beamed at them all. "They've got bacon in them," she said proudly, swinging her legs as she waited for her *mamm* to scoop up a big portion and dump it on her plate. "And cheese," she added.

Which explained why they had a yellow cast to them. Joy should've known. Jane loved cheese and put it in anything she made. She'd even tried to make cheese sugar cookies once in the bakery. Which had Joy sending her straight back upstairs to her coloring book—though Joy had been working on a cheese-straw recipe ever since.

"Sounds yummy," Joy said, placing the spoon back in the bowl and handing it down to Johnny B.

"Mamm?" Johnny said as he scooped out his own potatoes and passed the bowl to Chris. "Have you talked to the teacher about me going back to school in January?"

Joy's heart dropped. She hadn't talked to the teacher. She felt bad about manipulating and badgering Johnny B into going back to school. He would have to eventually; the state would make him. But if he wasn't quite ready yet . . .

Maybe they could do some kind of homeschooling, which she had promised herself that she was going to check into. Right after Christmas was over. Things were just so hectic right now. Between Christmas and trying to get the room ready, she felt as if her head might explode from it all.

"I haven't," she admitted. And it wasn't that she hadn't had any opportunities to talk with Nancy. She just never managed to use that time.

"Do you think you could talk to her this week?" he asked.

Joy stopped reaching for the corn bread that Leah had made to go with their supper and turned her full attention to her oldest son. "This week?"

"*Jah*." He nodded. "I want to make sure she's okay with me coming back in for half the year. And then being there next year. I thought about asking Uriah if he would make sure there's a ramp at the school that I could use to get in. We haven't had an opportunity yet to talk about it, but I thought maybe the back door would be the place. We could put a ramp there instead of the front, so it wouldn't bother the little kids any."

"Speaking as a little kid," Jane started, "a ramp at the front door wouldn't bother me one bit."

Johnny B smiled at his little sister. "Thanks," he said. Then he turned back to Joy. "*Jah*? So we'll talk to her this week?"

Joy nodded slowly. "And you're sure?" she asked. "You're ready to go back to school?"

"I guess you could say I'm ready."

"I don't want to talk to her then have you start kicking up a fuss come time to get back into class," Joy told him.

He shook his head. "I'm not going to do that. I'm going back to school in January, and I'm going to graduate. I'm going to have to use my mind to make a living, so I might as well start now."

Chapter 17

"Are you gonna be glad to get the space back?" Uriah asked. It was Monday midmorning, and the room was basically complete. The men had already started moving Johnny B's bed into the bedroom and the couch from the back porch to the living room where it belonged. The dining room table had been returned to the dining room, and all the boxes with all the knickknacks and books and things from the living room that had been stored in the dining room were now sitting in the middle of the floor. Not optimal, but on its way to being back to normal.

Joy smiled, but the edges of it looked a bit worn out. She still had a long way to go to get everything done, he knew.

"So the girls are doing okay in the bakery?" he asked. They had to have been doing somewhat okay, otherwise she couldn't have left them there alone and come up to supervise the activities going on inside the house.

"Rachel reminds me a lot of Leah. She works really hard and does everything that I ask of her. But I know she would rather be doing something else besides baking. But Rebecca . . ." Joy smiled. "Rebecca reminds me of me. She loves to bake, and it's a delight to have both of them there helping me."

"Good." Uriah couldn't help but smile in return.

"Where's Johnny B?" Joy asked.

Uriah waved a hand toward the entrance from the living room to the *dawdihaus*. "Simon and Thomas are showing him all the amenities. How to get in and out of bed, how to get in and out of the bathtub by himself. It's really a great setup. It's going to give him a lot of independence. I think that will help him not to worry so much about every little thing. The more he can do for himself, the less he will feel intimidated by asking someone to help with the things he can't do."

Joy nodded. "That makes sense, I guess."

He fell quiet as Johnny B came rolling through the extra-wide doorway that led from the *dawdihaus* to the main house. His eyes were wide with excitement. "Mamm, you've got to see this. It's so cool."

She nodded. "I have plenty of time to look at it as soon as everything's in place. You go talk to Simon and Thomas and see if there's anything else they might need to tell you."

He turned his wheelchair on a dime and rolled back into the *dawdihaus*.

Uriah shifted from one foot to the other. It was great that the room was done. It was great that Johnny B was so excited. It was great that Joy was getting her house back in order, and it was great that his girls were doing great in the bakery. Everything was great. And yet he had something else on his mind. "Can I talk to you for a second?" He took one step closer to her as someone came behind him sorting out some box or another as they did the final cleanup.

She nodded.

He shifted again. "Someplace alone," he clarified. He was uncomfortable even using that word.

"How about the kitchen?"

If he said anything else, it might appear strange, and he didn't want her thinking this was strange at all. "That's fine."

She gave him a quizzical look, then turned and led him to the kitchen. From there they could still hear everyone bustling around in the *dawdihaus* and the living room. Faint laughter and calls for orders floated in from the bakery downstairs. But it was the two of them alone. Just as he requested.

She turned to him, brows raised. "What is it?"

He didn't want it to be like this. There was a part of him that told him he should wait. Maybe invite her out to supper. Take her someplace nice like the Italian restaurant. Away from kids and workers and bakery orders, but he decided that was just the coward in him trying to put off what he knew he wanted.

He cleared his throat and reached for her hands.

She gave him a strange look. "Uriah, are you okay?"

He closed his eyes briefly, opened them again, and nodded. "Joy," he began slowly. Even as sure as he was of this, he was still having to work at it. "I know this may seem kind of sudden, but I'm positive this is the right thing."

"Uriah, what are you talking about?"

He squeezed her fingers with his own. "Will you marry me?"

She stared at him for a full twenty seconds. He counted them off as his heartbeat pounded in his chest. What was taking her so long? Where was the elated "*Jah!*"? Where was the jumping up and down, perhaps even throwing her arms around his neck and hugging him close? Where was all the excitement? Where was all the joy? Where was all the happiness?

"No." She pulled her fingers from his now slack grasp and stepped back. She took another step away, her gaze never leaving his. "No."

He stood that way, his hands out in front of him just as they had been when he held her fingers in his own, even though she was no longer there. He was so shocked he couldn't move.

Why not? his mind screamed. *Why not? Why not? Why not?*

But he couldn't bring himself to ask.

"I'm sorry," she said, and disappeared out of the kitchen. He could hear her footsteps rushing down the hall to her bedroom. A door closed somewhere in the house, and he remained standing there. Alone now.

This is what it feels like, he told himself. *This is what it feels like to have someone carve out your heart with a plastic butter knife.* It wasn't all stabbing, sharp pains that made him feel like at the next beat, his heart just might stop working altogether. He wasn't sure how, but in such a short time, Joy had come to mean so much to him.

But the truth was, it hadn't been a short time. Not really. He had known and admired and respected Joy forever. Only recently had he come to love her in a romantic way. And he did love her. He knew she cared for him. And she knew he would be a good provider. So why had she told him no?

He was alone now. He couldn't ask her. He couldn't tell her that he loved her. He couldn't tell her that if she ever changed her mind, she knew where to find him.

He thought he heard Johnny B call his name as he left the kitchen and walked to the front door, but he couldn't stop. He couldn't turn around. He had to keep walking. He had to get out of there. On numb legs that barely held him upright, he climbed into his buggy and left.

* * *

"I can't believe it's finally finished."

Joy nodded and smiled and pretended that everything was just fine, just as it should be. When everything was far from fine and nothing seemed to be the way it should be.

She stopped at the doorway of the new, finally complete *dawdihaus* and allowed Rachel and Rebecca to step inside ahead of her. Johnny B was waiting there to show them around.

The bakery was closed. Now she was just waiting, pretending, praying she could keep it together until she could once again escape to her room and be alone.

She could feel Johnny B's gaze on her, and she knew he had his own questions that he wanted her to answer. He had already asked her twice why Uriah had left in such a hurry, and she had told him twice that she didn't know. Finally she was forced to add that Uriah was a grown man, and he could leave any time and in any manner that he saw fit. But she could feel Johnny B watching her, as if he knew that she knew something and wasn't telling.

After ohhing and ahhing over the room, Rachel and Rebecca stepped back into the living room, smiling at their father's handiwork.

"Where's Dat?" Rachel asked.

Joy resisted the urge to sigh. Or growl. Or even just exhale in an exasperated manner. Why was everyone so concerned about Uriah? He was a grown man, wasn't he? He could find his way home by himself, and he could decide when he wanted to leave. And he could do it all without telling another soul his intentions.

But she knew she wasn't being fair. She was dealing with her own emotions, and they were tainting her perspective on the entire matter.

"I think he went ahead on home," Joy finally replied as brightly as she could.

There was no way she could reveal the truth: That he had asked her to marry him. That she had turned him down. That he had left upset, and then she had cried her eyes out.

Everyone would want to know why. Why had she turned him down? And if she didn't want to marry him, why was she crying? Except Joy knew that it was more complicated than that.

Rebecca and Rachel shared a look, part concern part surprise.

Did they know? She didn't think so. She couldn't imagine Uriah sharing something like that with them before it happened. As possessive of their father as the two girls were, if Joy had turned him down and they knew about it, she felt fairly certain they would be firing questions at her instead of staring at her like she had tulips sprouting out her ears. No, they didn't know.

"Did he say why?" Rachel asked.

Joy shook her head. At least that was the truth. Joy knew the reasons, but Uriah had not told her what caused him to leave so quickly.

She was splitting hairs, but so be it. She had her own struggles at the moment.

"Maybe he had an appointment at the lumberyard."

Now she was grasping at straws. Many more idioms and she would have to lie down and take a nap.

"Maybe," Rebecca murmured.

Rachel nodded but didn't look convinced. She turned to her sister. "I guess we should just go on home. See about supper."

"I suppose so," Rebecca said.

But she made no move to leave.

Uriah's girls were smart. They knew something was amiss. And they knew that somehow it stemmed from her.

Or maybe Joy was just being oversensitive.

No. She could see them looking at her, those questions in their eyes. Questions she did not have the answers for. Questions that if she did try to answer, her replies would not be well accepted.

They were eighteen and sixteen. They hadn't lived enough life to understand. Neither one of them had loved and lost. Neither one had fought their way back. Raised a family single-handedly, built a business from the ground up, literally. They wouldn't know what it was like to sacrifice a hard-won independence.

She cared for Uriah. She did. More than she was comfortable with. But what scared her the most was the thought of losing him—the idea that she could relinquish her independence to love and then lose it once more. She was older now. So much older. She couldn't fight that battle again. She had to hold her ground. Not give an inch. Love was too fragile to give everything to it.

Another heartbeat stretched between them, and Rebecca gave a small nod. She glanced at her sister, then looked back at Joy. "I'm glad the room is finally finished." Then she gave another nod and made her way to the front door.

Joy hovered there in the living room as the girls donned their cloaks and left.

"Something's up," Rachel said as they rode along home.

"You think?" The cold wind brushed across Rebecca's neck, stirring a couple of loose strands of hair and her untied *kapp* strings. She shivered and pulled her scarf a little higher under her chin.

"Don't get mad at me," Rachel complained. "I didn't do anything."

"Sorry," Rebecca murmured. She really shouldn't take it out on her sister. But something was wrong. Ever since they had gone to work at the bakery, their *dat* had waited for them, so they could all drive home together. True, they weren't actually in the same buggy, just a caravan of Lehmans driving home. "Maybe he had a stomachache."

"Maybe," Rachel said. But Rebecca could tell that she was not convinced. "And when was the last time he complained about a stomachache? Or a headache, or any kind ailment for that matter?"

"You're right." Rebecca tightened her grip on the reins. It was a cold night as winter descended upon them, and her gloves were slick against the leather. It was easy to lose your grip, especially when you had too many things on your mind. "Something happened between them."

"I agree."

"Do you think they had an argument?" Rebecca continued.

Rachel shrugged, the motion dislodging the quilt she had pulled around the two of them. She jerked it back into place before answering. "What would they be arguing about?"

"I don't know," Rebecca said. "I got the feeling she wasn't thrilled with the idea of a *dawdihaus*. Not after Dat originally promised just a room."

"But she's smart. She's logical. A *dawdihaus* is a much better option for Johnny B. Especially if he never walks again. Where's he going to live when he gets older?"

Rachel pressed her lips together, thought about it a moment. "I guess whoever's living in that house will take care of him. If he doesn't marry. So see? It is a better idea." But she didn't think Leah would one day take over the bakery from her *mamm*. Maybe Jane . . . Maybe no one and all of this would be for naught. Who knew? No one knew what God had planned for them.

"That's it?" Rachel asked. "You think that they got into an argument about his rooms?"

Rebecca turned it over in her mind. It didn't fit. "If they had argued about his rooms, I think he would've heard."

"Who? Johnny B?"

"*Jah*," Rachel said. "And he was too excited to have that sort of stain on the day."

"And now we're back to square one."

"I still don't think Dat had a stomachache."

"Me either."

They rode the rest of the way home in silence.

At supper that evening they were all glad to have their *dat* home. But Rebecca could see that his mind was someplace else. He barely touched his food. He mumbled his way through the Bible reading. Then he went outside to check the animals as he always did before he went to bed, but it was hours before he usually turned in.

He came back into the house, kissed them all good night, then went into his room. He closed the door.

Rebecca looked at Rachel.

The younger girls chatted around them, unaware of the seriousness of what had just happened.

They had tried to get him to talk all night. Did their best to drag him into the conversation. They had asked him how he was feeling. They had asked him if something was on his mind. Every time, he told them no. But it was right there for them all to see. Something was wrong. But neither Rebecca nor Rachel had any idea what it could be.

Chapter 18

She couldn't put her finger on exactly what it was, but something was off. After everyone left, Joy had walked around her living room. The couch was back in its normal place. The bookshelf was back where it belonged, all the books lined up like good little schoolchildren, just as they had been before. All her decorations and pictures had been returned to the walls where they belonged. There were no boxes in sight. The dining room table and chairs had long since been moved back into the dining area, and the grandfather clock had been dusted. And yet something seemed off.

Johnny B had been snugly relocated into the *dawdi-haus*, which Chris and Jane had immediately renamed the "Johnny house."

He had slept there last night, in the new bedroom, in his new bed. A triangular device had been installed in the ceiling where he could pull himself up and move himself into his wheelchair without any help. He had a bathroom where he could take care of his needs, he had a kitchen with counters that were lower, so he could reach them from his chair, and he had all his things that had once been in the room he shared with Chris. He seemed happy. Happier than she had seen him in all the months since he had fallen from the hayloft.

"You're quiet today," Rebecca commented as Joy slid another batch of Christmas cookies into the oven. It seemed like they had been baking nonstop all day.

She murmured something she hoped passed as a response. Then added, "I didn't sleep well last night."

At least that was the truth. As usual, Johnny B had turned off the baby monitor so she couldn't hear him. He could turn it back on if he needed help, but somehow having that connection to him made her feel better. And now having him in a completely separate part of the house was scary to her. She told herself he needed the independence and that she understood. But it was hard.

"I think it's strange having your house changed that much," Rachel commented. She was standing by the cash register waiting for the after-school rush to appear.

As if on cue Leah, Chris, and Jane came tromping down the steps from upstairs. Jane fairly skipped over to Rebecca and gave her a quick hug. Then turned her attention to Rachel and blessed her with the same.

Leah immediately began to don her work apron and get ready for her shift as Jane and Chris snagged a cookie. It was normal, just like always. Jane kissed her *mamm* on the cheek and started up the stairs again. But instead of following behind her, Chris leaned up against the work counter and nibbled his cookie as if it might be the last one he would ever receive.

"Something on your mind, Chris?"

He looked down at his cookie and shrugged, mumbling something she couldn't quite understand. That was another thing. She couldn't remember the last time he demanded be called Topher.

"Did something happen at school?" She looked from

Chris to Leah. Her oldest daughter merely shrugged. If something happened, Leah wasn't aware of it.

Chris shrugged again. "No."

"Why do I feel like there's something you need to tell me?" She tried to make her words ring without accusation. It was a hard thing to do, but he didn't seem to notice whatever blame came through. Whatever it was that Chris had on his mind, it had sure taken that chip off his shoulder.

He stared down at his feet. "Tell me a story about Dat." He lifted his eyes to hers. She could see the hope and desperation there. He needed to know something more about his father.

She never spoke of Rudy. Not because she didn't love him. The exact opposite. She couldn't speak of him and not be able to be around him. At least at first that's how it had been. Now things were easier. But just after he had died, it had been so difficult to even say his name. So she hadn't. But now she realized, in dealing with her own pain, she had neglected her son. Something she had never intended to do.

She glanced quickly around the bakery. Rachel and Rebecca were doing their best to pretend like they weren't paying attention. Leah was tying on her apron, still watching both of them closely. There was only one customer in the store. They were looking at the cake decorating book, trying to find the perfect design for their upcoming event. Joy took Chris over to the chairs they had behind the counter, away from the ovens, away from the cash register. "What do you want to know?"

His big, blue eyes filled with tears. "I don't remember him much. I would like to know anything that you might want to tell me. What was his favorite color? What was his favorite food? Did he like to play baseball? Could he swim? Did he go swimming in the lake? Was he afraid of the water? Or snakes? What about frogs?" His tears broke free and slid down his cheeks.

The questions came at her so fast she barely had time to register one before another was zinging in her direction.

"Blue," she finally said. She felt her own tears stinging her eyes. But it was *gut* to talk about him. Good to remember. "His favorite color was blue. His favorite food was spaghetti. He loved to play baseball. *Jah*, he could swim. He was not afraid of the water. He enjoyed swimming in the lake. He didn't like snakes but he wasn't scared of them, and he liked frogs. I think anyway. It wasn't something we discussed often."

He gave her a trembling smile.

"I'm sorry I never told you that before," she said. "He was a good father. He loved all of you so much. One time when you were just a baby you had a really bad ear infection. They don't know what caused it or why. But you couldn't even lie in your crib. You just cried and cried. For a solid week he held you in his arms at night. He slept sitting up so he could hold you up and you wouldn't cry."

Chris's expression was one of wonder and awe. "He did that for me?"

Joy smiled. "Of course he did. He loved you so very much."

"I love him too," Chris said. "Even though he's not here, I still love him."

"I wouldn't expect anything less," Joy said.

Chris nodded and wiped his nose on the sleeve of his shirt. Joy decided now was not the time to fuss at him for such manners.

"You okay?" she asked.

He sniffed but nodded.

The bell over the door rang, signaling the after-school

rush. She rose to her feet. "Are you gonna go upstairs with your brother and sister?"

He shook his head and took another bite of his cookie. A big one this time more like the Chris she knew. "I think I'll hang out here for a while."

She nodded, and went to check the cookies still baking in the oven.

Things were changing. Chris was changing. Johnny B was changing. And those weren't the only things. *Jah*, Uriah was no longer in the house. *Jah*, the construction was done. She had her living room back. All the furniture was where it belonged. Doorways were wide and everything was back to normal. And yet nothing felt quite right.

Chapter 19

Rebecca took a step back and critically eyed the icing rose that she had just piped.

"Very nice," Joy said.

Rebecca tilted her head in the other direction. "I think it's a little bit crooked."

The phone rang.

"I'll get it," Rachel said. She moved toward the avocado-green phone hanging on the wall. They had a cordless . . . somewhere. But Evie was bad about leaving it places it didn't belong. Most times it was hard to find before the person on the other end of the line hung up.

It was Friday, just before closing time. Evie had asked for the day off, and so they had switched. She had worked Thursday, and Rebecca and Rachel had taken her Friday. Rebecca didn't mind, since Joy did most of her bread baking on Monday, Wednesday, and Friday, so Rebecca didn't usually get to be a part of it. And she wanted to know everything there was to know about the bakery business.

She'd been dreaming lately about having her own bakery. What it would be like to own the shop, decorate cakes, make delicious bread and all the other wonderful treats that Joy had in her shop. The only problem was that if she did it in Paradise Springs, she would be in direct competition with Joy. That wasn't a nice thought at all.

"What you have to remember is right here, you have a single rose. When they are on the cake in bunches, a little imperfection is not nearly as noticeable."

Rebecca pursed her lips and continued to study the rose. She understood what Joy was saying, but she wasn't sure she liked the idea. Perhaps she was just a perfectionist at heart.

Rachel hung up the phone and came to stand next to them. "That was Dat. He said he wasn't going to be able to make it tonight."

Rebecca looked to Joy to see what her reaction to that news might be. But her face was impassive, blank as a napkin lying nearby.

"That's too bad," she said.

All week Rebecca had tried to figure out what had happened between Joy and her father. It was obvious something had, but no one was talking. She supposed it was none of her business, but she had a feeling both of them were hurting. She loved them both, and she honestly wanted to help.

"Why not?" Rebecca asked.

Rachel shrugged. "He said he had to stay at the lumberyard for something or another. Should we call off the dinner?"

"No," Joy said a little too loudly, a little too quickly. "I mean, I don't think so. We all have a good time. I can't see having everyone else miss out just because your father has to work."

Rachel seemed to think about it a minute. "We'll have to go get Ruthie and Reena from the house," she said.

"And Dat usually picks up the food on his way out here," Rebecca added.

Rachel turned to her sister. "I'll go get the girls if you go get the food."

"Deal," Rebecca agreed.

And that was how Rebecca found herself trotting into town on a cold afternoon to pick up Chinese food. She really didn't mind. She enjoyed the dinners with her cousins and her aunt. But it might be a little strange without Dat there.

She told herself she really wasn't spying on him when she went by the lumberyard. She had to drive that way to get to the Paradise Chinese Buffet. It was only natural that she look over. But she almost jerked the reins and stopped in the middle of the road when she saw his buggy wasn't there.

Jah, she'd been a little more interested in her icing rose than what Rachel had first been telling her about their *dat*, but she was certain that he said he had to work. At least she was certain that's what Rachel had said. Had her sister gotten it wrong? Or was her father avoiding Joy?

Rebecca picked up the food, and on the way back she studied the parking lot at the lumberyard once more, just to make sure his buggy wasn't hidden someplace where she couldn't see it from the road. But she knew better. She'd passed it too many times before. She knew where he liked to park and all the little places in the parking lot where a buggy could rest. He wasn't there. But why?

Seven excited faces met her in the living room as she walked in with the two bags of Chinese food. She took it immediately into the dining room, where their places had already been set for them to eat. Just nine. That one empty space seemed to mock her. Everyone prayed and started doling out food.

Rebecca took advantage of the noise and turned to Rachel.

"Dat wasn't at home, was he? When you went to pick up the girls?" She asked the question so that only Rachel could hear. Not that anyone at the table was paying attention to her. They were too busy eating wontons and spring rolls dipped in sweet-and-sour sauce.

"No." Rachel frowned. "I told you, he said he was working. Why do you ask?"

Rebecca paused for a moment. Should she tell her sister that their *dat* was not where he said he was going to be? No, she decided. No good would come of it. If their father had wanted them to know where he was, he would've told them. Yet it wasn't like their *dat* to lie. That was what bothered her the most.

"No reason," Rebecca said. She waved a hand around as if to erase the words she'd spoken. "Forget I said anything."

She missed him. It was as simple and as complicated as that. It just didn't seem like the same kind of family dinner without Uriah there. Joy was sure the kids missed him too, though they were chattering on like they always did. Probably because they were worried about the reasons behind his absence. She hoped and prayed it had nothing to do with her turning down his marriage proposal, but how could it not? She wished she'd been able to explain her reasons to him, but she had fled the room knowing that if she stayed a moment longer, she might end up caving and surrendering everything she had worked so hard for.

I'll call him tomorrow, she decided. It was a Saturday morning. He would be at work at the lumberyard, and she would be at work at the bakery. They both had a phone.

She would just call him. She could make sure he was okay, make sure he knew that she still cared about him. And hopefully she could get everything back right again.

They ate Chinese food until the kids all said they were about to pop. Joy had trouble swallowing even a few bites. But she did her best. She didn't want the children to know how much she missed Uriah being there.

"Everybody take your plates to the trash," Ruthie commanded pointing toward the kitchen. It was how they always did it. Eating off disposable plates and forks for easy cleanup. The only difference that night was that they were actually in the dining room instead of at the dining room table shoved into the living room, which included Johnny B's bed and the furnishings.

"We know what to do." Chris rolled his eyes at his cousin.

"*Jah*," Ruthie shot back. "And now's the time to do it."

For a moment Joy was afraid that Chris was going to shove his plate at Ruthie and tell her that if she wanted it in the trash so bad, she could take it there herself. He paused a second too long.

"Chris," Joy said, a warning in her voice.

He turned toward her. "She's not the boss of me."

Ruthie propped her hands on her hips and twisted her mouth into something akin to a frown. What was it Rebecca had called her? A tyrant. *Jah*, that really covered it.

"Regardless," Joy said, as patiently as she possibly could. "You need to take your plates to the trash, then we can go play games."

Thankfully he relented. And, she noted, once again his change of nickname wasn't brought up. Thank heaven for small miracles. It was one less thing she had to worry about.

"Let's team up for Dutch Blitz," Ruthie suggested. "Boys against the girls."

Chris scoffed. "That's not fair. There's only two of us and six of you."

"Okay then," Ruthie said. "We'll play Lehmans against Lehmans."

Chris rolled his eyes. "That doesn't make any sense either. We're all Lehmans."

Rebecca took that moment to step in. "I think she means the Uriah Lehmans versus the Rudy Lehmans, right?" She turned to her sister.

"That's right."

"I don't want to play," Chris said.

"Fine then," Ruthie said. She turned to Jane. "You're on my team."

Jane shook her head. "I don't want to be on your team. I want to be on Rebecca's team."

"But if we play youngest against oldest that won't work."

"Who said we were playing oldest versus youngest?" Chris shot back.

Ruthie turned to him. "I thought you weren't playing."

"I'm not."

"Ruthie." Joy picked that moment to intervene. She hadn't realized it before now, but Ruthie was a tyrant. She seemed to boss everyone around. Being the youngest of four . . . Well, Joy found it highly unusual. Jane usually went along with everything her older siblings did and said, learning from them and their mistakes as they all went along. But not Ruthie. She needed to lead them all. "Can you help me with something in the kitchen please?"

"We were just about to play," Ruthie protested.

"Rachel, would you get the cards out and get them shuffled? Then when Ruthie comes back you can start."

Rachel nodded and headed for the bookcase where the games were stored.

Ruthie lifted her chin at stubborn angle.

"Just for a minute," Joy said. "Promise."

She led Ruthie from the living room into the kitchen and across to the basement door.

"Where we going?" Ruthie asked.

Joy started down the basement stairs, the motion-sensing lights flickering on to help her find her way. "I made some special cookies today and we were going to try them tonight. But I left them in the bakery. I thought you might come down and help me bring them up."

That seemed to satisfy Ruthie, and she went downstairs without fuss.

It was the truth. Joy had made some special cookies, but they weren't necessarily for tonight. Still it was a good excuse as any to get the girl alone for a few minutes.

Joy stepped behind the counter and hooked her arm over her shoulder. "Come on back," she told her.

Ruthie inched her way behind the counters into the space where the workers usually were.

"Can you fold this box up for me?" She handed Ruthie one of the flattened boxes they used for pastries and such.

Ruthie nodded but looked at the box hesitantly.

"It's not hard," Joy coaxed. "First thing is we should open it so it has a hole, then just fold the flaps in until you have a box."

Ruthie did as Joy instructed. Her tongue stuck in the corner of her mouth as she worked.

"This is a special recipe," Joy said. "I got it out of a magazine when I was at the doctor's office last." She put one finger over her lips. "Don't tell anybody."

Ruthie nodded, her expression serious. "I won't. It's our secret. What kind of cookies are they?"

"They're oatmeal cookies, but they're made with white chocolate chips and dried cherries."

Ruthie wrinkled up her face. "Dried cherries?"

Joy nodded. "You know, like raisins are dried grapes but these are—"

"Raisin cherries."

Joy laughed. "That works. Here," she said, handing Ruthie a disposable plastic glove. "Put this on your hand and take these cookies and place them in the box. Count out two for everybody just in case."

Ruthie nodded, and started loading up the cookies.

"Sometimes it's good to be in charge, don't you think?"

"I suppose," Ruthie said. "But I'm little."

Like that stopped her. "Well, sometimes it's good *not* to be in charge." She didn't know how to broach the subject without alienating the poor girl. But bossing everyone around was surely not going to make her friends, now or in the future. "Some people have to be in charge a lot," Joy continued. "Like *mamms* and *dats*."

Ruthie filled the box of cookies and handed it to Joy. "I'm just like my *mamm*," Ruthie said. "Everybody tells me so."

Joy mentally did the math. The girl couldn't have been more than four when her mother died. And she probably remembered as much about her as Chris did of Rudy.

"Do you like when they say that?" Joy asked. "Do you like when they tell you that you're like your *mamm*?"

Ruthie stopped, considered the question for a moment. "*Jah*," she finally said. "I do. I want to be like her. Just like her."

Joy reached out and touched the girl's dark hair. "You look like her. You have her hair. And her eyes. And her nose." Joy dabbed a finger against the end of Ruthie's pert little nose.

Ruthie laughed.

"But you know you don't have to be in charge of everything in order to be like your *mamm*. Because you already are."

Once again Ruthie considered those words. But this time she nodded a little slower. "I guess so," she said, though Joy wasn't sure she was entirely convinced.

"I know so," Joy replied. "And I wouldn't tell you wrong."

Ruthie smiled at her. Heavens, the child did look just like Dinah. And Joy figured bossing everyone around and running the household like she thought a *mamm* would do was Ruthie's way of keeping her mother alive.

Then she thought about Chris coming in and asking her things about Rudy. Things that she never thought to tell him about his father.

"Did I ever tell you that your *mamm* used to make the best brownies?" Joy asked.

Ruthie looked up at her with wide eyes. "Better than yours?"

"Now don't go around telling everybody this," Joy started, "but, *jah*, hers were pretty good."

"What else did she like to bake?"

"She baked all sorts of things, but brownies were definitely her specialty. In fact, I think it was a pan of brownies that managed to get your *dat* to fall in love with her."

"I wish I had her recipe," Ruthie said.

"I bet it's in one of her cookbooks."

"Maybe," Ruthie said. "Whenever I'm looking through them, I'm not really thinking about making brownies. But when I find it, I can make brownies for everybody for dessert."

"You could do that one week for our family supper," Joy suggested.

"That would be fun," Ruthie said.

"How about we do this?" Joy said. "Let's let each person be in charge of something different."

Ruthie seemed to think about this for a moment. "Like what?"

"Well, you're going to be in charge of the dessert. Perhaps Rebecca can be in charge of the games. Johnny B can be in charge of the paper plates. Chris can pick out where we're going to get the food from. And on like that."

The idea was so foreign to Ruthie that she had to think about it for a moment before answering. "I suppose that would be all right."

"It would take some pressure off of you. You work too hard at these family dinners," Joy said.

"I don't mind," Ruthie said importantly.

"I know you don't," Joy replied. "But I do think you should enjoy yourself more."

Ruthie nodded. "I'll try, Joy," she said. "I will surely try."

"Mamm!"

It was a sound she wasn't used to. At least not in this situation. Johnny B was at the upstairs basement door hollering down at them. "We need you."

"Be right there," she called up to him. Joy turned back to Ruthie. "We better get back upstairs; it sounds like trouble is brewing."

And that was just what she had been afraid of when Uriah called and said that he wasn't coming. She was afraid of how she would handle all eight children. Even if two of them were practically adults.

"I'm just saying it's not nice to tease someone." Joy heard Rebecca's words before she even got the kitchen door shut. What had happened now? She hustled through the kitchen and back into the living room, Ruthie hot on her heels carrying the box of cookies.

"What is going on in here?"

Reena, who had tears streaming down her face, and Chris, who was red around the ears, both started talking at once. Johnny B and Rebecca joined the diatribe, each trying to explain a side of the story.

Joy held up her hands to stop flow of unintelligible words. "One at a time," she told them. She turned her attention to Reena. She figured since Reena was in tears, she deserved first say. "Reena, what happened?"

Reena hiccupped softly. "Chris said that he didn't like my doll."

"Nuh-uh." Chris jumped to his feet, the red from his ears staining his cheeks now as well. "I just said that you were too old for it."

"If it's mine, how can I be too old for it?" Reena shot back. She hugged her American Girl doll to her chest protectively.

Joy had to admit that Reena was a bit old to be carrying a doll everywhere, but who was she to say if it gave her comfort?

"I don't take mine all over the place."

"*Danki*, Jane. But I think this is between Chris and Reena." Joy turned back to the other two. It was true Jane had an American Girl doll. There'd been a time when she carried her everywhere and had tea parties and bought outfits and begged Joy to sew her a matching dress each time she sewed a new dress for Jane. But that had long since passed, and Jane was a good four years younger than Reena.

"Chris." Joy turned her attention to her youngest son. "You are entitled to your opinion, but you should not force it on someone else, especially if it might hurt their feelings. You owe Reena an apology."

He ducked his head and stared at a spot on the floor. "Sorry," he told her.

"*Danki*," Reena said, then she sniffed loudly.

"Reena, the problem with loving something like a doll so much that you want to carry it with you everywhere is that sometimes people think you might be too old for it. That doesn't mean you have to get rid of it, and it doesn't mean that it's a bad thing. Jane," she turned her youngest, "why don't you and Reena go upstairs and you can show her your American Girl doll? And maybe next week the two of you can play with them before supper."

"So I'm not too old for it?" Reena asked.

Joy had a feeling she would outgrow it soon enough. Soon she would be thirteen and taking part in more grown-up activities with other girls her age. And by then the American Girl doll would be forgotten, propped up on the dresser or stored under the bed wearing whatever dress she'd had on the last time she'd been played with. But that was a decision Reena needed to make for herself. No one else could tell her when it was time to stop playing with dolls.

Joy knew grown women who collected dolls and had them all over their houses. Most, of course, were *Englisch* women. She even knew of some who collected the old-fashioned Amish faceless dolls. To each his own, right?

"When you feel that you're too old to take your doll around, then you will stop taking her around. But until then she's your responsibility. You have to make sure she's dressed, you have to make sure she's clean, and you have to make sure that you don't leave her anyplace. It would be a shame to lose her. You've had her awhile, *jah*?"

Reena nodded.

"Okay then." Crisis averted. And if Reena wanted to haul her doll around for her own comfort, at least Joy had turned it into a lesson of responsibility. Though she hoped the girl was prepared for more teasing in the future if she continued the behavior, that was something Reena would have to realize on her own.

"Come on," Jane said. "I want to show you my doll." She took Reena's hand and together the two of them made their way up the stairs toward the bedroom that Jane shared with Leah.

"You can show her mine too while you're up there," Leah added.

"I've got an idea," Ruthie said just as the two girls reached the top of the landing. "We've all got American Girl dolls. Why don't we each bring them next week and we can show everyone our favorite dresses?"

Reena tucked her doll in the crook of her elbow and clapped her hands in glee. "That's a marvelous idea."

Chris groaned. "We're going to be flooded with girl things."

Joy chuckled. "We'll find some boy things to balance it out, so you and Johnny B can have something to talk about."

Johnny B rolled his eyes. "No, thank you. And I still want to be left out of the doll conversation as well."

"Maybe we can go out in the barn and play with the kittens," Chris added.

"I want to do that now," Ruthie said enthusiastically.

Rebecca and Rachel chuckled. "Me too," they said together. And dolls forgotten, they all tromped out to the barn to check the newborn kittens.

Joy had really been concerned about having all eight kids without Uriah there to lend a hand, but it was going just fine. All things considered, they were having a really good family night. The only problem was she really missed Uriah.

"Funny thing," Rebecca said the following day. Johnny B was set up in the office with Rachel supervising his work for the time being. So Rebecca took the opportunity to slip out and talk to her *dat*.

"What's that?" Her father looked up from the invoice he was checking. She had caught him between customers, which was a good thing. Saturday mornings at the lumberyard were fairly busy, even in the wintertime, when not nearly as much building was going on around Paradise Springs.

"We ate Chinese last night at the family dinner."

"You already told me that," he said, a hint of confusion creeping into his tone.

"*Jah*. But when I drove to town to pick it up, I passed by here, and I didn't see your buggy."

"That is funny," he started, "seeing as how I was here working on a big order until way after seven o'clock."

He said the words with conviction, but he didn't look her in the eye. To Rachel, that was as telling as it got. Something was definitely up. His words were not the truth. What did that mean?

She wanted to press further but couldn't bring herself to disrespect her father in that manner. Call him a liar . . .

She mentally shook her head. It wasn't something she was prepared to do over one family dinner. Her father had to have some other reason for not coming. Some reason that he didn't want them to know about. Why? She had no idea.

"I think I parked out back last night," her father explained, nodding as if he had somehow come to this great understanding.

"Maybe." Rebecca allowed him the excuse. She had looked in the back to see if her father's buggy was hiding somewhere, and she was confident that he had not been at the lumberyard when he said he was. But she couldn't question him further. He was a father, after all.

"Okay," she said. "I suppose I should go check on Johnny B and Rachel."

Her father nodded. Then the phone rang, effectively cutting off any more conversation between them.

"Paradise Lumber," Uriah said into the receiver as Rebecca moved away, back toward the office.

There had been a brief moment when he thought she might question him further about where he was the night before. He hated lying to her. He hated lying to them all. But it wasn't something he could do. He couldn't spend every Friday night with Joy, pretending like everything was just as it should be when it wasn't. And he surely couldn't tell his family—or Joy for that matter—the truth on that either.

"You know what they say . . ." Joy. Hearing her voice made his heart soar and his stomach hurt all at the same time.

"What's that?" he managed to croak.

"All work and no play makes Uriah a dull boy."

He sighed and pretended like he was tired from all that he had been doing when in fact he'd left work right on time, drove to the house, made a sandwich, and then waited for his kids to come home. *Jah*, big day.

"Some days are just like that," he said. "You know how it can be."

"*Jah*," she said. "We got a big order for Christmas in

yesterday. I don't know what I would do without Rachel and Rebecca there to help me."

"That's good," he said. And it was. But talking to her like nothing was wrong was breaking his heart. The sound of her voice reminded him of his folly. Of being foolish enough to fall in love with an independent woman. An independent widow. He might have had better luck with an independent young girl who hadn't yet tasted that success of life, that sense of accomplishment that comes after tragedy. When you know you're going to live through it. It did something to a person. It changed them. And once you knew you could survive . . . Nothing was the same again.

"Anyway," Joy was saying, "you are coming next week, right?"

Uriah gripped the phone a little tighter. "*Jah*," he lied. "Of course." But he couldn't tell her what excuse he was going to concoct now. It was too early. He had to continue to pretend that he was coming, right up until that moment he called to say he wasn't.

He hated the deception. But what else could he do?

"And you're okay?" Joy asked. She didn't have to voice the question for him to hear it in the words. He had asked her to marry him. She had turned him down, and he had barely spoken to her for a week. She wasn't worried about the marriage; she was worried about the relationship that they'd had previously. She wanted to make certain it was still intact.

"Of course." The lie slipped easily from his lips. It was a shame that he had lied so much these last few days that he could do it without hardly blinking an eye.

"And we're okay." It was a soft-spoken statement. But it weighed heavily.

Uriah turned away from the mouthpiece and cleared his throat. He could do this. "Of course we are."

That seemed to satisfy her for now. Though he had a feeling she would be calling periodically throughout the week to make sure he wasn't changing his mind. Yet in the end, he would have to. He would be forced to see her every other week at church, but other than that, he wasn't sure he could face her at all. A man could only do so much. He hung up the phone with his heart still broken.

Chapter 20

December passed in a blur of parties and gifts and snow and cold weather. But the saddest part of all was that Uriah hadn't spoken to Joy since the Saturday after he had asked her to marry him and she had said no. He thought there for a while, just after that call, she would dog him, make sure he was coming to all the family events. She hadn't, and now he supposed she understood that he needed space. She'd given it to him. And to think he'd believed his heart was beyond further breaking. How wrong could one man be?

He wanted her back in his life, and yet he knew that wasn't possible. Yet she was still there, hovering on the fringes. Rebecca and Rachel came home on Monday and Wednesday and smelled just like Joy. Like sugar cookies and yeast bread and something else—maybe vanilla—all wrapped up into one scent with just the hint of cinnamon. It was strange and familiar and poignant in the same moment. And he made his daughters take a bath as soon as they came in the house. He couldn't stand to smell it and think about Joy all evening.

There were other changes in his house too, and he felt he could only attribute them to Joy—perhaps because he'd asked his daughters outright. Somehow between the time that Johnny B's room was done and the middle of December, Uriah noticed that Reena wasn't dragging her doll around all the time. The precious American Girl doll now had a place of honor on her dresser upstairs and was dressed perhaps every other day or so. But Reena didn't bring her down to dinner, and the doll wasn't always in the buggy whenever Reena was. Reena had started to go outside and play more with her friends, and for that, he was grateful. When he asked her where her doll was, she told him that she had left it upstairs; that it was a good thing to keep, but that didn't mean she had to take it everywhere with her. He had been trying to instill that idea in her for a while and never could get the point across. He made a note to ask Rebecca and Rachel, but he had a feeling Joy was behind this change.

And Ruthie. Ruthie was no longer the mini household tyrant. Though sometimes when he came home things were in a bit of chaos because Rachel hadn't figured out what to cook on a Wednesday while Rebecca was at work and Ruthie was upstairs coloring instead of downstairs dragging out ingredients and bossing everyone around. One night he pulled her aside and asked her outright. She told him about a conversation she'd had with Joy about her mother. How her mother would always live inside her. Uriah wasn't sure what that had to do with anything—he had continually told his girls the very same thing since their mother had passed—but somehow hearing it from Joy changed Ruthie from six going on twenty-one to six going on seven. He liked the change, and yet it was a little sad that she had to change at all. She'd been that way for so long now. But he was glad Ruthie was back to being his little girl, and for that, he had Joy to thank. If only he could talk to her. If only he knew what to say.

* * *

December had brought many changes for Joy as well. Evie had decided that perhaps baking wasn't for her after all. She gave notice, but still came by a couple of days a week to spend time with Johnny B.

Since he had moved into his "Johnny *haus*," he had made one mention about never walking again or never having a life. Some days she even caught him smiling. That was a blessing, and she knew to count it. Sometimes she counted it twice.

At the end of the month, as planned, Rachel had given up her job at the bakery. Rebecca had stayed on, of course, but moved to the Monday, Wednesday, Friday shifts that Evie had previously worked. Rebecca's help in the bakery was another blessing. To Joy, Rebecca was just a more mature and grown-up Leah as far as hard work and enthusiasm were concerned, mixed with Joy's own love of baking. That love lifted everything. Neither Rachel nor Leah loved baking and cake decorating and all the little, tiny details: proper egg wash and sprinkles and fancy cuts and all the other things that made Joy's bakery different from the rest. Joy was so very glad to have Rebecca working in the bakery. It was another one of those double blessings she counted twice.

But Uriah. She didn't know whether to initiate a conversation with him or not. That November Saturday he had told her everything was fine, and she had told him that she understood. Even though she knew he was lying the whole time. Nothing was fine, and nothing was going to be the same again. So what was she supposed to say to him now? That she was sorry that she couldn't give up her independence?

She had tried those words once. She had practiced

them in the mirror and they had sounded so shallow that she knew she couldn't say them to him. Yet there they were. It was the truth. Yet she missed him. That was the truth as well.

He had found reasons all December not to come to the family dinners. A couple of times were weather related, so she really couldn't hold those against him. The kids still wanted to eat together, and Joy let them have their fun. Rebecca had used one week to have a cookie decorating class with the others. She wanted to try it out on them first before she took it to Joy as a permanent idea for the bakery. Everyone had had a great time, and Joy was considering the idea.

Nothing had been decided yet at the Whoopie Pie Widows Club. They put off determining how they were going to define "widow" until after the first of the year. Now that the time was here, a decision was going to have to be made. And soon. As in tonight.

"Are you back now, dear?" Katie asked.

Joy pulled herself from her thoughts and smiled at the older woman. "I just have a few things on my mind."

The woman patted Joy's knee and gave her a knowing smile.

"Are we going to take a vote?" Betsy Stoll asked, looking around the room. Joy liked Betsy. Smart as a whip and with a no-nonsense manner. She ran Paradise Apothecary and had an herbal remedy for almost everything. Maybe Joy should stop by there the next day and see if Betsy had something for her aching heart.

"How are we going to vote? A show of hands?" Sylvie looked around the room at the other widows. Honestly, Joy didn't care one way or the other. Truth be known, she cared about little as much as she cared about figuring out a way to get Uriah to talk to her again.

"It's hard to vote on this with the two of you sitting here," Elsie said. "No one's going to vote against you, even if they believe that they should."

Sylvie tilted her head one way and then the other, as if considering the words from all angles.

"We could write what we think on a piece of paper," Lillian suggested hesitantly. "Then put it in a hat. No one would know how anyone voted then. We could count the votes that way."

Millie and Sylvie shook their heads, incredulous smiles on their faces.

"You're not voting against us," Millie explained. "It's an informal group."

"That's right. We can run it however we like," Sylvie said.

"So we could say you have to have been widowed before in order to be in the club." Hattie looked around the room to see how that would be taken.

"I think that goes without saying, dearie," Katie said with of quick nod. "Widows group and all that."

"I guess what I mean is, all of us here have been married, and all of us here have had a husband who died. That makes us widows. But even if you get remarried, we have all still gone through the loss of a spouse. That's why we got together to begin with."

"Makes sense to me," Elsie said.

"So it would still be open to the members who could've joined before?" Sylvie asked.

"Like Callie Raber," Hattie put in.

Callie's husband had died last summer, and since then Hattie had been trying to get her to come to the meetings. So far she had been unsuccessful. Callie was fifty and childless, still reeling from her husband's accidental death and the fact that she was all alone now.

Millie nodded. "I like it." She smiled. "Not that I've

ever officially been a member of the group or anything. I probably shouldn't have a say at all."

The women all pshawed and pooed and flicked her words away with fluttering hands.

"You've been here long enough to be a member for sure," Katie said. And everyone nodded in agreement.

"It's decided then." Sylvie looked around at each person in turn, meeting their eyes and getting a nod in answer. "Everything is going to stay just the same."

"*Jah*," they all agreed.

"And we'll still hold the meetings here at the inn?" Sylvie looked to Millie for reassurance. The new dynamic between farm and B&B still seemed a little strange to the women.

Millie nodded. "I would love to have the meetings here each week."

"So nothing's changing?" Elsie asked with a slight frown. But that was Elsie. She seemed to find the cracks in everything.

"Right," Sylvie said in that no-nonsense tone of hers. "Everything's going to stay just the same as it is right now."

That was one thing Joy could be happy about. There had been far too many changes lately.

They had been baking bread all day. All sorts of loaves. Cinnamon bread, onion cheese bread, sourdough bread. Ciabatta and focaccia. They'd even baked some banana bread and some fruitcake which, despite the name, Joy considered to be questionably somewhere between cake and bread.

And all morning long Rebecca had been trying to gather up enough courage to ask Joy what had happened between her and Rebecca's *dat*. Something had happened.

Rebecca had the feeling that if she asked Joy, she would get the same sort of answer that she had gotten from her *dat*. That there was nothing wrong, followed by an indulgent smile as if to say, *Go on, silly child. Don't bother me with stupid questions.* But something had happened, and it had happened a while back. All the way back in November, just after Thanksgiving. Right about the time they finished Johnny B's room. Since that time, everyone had been busy with weddings and Christmas parties. They'd been busy enough that at the time, Rebecca wasn't sure if she was imagining the changes or not. There had been times when it seemed like it was so obvious, and others when it didn't seem that way at all. Like maybe she'd been imagining it. But one thing was certain: Her *dat* wasn't coming to the Friday night dinners anymore.

"Joy," Rebecca started as she took yet another tray of pretzel bread from the oven. It was the latest thing Joy was trying, and Rebecca was secretly thrilled that it had been her idea.

Joy looked up as she continued to wipe down the worktable.

"Do you still want to have the family dinners on Friday?" Rebecca plunged in. "Because I'm getting the feeling that Dat doesn't want to have them because he never comes anymore. He's always working late."

Joy's gaze dropped back to the worktable. She scrubbed a particularly stubborn spot. "If he said he's working late, then he's working late."

"Every Friday?" Rebecca asked. "That's virtually impossible. Something happened."

As she watched, Rebecca saw a line of color work its way from Joy's neck all the way to the roots of her hair. Whatever had happened, it had happened between Joy and her *dat*. Rebecca knew it as sure as she knew her own name.

"Are you not going to tell us what's wrong?" Rebecca asked gently. "I mean, everyone loved having the dinners, and it's just not the same when he's not there. You can't just let us flounder around and not understand."

Joy continued to scrub as if her life depended on it.

"Joy, please," Rebecca beseeched.

Joy stopped, her face still blazing red, and tossed the rag aside. "He asked me to marry him."

Rebecca's heart soared. "That's so exciting! That's perfect!" That was just what they needed. Maybe not what they wanted when they started out, but Rebecca knew that it was just what they needed now for certain. "The two of you will be so good together. Please tell me you're not waiting until the fall to get married. It would be so wonderful for everyone if the two of you got married now." That was also something she never thought she would say about her father, but it was true. It was also exciting, and it was all so perfect.

Until she ran out of words.

And suddenly, she realized that Joy wasn't talking. She wasn't smiling. She wasn't anything-ing.

"I told him no."

Rebecca opened her mouth to say something, but realized she had no response for what Joy had just told her. "You told him no?" It was all she could do, repeat what Joy had just said. "What do you mean, no?" She finally found her voice and the questions kept coming. "Why did you say no?"

Joy stared at her. Her mouth was pressed into a thin line. Her eyes held some emotion that Rebecca couldn't name, and her chin was held at a willful angle. "That's private."

Rebecca couldn't find fault with Joy for not immediately spurting out some excuse or another. But that didn't stop her from needing an answer. Needing a reason for things falling apart when it all seemed to be finally clicking into place.

She shook her head as if somehow that would bring everything back in line once again. "I don't understand. Do you not love him?"

Joy's chin raised another inch. "That's private."

"After everything he's done for you and your family?" Rebecca couldn't stop herself from pressing further. "Not even just Johnny B's rooms, but all that stuff with Chris. If it hadn't been for Dat, Chris would still be going around demanding to be called Topher. Johnny B's not nearly as unhappy these days. I don't know if it's the room or the fact that my *dat*'s been talking to him about different things. Did you know that Dat printed out some stuff for Johnny B, so that he knew that there was life after having a spinal cord injury? That there might be hope for him to have a family one day? With medical intervention, maybe. But it was the possibility. A possibility he hadn't known before. Haven't you noticed the change in him?"

Joy's defiant stance crumpled a bit. Her shoulders drooped; her chin dropped. Hurt flashed in her eyes.

This was not what Rebecca wanted. She hadn't told Joy all this to crush her spirit. Then suddenly she knew. Joy wanted to take care of these problems herself. Rebecca's *dat* stepping in undermined her authority with her boys. Never mind that his counsel helped; it was Joy's place and not Uriah's.

"I'm sorry," Rebecca said. She felt tears rising in her eyes and saw those reflected in Joy's own. "I meant no disrespect."

Joy nodded. "I understand." And then Rebecca's shoulders shook as Joy took her in her arms and hugged her tight. The dams broke and the tears fell.

Joy stood at the top of the stairs, pausing for a moment before stepping into her own kitchen. It was after five; the bakery was closed for the evening. Anything they sold now was on the honor system. She left some goods on a table just outside the customers' door with a shoe box to deposit the money in. Mostly day-old stuff that might've been tossed out otherwise.

Tossed out, tossed aside, kind of the same way she did Uriah. Not that she could admit to that. But she could see that Rebecca felt that way. The thought made her stomach ache. She had never meant to hurt her niece. She had never meant to hurt Uriah. She had never meant to hurt herself. And yet her heart was still breaking. Now she had even more to be heartbroken over. Uriah had become a beacon of hope in her sons' lives. Chris didn't walk around angry and defiant all the time now; Johnny B wasn't so sullen. *And* he was back in school, which Joy hadn't been sure would ever happen. Uriah had given her boys hope, and she was crushed. Because she wanted to be that hope. Yet it hadn't been her. It was Uriah. It was all about Uriah now.

Everything that Rebecca said had just made it all worse. So much worse. Joy should've been the one to see how to get Chris to accept his name, accept the changes in his life. She should've been the one to find Johnny B a job, settle him down, and make him realize that there was life after an accident. That life went on despite any fear that it might not.

She had wanted independence for herself, but she had wanted it for her family as well. Yet she hadn't been independent at all. She had relied on Uriah more than she had relied on anyone in all the years since Rudy died. To her, that meant she was losing her independence, whether she liked it or not. She didn't like it. She needed to get it back. One hundred percent.

Chapter 21

"Everybody settle down," Rebecca said that Friday evening at the next family supper. "We don't have long before Joy will be back."

"And that's why we're having a family meeting now?" Jane asked. "Because *mamm* is not here?"

Rebecca nodded and smiled at the young girl. "We have some things to talk about that are important."

"Things that you don't want her to know about," Ruthie guessed.

The younger kids would continue to ask questions until they ran completely out of time, so Rebecca decided to ignore that and continue with the business they needed to discuss.

"It takes for-*ever* to go get food," Chris complained before she could get even one word out. "We've got ages until she'll be back."

"It seems like it now," Rachel put in. "But she'll be back before you know it, and this is important."

Rebecca sent her a thankful smile.

"Rebecca already said that." Reena shot her sister a look.

"Stop," Rebecca said. The one word was loud enough

that everyone stilled immediately. "Listen, have you guys noticed that Dat isn't here?"

"Of course we've noticed," Johnny B said. "He has a lot of work to do at the lumberyard."

From the tone of his voice, Rebecca heard what he didn't say: That Johnny B believed the lie because of all the work her *dat* had done for him by building him a *dawdihaus*. Johnny B believed that Uriah took time away from the lumberyard to do him that good deed, and now he was having to work extra hard to make up for the time he was away. She wanted to tell him that wasn't the case, but she had to stay on topic for now.

"He's not had to work late," she said, though she suspected he had actually been staying at the lumberyard lately, ever since she told him that she hadn't seen his buggy parked there when she went to get Chinese food that first time. She supposed he could find something to do at the lumberyard even if he was the only one there. "He doesn't have to work that hard," Rebecca continued. "He can take a Friday night off and come to supper."

"Are you saying he doesn't want to?" Reena looked close to tears.

"I'm saying . . ." Rebecca tried again. "I'm saying that something is going on. And I think it's going on between our *dat* and your *mamm*."

"Like, romantically?" Leah looked hesitant to even say that last word.

"Maybe," Rebecca said.

"That doesn't make any sense." Johnny B slouched back in his wheelchair. "If they were being romantic, wouldn't he be coming over here more, not less?"

Rachel shook her head and for once Rebecca was glad her sister stepped in with an answer. "We believe something happened between them," she started diplomatically.

Rebecca had told Rachel about the marriage proposal, but she hadn't let Reena and Ruthie in on the secret. Just as she wasn't really certain Chris and Jane needed to know all the details. They were just too young to understand.

"Something?" Leah asked. "What do you mean *something*?"

Rebecca shook her head. "I don't know." But again she said the words knowing that the marriage proposal had to have been what split them apart.

"You know what?" she started again. "Just forget it. It doesn't matter." She shook her head, and the other seven children stared at her. "Leah," she said turning to the girl. "Can you help me with something in the kitchen?"

"So the family meeting is over?" Chris asked.

"That's right," Rebecca said. "I'm sorry to have bothered you. Go play or whatever until your *mamm* gets back with the food."

He got up from his chair and trudged toward the living room.

"That was kind of a dumb meeting," Johnny B said.

Rebecca could only shrug.

"Kitchen?" Leah asked.

Rebecca started toward the kitchen, snagging Rachel's arm on her way. Without missing a beat she dragged her sister into the kitchen along with her. Leah followed behind obediently.

They were no sooner out of the dining area and in the kitchen when Rebecca heard Ruthie say, "Let's go get the cards ready for Dutch Blitz." She paused for a second and then added, "If you want to that is."

Rebecca had pointed out to Joy all the changes that her *dat* had brought about in Joy's life, but Ruthie's new attitude was just one of the changes that Joy had brought to her family. Ruthie was still sort of bossy and liked to be in charge—or at the very least have her opinion and thoughts known—but she wasn't nearly as tyrannical as she had been.

"What are we doing?" Leah asked.

Rebecca nodded toward the door. "Go get Johnny B. And then close the door behind you when you come in."

Leah frowned. "Why?"

Rachel shot her an exasperated look. "Just do it."

Leah exhaled, albeit a little too heavily, but did as her cousin asked. "Johnny B," she called.

"What you want?" he grumbled from the dining room.

"Would you just come here?" Leah asked.

"Please," Rebecca called.

"Whatever," Johnny B said, but she could hear him wheeling himself toward the kitchen.

This was what Rachel needed. The big kids together helping steer the fate of the family. She had wanted it to be a family meeting, a family get-together with everyone involved, but now, looking back, this was something the little kids just wouldn't be able to understand.

"Shut the door behind you," Rebecca told Johnny B quietly.

He shot her a questioning look but did as she asked.

The minute the four of them were together in the kitchen Rebecca sucked in a deep breath and got down to business. "It seems our *dat* asked your *mamm* to marry him."

The look on Leah and Johnny B's faces were exactly how she imagined she had looked when Joy had told her the news.

"The only problem is Joy told him no."

* * *

"What? Why?" Johnny B felt the words zing from him like a bullet from a hunting rifle. He wasn't much on romance and love and all that sort of thing. Not like a girl would be. But Uriah and his *mamm*, they would be good together. He could see that. He didn't know why the thought even occurred to him, but he had this feeling that his *mamm* was kind of lonely lately. It'd been a long time since his *dat* had died, and then she had thrown all her energy into the bakery. Then once he got hurt, she seemed to spend all her time on him. She wasn't getting any younger, and he supposed it was time she spent a little of that time on herself. Not in a selfish way. Getting married wouldn't be selfish. It would be bringing the two families together. He wanted Uriah to be a part of the family. He thought that Leah might too.

So then why had his *mamm* told Uriah no? It just didn't make any sense. There was nothing wrong with Uriah. His mother wouldn't have allowed him to be in their house if that were true. Johnny B knew for a fact that Uriah had been invited to all the family dinners that they'd had since they started. It was just this last little bit when Uriah had decided not to come. So no, there was nothing wrong with him. That was dumb to even think about such a thing. Uriah was a good guy, and Johnny B wanted him around. Now they just had to figure out how to get him around without their *mamm* getting upset about it.

"What do we do?" Leah asked.

"I don't know. I've been thinking about something," Rebecca said. "Well, me and Rachel have been thinking about some things. And we've come up with one idea."

"I could pretend to be hurt," Leah said.

But Rebecca shook her head. "That's not right, to pretend

to be hurt and have our parents be worried about us. I was thinking more along the lines of a Demi Dawn party."

Demi Dawn was the newest thing in essential oils and herbal remedies. The idea had come to Rebecca the last time she'd been in Paradise Apothecary. Most of the things that Betsy Stoll carried in the store were homegrown and locally produced, but she did have a line of Demi Dawn lotions, soaps, and cleansers. According to the brochure that Rebecca had picked up, there was a lot more to it than those three items. There was a full line of bath care, baby care, and even clothes detergent. Everything was supposed to be better for houses with septic lines, like most of the Amish homes in the area had, and to be safer for the environment.

"I'm not sure your *dat*'s really into Demi Dawn," Johnny B said.

Rachel shook her head and to her credit didn't roll her eyes at her cousin. "We're not really gonna have a Demi Dawn party," she said. "We're just going to use the idea to get your *mamm* to come out to our house instead of being here for the evening."

"Why?" Johnny B asked, looking from Rachel to Rebecca and back again.

"I get it," Leah said. "That way you can get the two of them together without tipping Uriah off to what's going on."

Rebecca snapped her fingers and pointed to Leah. "You got it."

"So the Demi Dawn party is just a ruse?" Johnny B asked.

"That's right," Rachel said. "You and Leah bring Jane and Chris to our house. We four will already be there. Your *mamm* will come from the party and—"

"Wait, wait." Leah held up both hands. "How are we all

going to get there? I mean, Mamm will think that we are staying here. What are we going to tell her to get ourselves over there too?"

"I don't know. Tell her you're going bowling or putt-putt golfing," Rebecca said, obviously a little frustrated that she had been stopped mid-explanation. Or perhaps it was because she had been stopped mid-explanation with a problem that needed to be addressed.

"Putt-putt golf in January?" Johnny B shook his head at her.

"They are open year- round," Leah said with a small nod.

"Actually," Rachel said," I saw in the newspaper that Paradise Putt-Putt has a 'polar bear special,' and if it's under forty-five degrees, you can golf for half-price."

"I guess that would work," Leah said. But she chewed her lower lip as if she wasn't quite certain of the excuse.

"Then tell her you're going bowling," Rachel said. "You can bowl in any weather."

"So we tell her we're going bowling," Johnny B said.

"But instead of going bowling you come to my house. Your *mamm* will be there for the fake Demi Dawn party. Dat be there because he lives there, and we will all be there. Once everyone's together, we'll have ourselves a good old-fashioned family supper."

Whoever heard of having a Demi Dawn party on the same night as the prescheduled family dinner?

Joy pulled her buggy to a stop outside Uriah's house. She should've asked if he was going to be there. Then perhaps she could better prepare herself for what lay inside. Surely he had taken the younger kids to get ice cream or something. If that was the case, then she wouldn't have to face him. As it was, whatever waited for her inside his

house would have to be confronted soon. It was too cold
outside to linger in the buggy and wonder about things out
of her control.

With a fortifying breath, Joy set the brake and climbed
down from the buggy. She would've thought there would
be more carriages parked outside Uriah's house. She had
no idea how many people were invited, and she was a bit
early. Yet not so early that she would be the first one to
arrive.

The front door swung open, and Rachel came tripping
across the porch and down the steps.

"Joy!" she said. "I'm so glad you made it."

Joy smiled and continued unhitching her horse from the
carriage. She wasn't sure exactly how long the party
would last, and she preferred to shelter the beast in the
barn instead of leaving it out to weather the cold January
winds.

"Here," Rachel said, nudging her aside. "You go on in
and get warm. I'll take care of the horse."

"*Danki*," Joy said. "Where is everyone?"

Rachel waved a negligent hand in the air even as she
continued to unhitch the mare. "They'll be here shortly."

Joy stopped for a second, then shook the thought away.
It didn't matter that Betsy hadn't mentioned the party on
Tuesday at the widows meeting. That didn't really mean
anything. Nor did the fact that she was the first one to
arrive. Yet somehow she had the uneasy feeling that this
night was not what it had been advertised to be.

She paused only for a moment—just long enough to
take a steadying breath —before turning the knob and
stepping into the warm house. She wouldn't presume to
detail everything she thought she might see as she walked
in, but what she saw certainly didn't fall under any de-
scriptions of "party" in her thoughts. She had at least

expected a few balloons. A table set with paper plates. Perhaps even a huge crystal-looking bowl of punch, matching napkins, plastic ware, cute little cups, and instead she found . . . Uriah's everyday house.

Perhaps she'd gotten the date wrong. She turned to step back outside and ask Rachel if she'd somehow made a mistake. But the very thought of Rachel outside, unhitching her horse, affirmed that Joy hadn't been in error. She came when she was supposed to, yet the scene around her was anything but what she should have stepped into.

"Joy."

Rebecca.

Joy whirled around to face her niece. "If you wanted to have the family dinner night here, all you had to do was say something." She said the words even though she knew that surely wasn't the case. Her kids had gone bowling or some such. A family dinner would have required all of them to be there, not just Uriah's kids. "What's going on?"

"We kids got together and decided that we didn't like Dat not being at the family dinners."

"And you thought you would move it here and lie to me so I would come?" She shook her head, not understanding the logic behind it all. She didn't like being deceived.

"I'm sorry about the lie, but I couldn't tell you the real reason we wanted you to come. You know, a blind man could see that something happened between the two of you."

"Me and your *dat*?" Joy crossed her arms. She felt the need to wrap them around her body and hold herself together. "You know what happened."

"*Jah*, I do. And I also know that nothing will be resolved if he keeps avoiding you and you keep letting him."

"There's nothing to resolve." Joy frowned, not quite understanding Rebecca's reasoning. "There is no Demi Dawn party?"

Rebecca shook her head.

"I suppose your father didn't take the younger kids into town for ice cream or popcorn or something?"

Rachel shook her head again.

Behind Joy the door opened. She moved to one side to allow Rachel to step into the house.

Just then Uriah came down the hallway. "I don't know why I had to change my shirt—" He stopped in his tracks as he saw her standing there. "Hi, Joy."

She dipped her chin in his direction. "Uriah."

A tense moment stretched among the four of them until Joy could take it no longer. She swung her attention back to Rachel. "Where are the younger kids?"

Reena and Ruthie came skulking out of the kitchen. No doubt they had been standing near the doorway, listening to every word spoken. From the look on their faces, it was obvious that they had been in on this the whole time.

At least her own children had stayed out of the meddling. The thought had no sooner crossed her mind than she heard a buggy rattle outside. Her heart sank a little lower in her chest.

"I'm going to go out on a limb here and say that my children just arrived to back you up."

The four girls nodded.

Uriah looked from one of them to the other, his gaze skipping over Joy with quick efficiency. "What's going on here?" He gave them a moment to answer, but when none of the girls were forthcoming, he turned to his eldest. "Rebecca?"

"Just a minute," she said. "The others are here."

"I'll just go—" Rachel didn't finish the sentence as she slipped back out the front door probably to help Leah get Johnny B out of the buggy and into his wheelchair. A part of Joy knew she should put her feet into motion. She should go out and help. Another part of her wanted to make him stay in the buggy and to send them all back home. Tell them that whatever they had planned this evening had been called off.

"The others?" Uriah said. "Joy's kids?"

"*Jah.*" Ruthie took a step forward, pulling herself to her full height, which at eight was not much. "We want to have a family supper tonight, and that means everyone in the family should here. Including you."

Uriah looked to Rebecca for answers, but she seemed unable to give him one.

Joy took a step forward. "It appears they set up a charade tonight to make sure everyone was at this family dinner."

"A charade?"

"Yes, a charade. A fib. Call it what you want. But they devised a story to get the both of us here."

"They?"

Have mercy! She wished he would stop repeating one word of anything anyone said. Joy briefly closed her eyes and counted to five, hoping she could steady her rising anxiety and agitation. This was not how the evening was supposed to turn out. "Our children."

They must've planned it out well, for in no time at all, Leah was wheeling Johnny B into the house with Chris, Jane, and Rachel trailing behind.

Joy waited until all the kids were inside before she broke the news to them. "There's not going to be a family supper tonight. Though I do not appreciate your deceit, I do appreciate your feelings. However, this is not the way to go about it."

"I'm sorry," Rachel said. "We didn't know what to do."

"There's nothing you can do," Joy said, wishing Uriah would jump in at some point and help her. But he was standing still as a statue and so far had barely managed anything other than a one- or two-word response to everything said.

"But we got sandwiches," Leah said.

"*Jah*," Johnny B shot from his wheelchair. "We just wanted the two of you to talk it out."

"There's nothing to talk out." Uriah finally stepped into the conversation.

"Not from where we're standing," Rebecca told them.

"I think I should leave." Joy started for the door.

"No!" All eight kids shouted the word at the same time, but the most surprising thing to Joy was that she heard Uriah's voice in there as well.

"They have sandwiches," Uriah said. "The least we can do is eat one."

She supposed he was right about that, but he had been the one to start bowing out of the family dinners. He had been the one avoiding her. She was just trying her best to respect his decision, and since they were in his home, it only seemed right that she be the one to leave. "You sure?"

His expression was anything but convinced, and yet he nodded. "I'm sure."

Joy couldn't decide whether to address or ignore their children's hopeful faces. Just because they were having a sandwich together didn't mean things were going to go back to the way they had been before. That was the saddest part of all.

She missed Uriah. She missed her friend. And she was sorry that she couldn't be what he needed in their relationship.

It might go down in the annals of Lehman family history as the worst family dinner ever.

Joy couldn't find conversation to engage the children in, and anything that she wanted to say to Uriah needed to be said in private. So she ate her sandwich in silence.

Uriah too seemed to have no words. He slowly chewed each bite and switched his attention back and forth from whoever was talking at the time. The children chatted away incessantly, doing their best to cover up their parents' silence.

Joy was certain she had never in her entire life taken so long to eat half a hoagie and a small bag of chips. She somehow managed to choke it down. Anything so that she could get back into her buggy and go home. Where tonight she would probably cry her eyes out over the lost friendship, her inability to be in love, and her conflicting dreams for the future.

Once everyone finished their meal, the children jumped up without having to be reminded and gathered all the disposable plates and utensils and napkins, all the wrappers and the chip bags and the paper cups. In no time at all, they had everything back to normal. Though Joy knew there was nothing normal about the evening.

"*Danki* for supper," Joy said, nodding to the children. She knew they meant well. But it was time to escape while she still could. "I think it's time for me to go home."

She'd expected some pushback from the kids, but it seemed they had learned their lesson. They all just sadly nodded.

Somehow she managed to smile at them and keep her tears hidden as she tied her bonnet around her chin, grabbed her scarf and cloak, and headed for the door.

"I'll help." Uriah was on his feet in an instant, shocking all the children and even Joy herself.

"There's no need," she said. What was he up to? She was giving him what he wanted. He was the one who stopped coming to the family suppers. He was the one who couldn't seem to talk about this big white elephant in the room. Why was he trailing behind her?

He grabbed his coat and hat and opened the door. Joy stepped through, ignoring the hopeful, eager faces of the children.

Neither Joy nor Uriah spoke as they made their way toward the barn. She wanted so badly to ask him if his intention truly was to help her hitch up her buggy. It wasn't like she hadn't been doing it since she was ten years old or anything. Perhaps he was just trying to be gentlemanly after everything that had gone on between them.

Or perhaps he wanted to talk.

A few more steps into the barn and she wouldn't have to wonder anymore, but those steps seemed to take forever, as if they were being performed with some sort of fancy *Englisch* movie camera trick.

Then, finally, they were in the barn.

"I just wanted to say that I was sorry, Joy." Uriah's voice came softly from behind her.

Joy turned around, wrapping her cloak a little tighter around her as she did. "You started these family dinners, Uriah. Now I think it's time for you see them through. Regardless of anything that has happened between us, the kids need them."

He nodded without saying a word.

Silence fell like a storm cloud between them. It seemed harmless but crackled with electricity.

"Why?"

She had no answer. She cared for him; she couldn't deny it. Nor could she use the word love. Just admitting that she cared for him, even to herself, scared her silly. She had been a wreck when she lost Rudy. Such a wreck that she never thought she would recover. Everyone in Paradise

Valley thought she was so strong and determined, but if she hadn't opened the bakery, she might've just lost her mind. Yet she didn't want to tell Uriah that.

"Why do you want to get married again? I know you loved Dinah. And I know her death was crushing. How can you piece the tiny bits of your heart back together? How do you make it whole again and expect to give it to someone else?"

He shook his head, tears welling in his eyes. "I can't give you my whole heart. A part of it died with her, but that doesn't mean it's not still beating. That doesn't mean that life doesn't go on. It doesn't mean I shouldn't have happiness—and, for that matter, that you shouldn't either."

At his passionate words, her breath caught in her throat. She couldn't speak. She couldn't breathe. For a moment her heart stuttered in her chest.

Then he continued. "I know you have a broken heart. And I know that there's a part of your heart that will always belong to Rudy. I wouldn't be able to love you if it was any different than that because it's just a part of who you are. It's a part of life. It's a part of loving someone and losing someone."

It seemed after all these weeks of silence, the dam had finally broken and the words were tumbling free.

"I understand that you're afraid," he continued. "What are you afraid of? You've already lost so much, wouldn't it be nice to gain a little?"

For a moment it seemed as if he was about to wait for her answer. An answer she wasn't sure she could deliver. Then he shook his head and walked away.

Joy was left to go home by herself.

Chapter 22

No matter what she tried, or how hard she tried it, Joy couldn't shake Uriah's words. For days she couldn't get them out of her head. It seemed like every time someone said the word heart or broken, that's all she could think about.

And with Valentine's Day coming up, there were hearts everywhere. People were always talking about hearts. Joy worked in a bakery where there were tons of broken cookies. Whatever she did, she was reminded of Uriah.

So she was afraid. She wasn't ashamed of that. She had every right to be afraid. And she had every right to protect her heart. So why did she feel so bad?

She didn't know. She couldn't determine that. So the question dogged her constantly.

Even after all that had happened, Rebecca still retained her job at the bakery. Joy was glad about this for several different reasons, but mainly because Rebecca didn't allow all the trouble between Joy and Uriah to taint their relationship. They had become quite close in the last couple of months. Rebecca truly did have the same love of baking that Joy had. It was definitely a blessing to love this skill, for it could earn a woman a decent living.

Now that the Christmas rush was over, Joy moved Leah to working only Tuesdays and Thursdays and had Rebecca there full time Monday, Wednesday, Friday, and Saturday.

This new schedule gave Joy more opportunities to take care of business in town. Like today, when she'd gone for a yearly checkup. Something she hadn't done in . . . well, it'd been over a year, that was certain. Everyone was always telling her that she had to take care of herself for her kids. She tried the best she could, but sometimes there just weren't enough hours in the day to get everything done. Rebecca had taken some of that burden from her, and Joy was grateful.

As she came through the house, she could hear someone in with Johnny B. The door leading from the living room to the *dawdihaus* was usually kept open, especially when he had company. The voice was female and familiar. Evie seemed to have quite a thing for Johnny B. Joy just hoped that it didn't break both their hearts.

Johnny B continued to do strengthening exercises and was more involved in his own care these days. Joy knew he had accepted the "fact" that he would never walk again. She still wasn't so sure and prayed nightly for a change in his condition.

Since he had company, she didn't bother him to let him know that she was home. Instead she went through the kitchen and opened the door that led to her basement bakery. But when she got to the bottom of the stairs, she decided that Party in Paradise, the local party supply store, must have exploded inside her bakery.

She stopped, looked around, and managed to keep her gasp inside. There were a couple of customers waiting, but Rebecca was handling them all like a pro. Not only was she a baker, she was a born businesswoman. Which left Joy more time to stare at all the decorations.

Red. Pink. White. Everywhere.

Sparkly. Glittery. Shiny foil.

Streamers, paper lanterns. Hearts, hearts, hearts.

Rebecca looked up and caught Joy's stunned look. She obviously misinterpreted it for shocked surprise instead of shocked dismay, and her grin widened. She was proud of herself. Any other year—or perhaps for any other holiday—Joy would've said the place looked wonderful. Honestly, she had no idea where Rebecca found the time or the energy to do so much so quickly.

She must've had the decorations with her when she arrived that morning. But she had kept her plans a secret, waiting until Joy went to her appointment to execute the surprise.

"Rachel helped me," Rebecca said.

Joy turned her attention away from the display of glittery hearts on the back wall of the bakery. They were behind the cash wrap counter and above the worktable, but in plain view of anyone walking into the bakery or standing at the cash register. She believed she had heard it called a gallery wall and wondered how Rebecca had thought to organize the hearts in that manner.

The customers had all gotten their purchases and left, leaving the bakery to Joy and Rebecca.

"So?" Rebecca asked. "What do you think?"

What did she think? The whole thing was one big throbbing sore tooth named Uriah. Never before had she been one of the sourpuss people who said they hated Valentine's Day because they didn't have a boyfriend or a date. But this year it seemed she would join their ranks. Not because she didn't have a boyfriend or a date, but because everything about the holiday seemed to remind her of him. It was something she did not need.

"You don't like it?" Rebecca's tone plummeted. All the

excitement and enthusiasm that had vibrated off her since the moment Joy walked in vanished in an instant.

"No," Joy hurriedly replied. "It's beautiful. It's just—" She couldn't do it. She couldn't tell Rebecca how immature she felt over a holiday that would bring in money for the bakery. A holiday that was supposed to be just about fun and love and all good things. "It's beautiful." She bit back her own personal feelings and continued, "You did a fantastic job. Thank you."

Rebecca beamed. "And I made cookies too. Come look."

Joy put her feet into motion for the first time since stepping into the bakery. She moved automatically to the sink and began to wash her hands as Rebecca showed off her morning's handiwork.

"I know they're all just hearts. So I tried to do a little something different on each one. I made the red icing, but I figured I'd still use pink and white as well. And if I have time, maybe I can do some of that intricate work like I did on the Christmas cookies. What you think?"

The cookies were amazing. They were the size of Joy's hand. Each one was covered in a beautiful red royal icing and had all sorts of sprinkles on top—pink, white, red, and some even a little bit glittery with granulated sugar.

"I think they're beautiful." *I think I miss Uriah. I think my heart's going to break a dozen times before the middle of February comes and goes.*

"So how are things going with Uriah?" Millie asked Tuesday at the widows meeting.

Joy almost choked on the bite of whoopie pie that she had been trying to swallow when Millie spoke.

Katie, who was sitting next to her, jumped to her feet. She enthusiastically patted Joy on the back, as if that would somehow help her swallow past the lump in her throat. "I wasn't going to say anything, but I put real whiskey in that. I didn't know it would have such a kick."

Thankfully the attention turned her from Joy and Uriah to Katie and her honey cake whoopie pie.

"Real whiskey?" Lillian's mouth fell open.

"Well, that's what the cake recipe called for," Katie was saying. "And I didn't know what to substitute." She ended with a small shrug.

"I don't think you have to substitute anything at all," Betsy put in.

Katie just shrugged again.

"I'm with you," Sylvie said. "There's no substitute for the real thing. Besides," she looked around at all the shocked faces of the Whoopie Pie Widows Club members, "the alcohol cooks out and you're left with the flavor."

Katie nodded. "And I used our honey." Katie's brother Rufus Metzger was Paradise Springs's resident bee-keeper. His bees produced the best honey in all the valley as far as Joy was concerned. She not only kept the honey in her house for personal use, but she used it in the bakery as well.

Katie herself made all sorts of candies and treats with the honey her brother produced. She only did small batches and sold them around town, mostly as an impulse purchase on the counters of the Amish-owned businesses. Joy knew for a fact that there was a bowl of her candy at the hostess stand at the Amish buffet. As far as Joy knew, Katie didn't do it for the money, just for the love of pro-ducing treats. Joy could understand that. Once something became about money, even if it was something you loved to do, it changed things. Whether you wanted it to or not.

"It's fine," Joy said, finally managing to get the bite

from the middle of her throat down into her belly. "I just got choked, that's all."

She smiled and looked around at her friends as if to reassure them all. "Really." She took another bite to prove she was telling the truth.

"Were the two of you getting close?" Lillian asked. For a moment Joy didn't understand what she was talking about. Then, like the crash of a ton of bricks dropped from above, she realized. Uriah.

Before she could respond, Elsie jumped in. "I heard you guys are having these family dinners."

Hattie nodded. "I heard that too. At the same time, of course, and I thought that was just amazing. All of you getting together and eating supper. Just sweet." She smiled in that encouraging way she had. That was just Hattie. Always looking on the bright side of anything, not realizing that those dinners had led to Joy's broken heart. Of course, no one seated around eating whoopie pies, drinking coffee or tea, and socializing over nothing knew that she was brokenhearted. She didn't need to tell them.

"We put the dinners on hold for a while." She sent a trembling smile to the rest of the ladies and hoped they believed her. Even though it came from her own lips, she wasn't sure she believed it either.

"Oh, no," Lillian said with a worried frown. "Why? What happened?"

Joy shrugged as if it were no big deal at all, when in fact it was a big deal. Perhaps the biggest of deals. "We were just getting busy and all. It's hard to do that every Friday."

"Why?" Elsie gave her a hard stare. But that was just Elsie, kind of intense and definitely not one to try to smooth over harsh words and unafraid of stirring attitudes. "Don't you eat every Friday?"

When she put it like that, any argument that Joy had

disintegrated in a puff of smoke, like stepping on a mushroom that had gone to spores.

"And the girls," Joy finally said. "Rebecca and Rachel are both running around, so they don't always want to be there. Maybe we'll have another one someday. But not every Friday like we were doing there for a little bit. It just got to be too much." That sounded like the time, effort, and energy put into dinner for ten people was more than they could handle, not the fact that Joy's heart broke every time she saw Uriah. And she was sitting next to Katie, who had ten children and somehow managed to feed them every night, not just on Fridays. Thankfully no one brought that up.

"How is Imogene liking living in Paradise Hill?" Betsy asked.

Katie's daughter, Imogene, had recently married Jesse Kaufman, twin brother to Astrid Kauffman, the almost-secret undercover romance author who lived in Paradise Hill. Astrid didn't write under her real name. Joy had heard that her editor felt her name sounded too *Englisch* and asked her to write under her middle name, Rachel.

When Joy had found out they had a romance writer in their midst she bought one of Astrid/Rachel's books and read it. It was a sweet story with Amish characters and lots of details about Amish life, but she had to admit that it was a little over the top. Some of the things were a bit much for her, but she supposed that was just fiction. Life was so much harder.

The rumor around was that Imogene had hired Astrid to help find someone to marry so that she would have a man to help her raise her rowdy twin boys. Joy had no idea how much of this was true. The fact that everyone believed that Astrid was a matchmaker and not necessarily a romance writer was the first part of the story that people got wrong.

But whatever the truth was, Imogene fell for Astrid's brother, and Astrid fell for Ira Hostetler, the man she'd been trying to set up with Imogene.

Joy mentally shook her head. It just went to show that people shouldn't meddle in love. That should all be left up to God. He would take care of things. If that was what a person truly wanted. And prayed for. And hoped for. And wanted.

So lost she was in her thoughts, Joy started when Katie's hand rested on her knee.

"You okay, dear?"

Joy nodded. What else could she do? Maybe she wasn't okay today, but she would be okay soon. Surely she couldn't go through her entire life pining for something that she couldn't have, constantly torn between two loves. *Two loves and her need for independence,* a little voice inside her head corrected. The two loves could be reconciled; it was her fear of loss and her need to be in control that was standing in her way.

"Being heartbroken is a terrible thing," Katie continued.

Joy looked up and met her clear blue eyes. Her questions must have shown in her own, for Katie kept going, "It's written all over your face." Then she seemed to consider that for a moment. "It's obvious to me because I've seen it on my own face so many times." She shook her head as if she were falling headfirst into her own thoughts.

Joy supposed she hadn't thought about Katie's situation much. Just that she was a widow. After all, she was a member of the Paradise Springs Widows Group. But it was more than that. Katie had been married three times maybe . . . Joy couldn't remember. It might've been four. And for however many times she had been married, she had been widowed that many times as well. *Jah*, she had ten children spread among her husbands. And it was believed she was kin to almost everyone in the Valley, be it by blood or marriage.

Three husbands? Four husbands? That was a lot of heartbreak.

"How did you do it?" Joy asked quietly.

Katie bent her head close to Joy. The other chattering ladies in the room were still there, but somehow seemed separate from this connection with Katie.

"Did you ever try to ride a horse?" Katie asked. "What about the first time you made a cake and it was a total failure? So bad the dog wouldn't even eat it." The look on her face was so serious, and yet Joy couldn't stop a small chuckle from escaping her.

"I remember."

"Did you quit baking that day?" Katie asked.

Joy didn't bother to answer. She knew where Katie was going with this.

"And did your *dat* make you get back on that horse?"

It wasn't actually the answer Joy wanted. It was so cliché. So trite. When you fall off a horse you get back on. It sounded easy enough, but it was far from simple, and yet about as simple as it got.

"Love is special," Katie said. "I don't think I need to tell you that. You know. I saw you and Rudy together." Katie grinned, revealing a missing molar on one side. Somehow that made her smile even more charming. "Having a love like that once is so special. But if you're offered that love a second time—" She broke off and shook her head. "It seems like such a waste if you don't grab onto it with both hands."

"And how do you get through the loss? How do you manage to get through that?"

Katie's eyes sparkled. "How do you not?"

* * *

"What are you wanting to go to town for again?" Leah asked as she tied her apron around her waist.

For two days Joy could think of nothing else but Katie's words. *How do you not?* They floated around her head when she was trying to talk to customers. They floated around her head when she was trying to decorate cakes. They floated around her head when she was cooking supper, when she was getting ready for bed, when she was trying to go to sleep. *How do you not?* Those four little words seemed so effortless. And yet they held the answer to everything. *How do you not?* How do you not continue to live? How do you not fall in love? How do you not keep going on?

"We're out of . . . almond flour." It was such a lame excuse, but it was the only one she could think of. Wasn't that what she had told Leah before? She couldn't remember. "Rebecca is wanting to work on some gluten-free cookies."

Leah jerked a finger over her shoulder "There's some more in the pantry." She started toward it, but Joy stopped her. "There's not enough." Again, lame. But what else could she say? She needed to go to town. She needed to see Uriah. Maybe, just maybe, they could give this a second chance.

"Oh." Leah stared at her a moment, then nodded. "Okay. Well, go to town then, and I'll take care of things here."

Joy could feel her daughter's eyes on her as she made her way up the stairs and into the kitchen. She could almost hear the questions racing around in Leah's brain. But she couldn't answer them. Not yet. She had to talk to Uriah before anything could change. She'd hurt him; she knew she had. The terrible thing about it was she hurt herself as well. And yet she wasn't sure this would work. She didn't remember love being so scary. When did it get so scary? Wasn't it supposed to be happy and joyous and amazing and fine? So why was she filled with angst, scared to death, worried about every little thing? That in itself worried her. If love was supposed to be such a happy time, why was she not having a happy time?

She admitted it, if only to herself. She had fallen for Uriah. He was a kindhearted man. He was a good man. And she loved him. And she needed to tell him so. Right now. Before the gulf that she had dug between them got too big to cross.

She hitched up her mare and rode to town, one foot tapping all the way there. To say she was nervous was an understatement. But if he cared for her the way he claimed he did, he would be happy to see her. They could get over the one little problem of the one little turned-down proposal. Uriah was a fair man. He wouldn't hold a grudge.

Sure, he was hurt. But surely a change of heart could smooth over any ruffled feelings. Heaven help her, she hoped so anyway.

She pulled her mare into the lumberyard and tied her to the hitching post. Then she smoothed her hands down the front of her dress. Maybe she should've changed before she came. She should've worn her blue dress. It was one of her best. She didn't normally wear it to work because . . . well, it was work. Maybe she should go home and put it on first before she—

Get ahold of yourself. Five years from now no one would know what dress she wore that day. She just needed to get in there and talk to Uriah. Smooth over any bumps in the road, any problems that lay between them. Make this right.

She studied her reflection in the rearview mirror on the side of the carriage. Her color was high. There was no need to pinch her cheeks to bring a blush to her face. She ran a finger down each side of her prayer *kapp*, assuring everything was right where it belonged. Then she sucked in a fortifying breath and marched to the door of the lumberyard. She stepped inside with a purpose and stopped.

All eyes swung to her. Uriah was behind the counter with a guy she didn't know. An *Englisch* man who obviously worked there. Thomas Kurtz stood on one side of the counter, along with two *Englisch* men she didn't know and an Amish man she'd never met before. And they were all staring at her.

"I'll be with you in a minute," Uriah said, all businesslike and stern.

Of course he was putting on a front for the men watching his every move. Apparently it had gotten around town that she and Uriah had been seeing a lot of one another. That shouldn't have been big news; after all, they were kin by marriage. But that was the problem with a small, mostly isolated community. Any happening was a big happening.

"*Danki*," she said, and gave him a businesslike nod in return. She crossed her arms and stood to one side, waiting before her turn to talk to him.

It took everything she had not to tap her foot—not with impatience, but with the nervousness that was coursing through her. Waiting was an excruciating pastime. And it seemed to take forever before he got Thomas out of the way. Then he turned his attention to the two *Englisch* men who thankfully worked together. She didn't pay much attention as they signed whatever papers, showed him whatever invoice, nor while he ran the credit card. Then they too stepped out of the lumberyard office, leaving just her, Uriah, and the *Englisch* worker.

"A minute?" Uriah said pointedly to the young man.

He looked from Uriah to Joy and back again, a knowing light dawning in his eyes. "Of course." A second later he was gone.

Finally, *finally* she was alone with Uriah.

"So what can I do for you?" Again with a businesslike manner. Was he afraid someone was listening to him?

"I just came to see how you are." Somehow in the time it took for him to get rid of the customers in front of her, her courage had waned to nothing. Or maybe it was that curt businesslike manner of his that had her rethinking her reasons for coming.

"I'm fine," he said. But he didn't sound fine; he sounded . . . angry. Where there was anger, there were usually feelings bigger than anger. But was she willing to take that chance? She'd lied to Leah about needing almond flour, driven all the way into town, only to get here and find that maybe things weren't exactly as she thought they were.

Maybe she should test the waters a bit more. She searched her brain for some other reason for her to be in town, a reason other than simply to drop by and tell him that she loved him and had perhaps changed her mind, and if he had it so in his heart, that they could maybe get married and forget the proposal that she turned down. And when she thought about it that way, it sounded ridiculous.

"I was thinking maybe we could have a second chance at the Friday night suppers. I guess a second second chance," she clarified. They'd already had one failed attempt.

But the smile he gave her was sad, remorseful, and just a tiny bit bitter. "Sometimes you don't get a second chance at a second chance."

* * *

It was all lost. She'd blown it. She'd been stubborn and prideful and fearful. She had not trusted in Uriah, or the Lord, or even in herself. She thought she was running things, and that just went to show that it was better to live your life taking a few chances instead of trying to protect your heart at all costs.

"So are you going to tell me what happened?"

Joy looked up from rolling out dough and tried to form her expression into something akin to confusion. She had a feeling she didn't succeed. "What you mean?"

"I don't know what happened," Rebecca said. "But something happened. Dat came home in a mood yesterday when he got off work at the lumberyard. And here you are today acting the same way. Sure makes me think that something happened. Now, are you gonna tell me or not?"

Joy wasn't sure she could recount the story without crying. But she needed to get her emotions together. She had done this to herself. She had blown her chance, and she had no one else to blame. No sense crying over that. Sort of like spilled milk she supposed.

She recounted to Rebecca about going into town the day before and thinking she might spill her feelings to Uriah.

"What feelings?" Rebecca raised a brow with a knowing look.

"Are you really gonna make me say it?" Joy hated the wobble in her voice when she asked the question.

"I am. If you can't say it to me, how can you say it to him?"

Joy shook her head. "I'm not gonna have the opportunity now."

"Do it anyway," Rebecca instructed.

"I love him," Joy said. "Are you happy now?"

Rebecca shook her head. "First of all, of course I'm happy, and second of all, why would having you admit that you're in love with my *dat* make me happy? Especially when the two of you can't seem to get it together."

"I don't know," Joy said. "It's just something you say, I suppose."

"So you go to the lumberyard, and you're gonna tell him your feelings, but I'm guessing you didn't." Rebecca raised one brow in question.

"*Jah*," Joy said. "He was very . . . cold with me. I could tell that he didn't really want to talk about it."

"He was at work."

"Fair enough," Joy said. "But I figured there might be less people at the lumberyard than there are at home. Less people who care about our relationship."

"Agreed."

"So I asked him if we can have Friday night suppers again, you know, for everyone. He basically told me no."

"He's hurt. Understandably so."

She didn't need Rebecca to tell her that. She had seen it on his face and in every move he'd made since that day.

Joy shook her head in exasperation and defeat. "I messed up."

"It's not lost until it's lost," Rebecca said.

These kids with their New Age sayings. "What exactly does that mean?"

Rebecca smiled, and Joy could see the gleaming light of a plan forming in her eyes. "Just leave it to me."

Joy wasn't sure what Rebecca meant by that, but she had no other plans. She supposed it was a little like trusting God, but on a smaller scale. And she'd trusted God this far, she could put her faith in Rebecca too.

Chapter 23

By the time three o'clock hit on Valentine's Day, Joy thought she might collapse. They had done a booming business all day long. Joy wished she had called Evie to see if she might work just the one day to help them. But how was she supposed to know sales would skyrocket?

A lot of that she could credit to Rebecca and her new ideas for things to sell in the bakery. Joy was a good baker, and she enjoyed it. She paid good attention to the little details that made things very special. Rebecca was a good baker and paid attention to details, but she was more creative. The first thing she came up with was a cute heart cookie with the center cut out. That hole was filled with strawberry candy. When they put it in the oven and baked it, the cookie came out looking like stained-glass. Everyone was going crazy over them. She also made chocolate hearts, which really weren't baked at all, but everyone was having a good time eating and sharing and adding them to whatever order they had. Not to mention the other elaborate Valentine's Day heart-shaped sugar cookies that were extravagantly decorated to be valentines themselves. They were fine and innovative and different. It seemed like everyone in town was ready for different.

"Before you put on your apron, go get your brother and sister."

Leah looked up at Joy in confusion. "Jane? Chris?"

Joy nodded and handed a customer their cookies. "Thank you so much. Happy Valentine's Day. Enjoy those." She ended with a smile, then, "*Jah*," she replied over one shoulder. "That would be them."

Ever-dutiful Leah ran upstairs to get Chris and Jane. Between the five of them, they managed to keep the store going through the rush all the way up until closing time, partly because Rebecca came up with the idea to break up some of the sugar cookies and take the pieces around to the waiting customers. That way people could try a sample of those and some of the other treats they were selling before they even got to the counter. Bringing the samples around was Jane's job, and Joy was fairly certain it had increased their sales by at least ten percent. Never in the history of her bakery had she had a day like this. Not even at Christmas.

Joy turned the *open* sign on the door to *closed* and locked it for the evening. Then Rebecca grabbed her arm. "I just want to warn you before you go upstairs: Dat's up there."

Great. That was just what she needed after such a busy day. Uriah. Valentine's Day and Uriah was upstairs. "Why's he here?"

Rebecca shrugged. "He came to look at something in Johnny B's 'Johnny *haus*.' I heard him mention that the kitchen faucet dripped or something. Johnny said it was keeping him awake at night."

"*Jah*." Joy had heard all about it. And she had known that as soon as Uriah found out, he would come over and check it out. So she told Johnny B to put a towel down underneath the drip, so it wouldn't make noise. Obviously he felt it really needed to be fixed and had called Uriah.

Okay, so maybe it did.

Joy just wasn't sure she was up for Uriah tonight. On Valentine's Day. But she couldn't blame anybody but herself for her broken heart.

"*Danki*," she said.

Rebecca gave a small nod. Then the five of them trudged up the stairs, the kids leading the way.

Joy was bone weary as she stepped into the kitchen and closed the door behind her. Immediately something caught her attention.

What was on the floor? She opened her mouth to call for Leah to see if the girl would sweep up the mess. She had a feeling her daughter was about as tired as she herself was. Then she looked at what was lying there. Flower petals. Blood red, beautiful, velvety, rose petals. They made a trail all the way from the basement door out into the living room. From where she stood, she couldn't see where they went from there. What were they doing? Or maybe what had they been doing? She looked again through the kitchen door and saw more red in the dining room. Garland and maybe some bunting. And somehow she knew the flower petals meant more than just a mess. She stopped in her tracks and looked at Rebecca.

"Surprise," Rebecca said.

Surprise? What did that mean?

"Go on." Rebecca nudged her toward the dining room.

Joy stepped inside and saw the table set, but only two places. White candles flickering, red tablecloth, little foil confetti hearts. Since there were only two places ready, she knew right away that they were meant for her and Uriah. Not that she thought it was going to matter.

She turned back to Rebecca to protest just as she heard

Uriah say, "I don't really do electrical work. I can't imagine that I would be able to help with the light in here."

He stepped inside the dining room and stopped in his tracks.

Of course there was nothing wrong with the light fixture in the dining room. That was just Johnny B's way of getting him into the room for the surprise dinner.

Uriah turned back to Johnny B who, just as Rebecca had said to Joy, calmly intoned, "Surprise."

Joy was glued in place. She wanted to walk away. She wanted to take a step closer, but she couldn't move at all. She could only stand there, waiting to see what his reaction might be. What if he thought she set it up? Would he be angry? How would she explain that she too had been sucked into this plan, which obviously their kids had devised?

Uriah looked at the table. He looked up at Joy and stopped.

He turned back to Johnny B. "I'm not dressed for a romantic dinner."

Joy's stomach clenched. He was basically in his second home. And he was worried about how he was dressed for dinner? It was obvious: This was his way of getting out of having dinner with her at all.

She looked down at herself and gestured toward the front of her dress. "I'm not either." She started to turn to leave, but Rebecca blocked her path.

"Are you gonna be this stubborn for the rest of your life?" Rebecca asked. "Are you just going to keep walking away? Are you just going to keep making excuses?"

Joy stopped, turned around, unable to look back at Uriah. This was all her fault. She'd messed this up so badly. She had made so many mistakes.

"I'm sorry," Uriah said.

She closed her eyes. This was it. This was the time when he said he wasn't doing this anymore. That he'd had enough. He was going home.

"I've made so many mistakes," he said. His voice was quiet and solemn. "I rushed you."

She shook her head, still unable to face him. "I was prideful."

"You were scared. I should've seen that."

"Why don't y'all sit down and eat?" Rebecca said. She clapped her hands, and Rachel suddenly appeared with the platters, Chris behind her with a salad.

Joy stepped to one side to allow the children to enter. Her knees were shaking. Her hands were shaking. And she wasn't sure she'd be able to eat a bite until they got all this out. But the kids seemed to feel that if they sat down to eat then maybe things would work out after all. "I think it's safe to say that we both made our share of mistakes."

"Maybe it's time for a second chance?" Uriah said.

Joy smiled at him. "I thought we were the second chance." They'd both had a beautiful love once, a love that had lived on even though their spouses had died. God had brought them together only to have their own stubbornness and pride keep them apart.

"Maybe," Uriah said. "Or maybe this is our second chance at a second chance."

"You should sit down and eat," Ruthie said appearing next to Johnny B's wheelchair. "Why aren't they sitting down to eat?"

"Wasn't that the plan?" Reena asked. "We get them in here to eat, and they would talk?"

"They are talking," Jane pointed out.

"A second chance at a second chance," Joy said. "That sounds like a fine idea."

Uriah nodded as Joy pulled out her chair and sat at the table. "I think so too," he said.

The kids breathed a sigh of relief and began to serve their meal. "See? It doesn't matter if you're dressed for a fancy dinner or not. None of that stuff matters," Rebecca said. "The only thing that matters is—"

Uriah looked to Joy; their gazes locked. "The two of us," he said.

"The ten of us," she returned.

His smile was blinding, and the cheers from the kids was almost deafening. And Joy had never been happier.

A second chance at a second chance was just what they all needed.

Epilogue

Elsie Miller hated to admit it, but weddings made her sad.

They shouldn't. They should reflect a happy time, the joining of two lives. And then spring weddings . . . they were the saddest of all. A pair of hopeful hearts that couldn't wait to be joined to each other.

And that's where she was. At the spring wedding of Uriah Lehman and Joy Lehman.

It was wonderful that the two had decided to make their family one. But that wonderfulness was overshadowed by the fact that life was so unpredictable. Anything could happen at any time to destroy the happiness the two had found together. She didn't like having such negative thoughts, so the minute they crossed her mind she turned to the Lord and said a prayer.

Elsie prayed a lot these days.

"So how long do you think we have to stay?" She turned to her cousin, Hattie Schrock. The two of them owned Poppin' Paradise Popcorn Shop, which was on Main Street in Paradise Springs. Elsie enjoyed working with her cousin, even if at times they seemed as opposite as bookends.

"I want to stay for a while longer."

Of course she did. Elsie rolled her eyes. "Of course you do."

Thank goodness that second weddings didn't last nearly as long as first ones. They tended to be smaller, with this second wedding being the exception. Lord only knew how many people had gathered in the bonus room on top of Joy's barn.

Elsie supposed so many were in attendance because spring was in the air and everyone was feeling renewed and refreshed. She could hope—and pray—that everything turned out fine for the newlyweds.

Like the rest of the widows group, Elsie had heard the story of how Joy and Uriah's kids had brought them together. It seemed that each of them—Joy and Uriah—was being prideful and stubborn and unable to tell the other of their feelings. Elsie could relate. She couldn't imagine putting herself out there like that again. The first time was bad enough.

"I wonder how the girls feel about moving over here?" Elsie said. She dipped a carrot stick into the creamy ranch dip and ate it. She thoughtfully chewed, waiting to see if Hattie had any comment on the matter. She wasn't disappointed.

"They'll have plenty of space as soon as the new addition is built on."

Uriah had no sooner got Johnny B's *dawdihaus* built that he began to build extra rooms onto Joy's house for his girls. Just two more rooms, but Elsie had to admit that the house was beginning to look a bit mishappen. Or maybe it was just that she remembered it differently and the changes were jarring.

"Besides Rebecca is probably gonna get married in the next couple of years, don't you think?" Hattie continued.

Elsie shrugged. She didn't keep up with such things,

even if her cousin did. Elsie knew that Rebecca, Uriah's oldest, had put in to go to baptism classes this year. That meant she would be joining church in the fall. After she joined the church, she would be able to date and eventually marry. According to Hattie, Adam Yoder was first in line.

"I'm kind of tired," Elsie said. "And my feet hurt."

Hattie nibbled on a piece of cheese but didn't turn her attention from the milling crowd as she spoke. "Give it to God," she murmured. It was her standard response.

Elsie scoffed. "You can't give it all to God."

"Not true." Of course that's what Hattie would say. Elsie could have said for her if she had been in a mean-spirited mood. Thankfully she wasn't.

"You shouldn't bother God with the trivial stuff." Elsie had said those very same words too many times to count. Honestly, why did God need to get involved in everyday inconveniences? He surely had better things to do with His time than worry about Elsie's aching feet.

"If you can't trust God with pickle jars, how can you trust Him with money?"

Elsie harrumphed. If she had heard her cousin say that once, she had heard Hattie say it a hundred times.

"You know, you could use a little positivity in your life," Hattie said.

"What's positivity got to do with me?"

But Hattie was on a roll. "People get along without positivity day in and day out," she continued. "But are they successful? Happy?"

"I don't know about happy, but there's one who's successful." She nodded toward Christian Beachy.

"If I had to live with Malinda, I'd be grumpy too," Hattie said uncharitably.

Elsie just shook her head. "Some of us are happy just the way we are."

"Is that so?" her cousin asked.

"It is," Elsie countered.

Hattie frowned at her. "You can't honestly believe that a man as grumpy as Christian Beachy is happy."

Why would he not be? And frankly Elsie was getting a little worn out from all of Hattie's talk of positivity and happiness. Just where did she get these ridiculous ideas? "Want to bet?"

"I do believe gambling is a sin," Hattie shot back.

"Not for money," Elsie continued, frowning at her cousin. "How about chores?"

"Chores? Like the dishes?"

"Work chores," Elsie said, her plan beginning to take shape. If there was one thing she hated more than Hattie's can-do attitude, it was scrubbing the copper vats they used in the popcorn shop.

"Like?"

"Like if you can't change his attitude in the next sixty days, you'll scrub the copper vats at work. For a year. All by yourself."

"And if I can change it?"

Elsie did her best not to scoff at the idea. She was going to win this one hands down. "Then I'll scrub them." But that was never going to happen.

Hattie glanced over at the happy couple. "Sixty days you say?"

"Sixty days," Elsie repeated.

Hattie turned to her with a somewhat of a triumphant smile. She stuck out a hand to shake. "You're on."

RECIPES

Caramel Apple Whoopie Pies

Ingredients:

- 2 cups brown sugar
- ¾ cup butter, softened
- 2 large eggs
- 1 teaspoon vanilla
- 1½ cups applesauce
- ¾ cup whipping cream
- 2¾ cups flour
- 1 tablespoon ground cinnamon
- 1 teaspoon baking powder
- 1 teaspoon baking soda
- 1 teaspoon salt
- 1 can Caramel Condensed Milk, for filling (or make your own; see Joy's Dulce de Leche recipe)

Instructions:

Preheat the oven to 350°F.

Lightly wipe cookie sheet or whoopie pie pans with oil.

In a large bowl, beat together the brown sugar and the butter until creamy. One at a time, add eggs, vanilla, applesauce, and cream. Beat until well mixed.

In a separate bowl, sift together flour, cinnamon, baking powder, baking soda, and salt.

Add to the applesauce mixture. Beat on medium until mixed.

Scoop batter into the prepared pans.

Bake 6 to 8 minutes.

Remove from the oven and let cool completely on a cooling rack.

Spread one half of the baked whoopie pies with Caramel Condensed Milk. Top with another apple cake.

Or use the Joy's Dulce de Leche recipe for filling.

Joy's Dulce de Leche

Ingredients:

    1 can of sweetened condensed milk
    Room-temperature water

Instructions:

Remove the label off the can.

Place the can of sweetened condensed milk into a pot right-side up. Make sure you use a pot with lid.

Cover can with room temperature water, making sure the water level is at least 2-inches above the can lid.

Bring the water to a very light boil over medium-high heat. Reduce heat to lowest setting and allow to simmer for 3 to 3¾ hours. For thickest texture, making sure can is completely covered with the water always.

(If some of the water evaporates during the simmering process, add more hot water to keep the can submerged. If you have placed the lid on your pot you shouldn't have to add water.)

Once it has simmered the desired cooking time, remove the pot from the heat. Leave the can in the water to cool to room temperature. This will make the thickest dulce de leche for your filling. Store unused dulce de leche in the fridge in a glass jar.

Note: Do not try to open cans while still hot, as the hot dulce de leche may spew out because of the pressure.

Joy's Dr Pepper 'Pop Roast'

Recipe has been formatted for a family of four (or less with leftovers).

Ingredients:

- 1 large beef roast of your choice (2 to 4 pounds approximately)
- 1 tablespoon olive oil
- 4 medium potatoes, chopped
- 1 medium onion, chopped
- 1 large carrot, chopped
- 1 stalk of celery chopped
- ½ green bell pepper sliced
- 1 can Dr Pepper
- 1 can cream of mushroom soup
- 1 package of onion soup mix
- 2 tablespoons minced garlic
- 1 generous pinch of red pepper flakes

Instructions:

Oven method (*Joy's method*)

Preheat the oven to 350°F.

In a large frying pan, heat olive oil and sear the roast on both sides.

Add salt and pepper to taste, then place in large roasting pan.

Place chopped vegetables around the roast. (I always put the carrots in the bottom because it takes them longer to cook.)

Whisk together Dr Pepper, mushroom soup, onion soup mix, garlic, and red pepper, then pour over the roast.

Cover with foil and place in preheated oven.

Cook for 4 hours or until the roast is tender and pulls apart easily.

Slow Cooker Method
(because who has time to babysit a roast for 4 hours?)

Pretty much do everything the same except place it all in your slow cooker and let it cook for 7 to 8 hours on low.

Joy's Joyous Strawberry Scones

Ingredients:

  1 cup of chopped strawberries
  2 tablespoons granulated sugar
  2 cups all-purpose flour
  2 teaspoons baking powder
  Pinch salt
  6 tablespoons cold butter cut into pieces
  2 large eggs
  ⅔ cup milk

Instructions:

Preheat oven to 400°F.

Line a baking sheet with parchment paper and set aside.

In a small mixing bowl, sprinkle 1 tablespoon of granulated sugar over strawberries and mix until completely coated. Set aside.

In a medium-sized bowl, sift together flour, baking powder, and salt. Add butter pieces and cut in with a fork (or a pastry cutter) until all ingredients are well combined.

In a large bowl, whisk together 1 egg and ⅔ cup milk.

Add contents of medium-size bowl (flour-butter mixture) to the contents of the large bowl (milk-egg mixture). Mix with a wooden spoon.

Add strawberries and continue to mix until a dough starts to form. (If needed, add a bit more sifted all-purpose flour. Depending on the size of your egg, the dough might be too sticky unless you add more flour.)

Turn out onto a clean working surface dusted with flour. Knead until smooth.

Place mixture onto lined baking sheet, forming it into a circle. (Should be around 8 inches in diameter.)

Use a pastry cutter (or a serrated knife) to cut the dough into eight equal pieces. Separate and line them up on the prepared baking sheet.

In a small bowl, whisk 1 egg and brush the top of each scone. Sprinkle top with granulated sugar.

Bake for 15 to 20 minutes or until top is golden brown. Allow to cool before serving and enjoying.

Visit our website at
KensingtonBooks.com
to sign up for our newsletters, read
more from your favorite authors, see
books by series, view reading group
guides, and more!

BOOK   CLUB

BETWEEN THE CHAPTERS

Become a Part of Our
Between the Chapters Book Club
Community and Join the Conversation

Betweenthechapters.net